SADDLE UP, CITY GIRL

JILL WESTWOOD

"You find out who your real friends are when you're involved in a scandal." Elizabeth Taylor

CHAPTER 1

LAUREN

"*L*auren! Lauren! Eyes over here!"

Photographers shouted my name as I stood in the designated red carpet area in front of a backdrop. Shoulders back, hand on left hip, right knee bent slightly—I knew the drill. After being a reluctant celebrity for five years, I may have had the pose perfected, but I still didn't enjoy doing it, especially not when my "husband" had his arm around me, pulling me against his side. In my head, I counted to ninety. A minute and a half was an acceptable amount of time before walking away. Counting also gave me somewhere to go in my head so I wouldn't obsess about whether I had lipstick on my teeth or a stray chin hair only a high-resolution camera would catch. Or the fact that my husband was touching me in places that felt too intimate now that we were estranged. Maybe if I'd experienced fame when I was a young woman, I'd be better at it by fifty-two.

My husband, Frederic, or Freddy, as the world knew him, dazzled the photographers with his ultra-white veneers and chiseled jawline. God, how handsome I thought he was before I knew what ugliness lay beneath the shiny surface. Good looks definitely weren't enough to make up for the deficiencies in his character, but most of the world didn't know the true Freddy or the real me. They saw what was in front of the camera—a picture perfect middle-aged couple attending a fancy schmancy event in New York City. Lucky us.

As we left the press area and walked into the main event in my sister's opulent new hair salon, he lowered his head, still smiling, and whispered in my ear, "I detest this bullshit."

At least we had that in common.

People might think he was whispering sweet nothings, but no, we didn't do that kind of thing anymore. Hadn't exchanged loving words in more than a decade. To maintain the charade, I gave my head a toss and laughed quietly, as if we were sharing an intimate joke. Maybe I'd become as fake as he was.

"You'll put up with this dog and pony show if you want to get your next check from me." I slid my hand into his as I spoke. He had the skin of a man who moisturized religiously. "Just two hours of your time is all I'm asking for this evening. Then you're free to go out and carouse and do whatever it is you do when you're in New York."

When we legally separated three and a half years ago, state law required me to continue supporting Freddy because supposedly he'd been the primary caregiver for our two children instead of working outside the home. In reality, we'd always employed a nanny so Freddy could parent when he damn well felt like it and use the rest of his free time to pursue his sailing hobby, as well as beautiful young women he met along the way. I worked my ass off to afford the lifestyle we enjoyed, and what did all my long hours at the office and lost time with my sons get me? A huge monthly alimony payment to him. On top of what I had to pay Freddy after the separation, I offered to throw in a hefty bonus if he agreed to two stipulations:

1. Keep our separation a secret.

2. Attend at least two public events with me per year.

It wasn't a bad gig for a European playboy, one who was tangentially related to royalty and was spending his fifties gambling, sailing, and sleeping with women half his age. Somehow, we'd managed to keep our marital issues on the down low, probably because he did his partying in places like Ibiza and San Tropez, not Manhattan.

The party I was forcing him to attend was incredibly important to me. My twin sister Tori and I were co-owners of a high-end matchmaking business called Ms. Match, which, five years ago, spawned a reality show of the same name. Tori was the company's head matchmaker and star of our TV show, while I preferred to stay behind the scenes as our chief financial officer, making as few on-screen appearances as possible.

As if Ms. Match weren't time consuming enough for her, Tori had recently started a salon with her friend Jenna, and now they'd added a haircare line to their empire. Tonight they were having a celebration at their salon in SoHo to launch their new product line, and if there was one person who always got my support and loyalty, it was my sister, which meant Freddy was going to show up for her whether he liked it or not.

We walked into the salon, and Tori greeted me with kisses on both cheeks.

"Hey, Lolo! You look beautiful." Like the rest of my family, she still used my childhood nickname.

"So do you." I looked her up and down, taking in her fierce tangerine colored body-con dress that accentuated her curves and contrasted with her long dark hair that fell almost to her waist. "That dress is absolutely gorgeous on you."

She loved bright colors and bold prints, and I was wearing my favorite shade too—classic black. We hadn't dressed similarly since my mother lost the battle to pick out our clothing for kindergarten.

"Thank you so much for coming tonight." Tori turned to Freddy. "Hello, Frederic. You're looking well-rested, as always."

Freddy ignored her dig. "Bonsoir, Tori. You look fantastique in that dress."

She did look amazing. Even with the stresses that came from running multiple business ventures, she'd never been happier or more radiant in her life. Some of that had to do with her boyfriend Nick, the first man she'd ever dated who was actually worthy of her. He was a childhood neighbor and friend with whom she'd reconnected last Christmas, all thanks to me, and they'd been inseparable ever since. Now they were contemplating getting engaged, and it was possible my sister would soon become the stepmother to his three teenage daughters. For Tori, life was always about new adventures, while I was the pragmatic twin, less prone to taking risks or walking the untrodden path. At fifty-two, I could see the road ahead of me stretching all the way to the retirement villa, and there was nary a bend or bump in it. The scenery was the same for miles and miles...

God, I needed a drink.

Reluctantly, Tori accepted kisses on both cheeks from my "husband" because, although she despised him for cheating on me, she went along with our deception for my sake. The only other people who knew about our faux marriage were our brother Rocco, his husband Jamison, my two adult sons, and the divorce attorneys who wrote the separation agreement. My mother was aware Freddy and I largely lived on different continents but she never asked why, which was fine by me.

"Freddy," Tori said, "since you never like to pay for anything, you'll be happy to know there's an open bar this evening." She squeezed my shoulder. "Grab a champagne and say hi to Rocco and Jamison. They want to see you." She pointed toward our brother and his spouse, who were both dressed in dapper suits.

"Will do," I said. "And congratulations, the place looks amazing."

"Thanks, sweetie. I have to mingle and promote. Catch you later?"

"Of course." I blew her a kiss. "Knock 'em dead, sis."

Before opening the salon, Jenna and Tori gave it a complete transformation from a rather grim discount mattress store to what was now a gleaming vision in white and gold with soft pink and coral accents. Clearly, Tori had selected her dress color to match the salon's decor, which was typical of her relentless attention to detail. She and Jenna had gone big in the literal sense when they designed the place—bold light fixtures descended from the ceilings like clouds, oversized velvet settees anchored the vast waiting area, and huge gilt-framed mirrors bounced light around the room. If I'd placed all of that in the salon it would have looked like a bordello, not a feminine, playful retreat from the sharp edges of the city. I had no doubt they'd book up months, if not years, ahead.

Seeing my sister promoting her new business made me think about our beginning as partners and how far we'd come. Fifteen years ago, Tori asked me to help her start up a small, elite matchmaking service that focused on an extremely wealthy clientele. We opened the doors of Ms. Match with a bank loan, a strong work ethic, and not much else. Now we were worth millions, and Tori was still expanding her brand. We'd recently announced that this would be the final season for our TV show because we both felt it had run its course, and then we received an unexpected offer—a media company wanted our entire catalog for their streaming service. My personal life was nothing to brag about, but professionally, I was a huge success. After Freddy and I parted ways, I decided you can't have it all, and I should stop missing the things I lacked—like a romantic relationship —and be grateful for my privileged life. Gratitude was easier to come by when I didn't have to deal with my husband in person.

I plucked a champagne flute off of a caterer's passing tray and took a fortifying gulp.

"That champagne is probably cheap garbage." Freddy perused the room. "And who did the interior design? It looks like a little girl's birthday party exploded in here."

I ground my teeth so hard that my jaw popped. "You should mingle on your own."

He huffed like a petulant child. "You dragged me here and now you don't even want to talk to me? What's the point?"

I glanced over at Rocco and Jamison, who smiled brightly at me. Only me. I wanted so badly to join them, but I didn't want to inflict Freddy on them. No point in ruining everyone's fun.

"You know why I need you here," I said. "It's supposed to be a win-win. You get more money, and I get credibility."

I didn't feel like I was winning, but there was nothing I could do about that for the moment. People liked to see their matchmakers in loving, healthy relationships, and, unfortunately, that hadn't been the reality for the Cozzi sisters. Until recently, Tori had spent her entire adult life as a serial monogamist, dating men who didn't deserve her. I'd married Freddy, a serial cheater, who I stayed legally bound to for the sake of our children. The truth about our love lives would destroy our reputation as matchmakers and make me prey for the paparazzi. The thought of our sons seeing their parents' marriage dissolution play out in the press was enough to make me sick to my stomach.

"Go get some alcohol," I suggested. "Free drinks, remember?"

"I can afford to buy my own drinks." I was afraid he'd

stick to my side all evening, but his eyes drifted over to the bar and he relented. "Fine. I'll mingle."

Grateful to be shed of him, I joined Rocco and Jamison who were standing in the reception area near one of the giant couches. The crowd was growing by the second, and I had to turn sideways to scoot through a group of people. Someone's glass tipped onto my shoes, dousing my toes with champagne. Fantastique.

"Hey, sweetie." Rocco gave me a kiss on the cheek. "I see you brought your French handbag with you."

I looked distractedly at the tiny Coach bag on my arm before I realized he was talking about Freddy. "Very funny."

Jamison smacked his husband's arm. "Ignore him. He's off gluten and it makes him cranky."

"Seriously, though…" Rocco glanced over his shoulder and lowered his voice, "if you ever need to get rid of him, I'll help you hide the body."

I snorted and took a swig of champagne. The bubbles tickled my nose, bringing on a sneeze that I successfully suppressed. "Thanks. I'll take that into consideration next time I'm feeling homicidal."

The three of us watched Freddy lean against the bar that was set up for the event. He was already flirting with one of the bartenders, who looked about half his age.

"It's not worth doing prison time for him," I said.

When Freddy sauntered away from the bar with his drink in hand, the bartender's eyes tracked his movements. He was still trim and suave at fifty-three, and it wasn't the young woman's fault she was ogling a married guy because he never wore a wedding band, even before we separated. His excuse was that European men didn't wear wedding rings, which was either true or one of the convenient explanations that he was so good at finding for his behavior.

"Look at him." I nodded my head toward Freddy. "He has no problem picking up women wherever he goes."

Rocco and Jamison exchanged side-eyed glances.

"Honey, you'd meet someone else if you divorced him," Jamison said. "You're gorgeous, funny and smart, not to mention loaded. You don't need him."

"Tori is all loved up now," Rocco added. "While the media is focused on her new relationship, this is your chance to dump Freddy."

"Did I hear my name?" Tori appeared at my elbow.

I swiped my thumb over her cheek where someone had left a lipstick kiss mark. "I thought you had to talk to other people?"

"I said that because I can't be around Freddy without wanting to kick him in the nuts." She leaned in and stage whispered, "Now, what are we talking about?"

"I was telling Lauren she needs to get rid of him once and for all." Rocco cupped his hands around his mouth and hissed, "Divorce."

"We want her to be free to meet someone else," Jamison chimed in.

"Meeting someone else is the least of my concerns." Seeing their raised eyebrows, I added, "Seriously. When we get divorced—which we will eventually—I'm going to be too busy dealing with a media cyclone to think about dating. I'll probably have to hide out in my apartment for a year."

"Then why not get it over with now?" Rocco asked. "The longer you wait, the more years you lose."

I sighed and stared into my empty glass. "If you're trying to make me feel better, it's not working."

"We're not trying to gang up on you," Rocco said, "but we've been worried about you. You've lost your Lauren sparkle."

"Thanks a lot!" I looked around for another tray of champagne glasses.

"What we're saying," Jamison added, giving his husband the stink eye, "is that you seem to be stuck in neutral. Your kids are out of college and starting their careers. Tori has this new business venture with Jenna. Freddy is doing his sailing thing in Europe. And you're just… "

"A loser?" I supplied.

Tori put her arm around me. "No one said that, honey. Look at you in this sexy dress! You're stunning and—" She looked over our heads. "Oops, they're summoning me. Time to shine!" And with that, she was off.

"Our sister loves a stage," Rocco said as our eyes followed Tori across the room.

"I'm not like her, you know," I said defensively. "I don't need a million projects, and I hate being in the public eye."

"We know," Jamison said. "We just love you and want to see you happy."

I bit down on my lip to keep myself from tearing up. My emotions were so close to the surface these days. "I'm in a down phase and feeling a little burned out. It will pass."

Liar. I'd been in close contact with my financial advisor in the past few months to figure out when I could retire. I used to think I'd work until death because I loved my job so much, but now…something was shifting inside me and the more I fought it, the harder it tugged. The walls of my office were closing in on me. My apartment felt like a cage. If I didn't make a change soon, I was going to suffocate.

"Maybe you need to move to a new apartment," Rocco said, as if reading my mind. "A new space, a new outlook. Somewhere with a nice big soaking tub where you can wash away all thoughts of that idiot ex-husband of yours."

I gave him a dubious look. "He's not officially my ex yet, and that's a lot to ask of a soaking tub."

"Welcome, everyone!" Tori's voice claimed the room, her rich alto amplified by the mic she held in her hand. She and Jenna stood in front of a pink curtain that blocked off the back of the room. "I'm Tori Cozzi, as most of you already know, and this is my business partner, Jenna Rossolino.

Thank you for coming here tonight to support us in the unveiling of Jentori Haircare. We're thrilled you're here with us. Your support means so much, and we hope you bring home some samples of our products so you can look as fabulous as we do."

The crowd laughed at her joke and, with a hair toss, she handed the mic to Jenna, who also looked incredible in a short gold dress topped with a leather moto jacket. She'd styled her dark hair to perfection in a sleek shoulder-length bob.

"Thanks, Tori." Jenna's voice wavered slightly. "We believe in these products because we helped create them. Yes, there are lots of haircare lines on the market, but many of them make promises they can't deliver. A lot of them are bad for the rest of your body too. Jentori is free from dangerous chemicals, one hundred percent vegan, ethically sourced, and"—she lowered her chin and dropped her voice into a conspiratorial tone—"to be blunt, this shit is going to make your hair look amazing."

The crowd clapped and cheered, and, off to the side, there was Nick gazing at Tori with such a fierce look of admiration and love that I felt both delighted for them and bereft that I'd never had anyone look at me that way in my entire life. I'd been married over two decades, and I'd never been sincerely adored that way. Maybe I never would.

Jenna handed the mic back to Tori. "Without further ado," she said, "let's unveil the products!"

Tori pulled a string to make the curtain behind them drop to the floor. Sure enough, we could all see a table stacked with haircare products in gorgeous pink and gold packaging. But no one was looking at that. Instead, we collectively gasped and stared at the couple making out to the side of the table. The woman had both hands inside the man's unbuttoned pants and was clearly doing a job that had nothing to do with salon work.

Sensing their audience, the couple froze in what must have been an unplanned sexual tableau. I blinked several times, thinking I could clear the error in my vision. That couldn't be Freddy and the young bartender standing there in flagrante delicto...

I shrieked and covered my mouth as Jamison and Rocco swung their heads towards me. Time felt suspended, and then pandemonium broke loose. Media cameras flashed as guests whipped out cell phones. Freddy zipped up his trousers, and the bartender spun around to put her back to the crowd. White noise, like the din of a passing train, filled my ears as I stood paralyzed in horror.

The bartender pushed her way through the crowd and ran straight out the front door, shirt still unbuttoned as she clutched it closed. Cameras flashed and people started shouting at me. I couldn't process any of their words.

As Rocco put a protective arm around my shoulder and ushered me toward the back of the salon, one thought ran through my head.

My life was over.

CHAPTER 2

LAUREN

*S*tanding outside the Laramie airport, I felt like something must have gone amiss. After taking a flight to Denver, then catching a smaller plane to Wyoming, I expected a private car to be waiting for me. None were in sight. In fact, I didn't see any hotel vans picking up passengers. I set my bags on the sidewalk and shaded my eyes against the bright sunlight, searching for my ride. Surely they hadn't forgotten to send someone for me?

Photographers set up camp outside my apartment building the morning after the party at Jentori, the scene of my ultimate humiliation. They were also congregating outside our office building and Tori's apartment, in case I tried to retreat there. Their pursuit of me had induced paranoia and panic attacks, and I started staying inside all the time with my blinds down. Tori finally had her assistant, Sully, book a trip for me out west at a remote resort and spa so I could lay low somewhere comfortable until the brouhaha died down in New York.

It felt cowardly to let the press run me out of town, especially when I was the victim, not the criminal. Of course, Freddy had left New York immediately. He was already in the South of France "licking his wounds," which was a euphemism for "drinking alcohol out of a model's belly button."

A black sedan pulled up to the curb, but before I could inquire if they were there for me, a young woman came outside and stepped into the car. I sighed and looked around but there was no taxi stand or sign for hotel transportation in view, and as I waited for someone to claim me like lost luggage, I grew more nervous. It looked like I was going to have to call the resort and find out what was going on.

"Unbelievable," I muttered under my breath. Or not so unbelievable considering my luck lately.

Emotionally exhausted and coasting on self-pity, I pulled out my phone to search for the resort's phone number. At that moment, a well-worn Suburban with filthy mud flaps roared past me at a dangerously high speed. The driver slid up to the curb and lurched to a halt. If this was how people drove around here, it was a good thing I hadn't rented a car to drive to the resort.

A man stepped out of the desperately dirty vehicle, yanked his t-shirt over his head, balled it up, then tossed it into the far depths of the backseats.

Ew. But also...wow.

For a man who looked to be around my age, he was in great shape—muscular back, broad shoulders, toned arms. Interesting...

I stared with growing curiosity as he took a new t-shirt from the front seat and slipped it over his head, his muscles flexing as he slid his arms through the holes and pulled the fabric to his waist. Then he grabbed a tan cowboy hat from the dashboard and put it on before slamming the driver's side door. Mesmerized by this display of casual masculinity, I finally dragged my gaze away so I wouldn't get caught gawking. Out of the corner of my eye, I saw him walk toward me, and my heart rate quickened. Shoot. Had he seen me watching him?

"Howdy, ma'am."

He was definitely speaking to me because I was the only one in the vicinity, so now I had to turn back and look at him again. Damn. He had the faded jeans and worn-in boots to pull that whole rough-and-ready look together.

"Hello." I gave him a tight, closed-lip smile that said I was being pleasant, but wasn't interested in whatever he was about to offer. Then I snapped my eyes back down to my suitcase. As a wary New Yorker, my guard went up when male strangers approached me, no matter how sexy they might be. Ted Bundy was handsome too, and look how that turned out.

"Are you heading to Silver Sage?" he asked, stepping closer to me.

And now I felt silly. "Oh. Yes, I am, actually." I finally noticed that under the dirt on the green SUV there was faded white lettering that read Silver Sage Ranch. "Are you here to pick me up?" It was a stupid question that I regretted the second it was out of my mouth.

"I sure am." He strode toward me, extending his hand for a shake, while I fanned my overheated face with my phone. "Matthew Hart, owner and manager of Silver Sage Ranch. Please excuse the dirt on the vehicle and"—he looked down at his jeans—"on me. A fence needed mending this morning, and I didn't have time to change after seeing to it."

Owner? That was a surprise. Didn't they have someone lowlier who could shuttle guests to the ranch, not to mention deal with fence repairs? I took a moment to drink him in— lean body, chiseled jaw, chestnut hair streaked with silver at the temples. His denim-blue eyes were the same color as his jeans. If Tori were here, she'd make a joke about forgetting the truck and riding the cowboy, but I was in this alone.

"I'm Lauren Wagonblast," I said, using my new alias. "Nice

to meet you." He clasped my hand in a firm grip, the calluses on his fingers playing roughly against my skin. I ignored the little tingle that shot through me at his touch because, seriously, I wasn't falling for his humble cowboy act. He was probably wearing that hat to play a part for the sake of a tourist.

"Nice to meet you, Mrs. Wagonblast." Amazingly, he didn't crack a smile at the ridiculous last name Tori had given me when she had Sully arrange my stay at the ranch. Next time, I was making my own reservation.

He walked around to the back of the SUV and opened the door to the trunk area. "Are those your only bags?"

I looked down at my carry-on bag and oversized suitcase on wheels. "This is it. The bigger bag is really"—he easily hefted the sixty-pound suitcase the airlines charged me extra for and tossed it into the back of the SUV—"heavy."

Not for him, apparently. He placed my smaller bag on top of the bigger one and slammed the two back doors.

"All set?" he asked.

I blinked up at the man in front of me, backlit with sunlight, and wondered what the hell I'd gotten myself into. He could be driving me anywhere for all I knew. Maybe he wasn't even from the resort, and I was being kidnapped and taken north or south over the border, never to be seen again...

I seriously needed to get a grip.

He took my hesitation the wrong way. "I promise the car is cleaner inside than out."

"No, it's not that." Okay, that was an issue, but I didn't want to seem prissy. "I was wondering if there were other guests coming with us?" I looked behind me but, alas, there was no one coming out of the doors of the airport.

"Nope, only you."

Only me and this stranger who could clearly overpower

me if he chose to do so. He had the correct name on his truck, but something about this situation still felt off.

"Alright then. Let's go."

As we drove down the highways of southeastern Wyoming, I found out what was meant by big sky country. Previous ski trips to Colorado hadn't prepared me for the vastness of the Wyoming landscape. Three-hundred and sixty degrees around us was an impossibly blue sky dotted with puffy white clouds that Bob Ross himself could have conjured. There was open land as far as the eye could see, dotted with conifers and low-growing scrubby bushes. Here, the trees didn't obstruct one's vision like they did on Long Island, where I grew up. You could see far and wide, all the way to the foothills of tawny, rugged mountains in the distance. Behind those stood what Matthew told me were the majestic Sierra Madres, capped in white even in the summer.

At one point, we passed a sign for a town called Elk Mountain, population one hundred and fifty-one. I'd been to Peloton classes with nearly that many people.

"It certainly is sparsely populated out here," I said, stating the obvious.

"That's the beauty of Wyoming. The cows outnumber the people. Kind of like subway rats in New York City."

I pointed a finger at him. "Hilarious, but I actually read a report that said the rat population is only one-third of the human population in the city."

He laughed and glanced over at me. "I stand corrected on that score. Cows are so much nicer than rats though, so it's not a fair comparison, anyway."

I tilted my head to the side. "Are they though?"

"Wow, not a cow person, I see."

"And you're not a city person, I guess." My voice had taken on a teasing, almost flirtatious tone.

"My trips to Manhattan have always been enjoyable. Couldn't live there, though. Not when this place exists."

At that moment, we were passing by a field full of grazing horses. "It really is beautiful. I knew it was pretty, but I never expected it to be…stunning."

Again, my words felt inadequate for the occasion. This trip, which began out of necessity, was feeling more like a vacation, one that was very much needed in my life.

"I'm glad you can appreciate it," he said. "Not everyone does. Some don't like feeling landlocked. Others find Wyoming too quiet and remote from everything else."

"I definitely don't mind the peace and quiet right now."

No more paparazzi stalking me and well-meaning fans stopping me in the street to hug and console me. Being hugged by strangers was way outside of my comfort zone. I only hoped the other guests at the ranch would be discreet and leave me alone. Typically, people at exclusive resorts were there to escape and recharge, not to bother other wealthy people, so I didn't expect it to be an issue.

"Just curious," he said, "how did you hear about us?"

"My sister found you. I told her I wanted to go somewhere I wouldn't be bothered for a while, and she did a little research and found Silver Sage."

"Have you ever been out west before?" he asked.

"No, but I used to ride horses as a kid, and I think that was on her mind when she made the reservation."

"Is that right?" He was driving with one hand, looking like he could navigate these roads blindfolded. Traffic certainly wasn't an issue.

"It's been a very long time since I've ridden." I didn't want to make myself sound like some kind of expert. "As a preteen girl, I was obsessed with horses. Quite a cliche, I guess. I read all the horse books in my school library and watched *Black Beauty* about ten times, and then I begged my parents for riding lessons.

They let me do it for a couple of years until it got too expensive." The riding lessons had to stop when my father was laid off from his job, but Mr. Hart didn't need to hear that aspect of the story.

"My daughter is obsessed with horses too," he said. "We'll get you back in the saddle again. There are beautiful trails at the ranch. You'll love it."

Back in the saddle again. I needed that in more ways than one. I separated from Freddy three years earlier, but we hadn't been intimate in much longer than that. Honestly, I hadn't even had a strong desire to be with a man, and I started to think my peri-menopausal body was closed for business. It was my gynecologist who convinced me to take measures to keep everything healthy and in working order down there by using the proper medications and supplements.

"You never know," she'd said. "At some point, you might want to become sexually active again. You're still a young woman, and you want to have all your options, just in case."

Her words had made me laugh inwardly at the time because I definitely didn't feel like a young woman, and my options were, due to my own choices, quite limited. You can't publicly date when you're in a sham marriage, not unless you're Freddy cavorting freely around small European beach towns. Even if I were single, finding someone appropriate to love after fifty wasn't a simple task, which was why so many older people hired matchmakers in the first place.

Now here I was, driving through rural Wyoming with a handsome stranger and thinking about my vaginal health. I guess celibacy wasn't feeling as appealing anymore. Not that I was going to do anything about it on this trip, but experiencing sexual attraction to a man was a good start. I peeked at Matthew, and a powerful urge to put my hand on his muscular thigh seized me. Where the heck did that come from?

I clenched my hands together on my lap just in case they

got any funny ideas. Obviously, I would never fondle the leg of a man I'd just met, but the fact that I'd even thought about it was scary and exhilarating. As we rolled along a stretch of lonesome highway, I became intoxicated by the Suburban's manly smell of sweat and leather. We were sitting together on a bench style front seat. Did Matthew's lady sit in the middle, her leg pressed up against his, the two of them all cozy and snuggled up? Could people have sex right here in the—

"You doing okay?"

His words broke me from my reverie. If I was lucky, he wouldn't notice the flush on my throat and cheeks.

"A little warm. Is it okay if I crack the window for a minute?" I asked.

"Sure."

Clearly, I needed to make conversation to keep my mind from wandering. "How long have you owned Silver Sage?"

"My parents bought it in the eighties," he said, "and almost two years ago I took over as manager. My sister and brothers followed other paths in life, but I wanted to keep the ranch in the family."

I took a swig from my water bottle. Maybe all of my fantasizing resulted from dehydration. "Do they live in Wyoming?"

"Only Sam, my youngest brother, still lives out here. He's our local veterinarian. Faith, my sister, lives in Texas, and my brother Bowie lives in Alaska." He turned the truck onto another long stretch of road that looked exactly like the one we'd been on.

I couldn't imagine living far away from my siblings. Tori was my other half and business partner, and Rocco was a best friend and confidante. Success and fame made it harder to trust people because you never really knew what they wanted from you, but with my siblings, I never had to question their loyalty.

"And are your parents still at the ranch?" I asked.

"They died in a car accident a while back. That's why I'm running it now."

I sat with the feeling of that loss, giving it the moment of silent reflection it deserved. "I'm so sorry. I lost my dad quite suddenly, and it was a shock, but losing both of your parents at once must have been a nightmare."

"It was hard," he said, "but being at the ranch makes me feel closer to them. I'm continuing their legacy, which is very important to me."

"I'm amazed you took over the family business by yourself. My sister and I own a company together, and I don't know what I'd do without her."

He glanced over at me. "Is that right? What kind of business are you in?"

I considered lying, but wasn't quick enough on my feet to think of anything other than the truth. "We own a matchmaking service."

"Really?" He appraised me with fresh eyes, as if I'd surprised him. "I didn't even know those existed anymore, what with online dating."

I wasn't offended. What would a guy from rural Wyoming know about elite Manhattan matchmakers? It was probably as foreign to him as something like rodeos were to me.

"Being on the dating apps is hard, and Stanley Cup winners and airline CEOs don't necessarily want to post their photos for all to see. Many high profile people prefer being set up by professionals. We background check every client to weed out the creeps and the scammers, and we do in-depth interviews and even conduct mock dates to give them tips. It's a process." An expensive process that most people couldn't afford. "My sister is actually the matchmaker. I'm the CFO, the numbers brain."

"Oh, so this is matchmaking for millionaires."

"And billionaires." I wasn't bragging, only stating facts, but I could see the slight shift in his expression. "Since it's our company, we can choose who we work with. If our clients don't treat other people with dignity and respect, we part ways with them."

The last thing I wanted to do was get into a big discussion about work, but when people found out I co-owned a match-making company, there were always questions. I could never get away from my job and, in some ways, that was my own fault. I had cultivated little in my life besides my career and my role as a mother. Who I was beyond those two things was becoming a question I wanted to answer.

"Sounds like you offer an important service, then." He drummed his fingers on the steering wheel. "Online dating doesn't really work so well in small towns. You'd probably just end up on a date with your neighbor or cousin. People tend to meet the old-fashioned way here."

"At the bar?"

He chuckled. "At the bar, definitely. Or church. My sister met her husband at college. A lot of folks marry their high school sweethearts."

"I think those are ideal ways to meet someone, if you can. In a big city, it can be hard to connect with other single people, although it seems like it should be the opposite when there are so many options."

"Women have a saying about meeting a man out here."

"Tell me."

He tilted his head. "The odds are good, but the goods are odd."

I smiled as I processed his meaning. "Is that so?"

"I can only speak for myself, but I don't think I'm that odd. Now my brothers are another story."

I laughed again, then waited anxiously for him to ask how I met my husband. Yes, I was alone on this trip, but I was wearing a diamond engagement ring and a wedding band on my left hand, and there was nothing I wanted to talk about less than how I met Freddy. Shifting in my seat, I slid my hand under my leg to hide the ring and hopefully ward off any questions.

Fortunately, Matthew Hart and I were both comfortable riding in silence, and that's exactly what we did for a good twenty minutes. Occasionally, I'd sneak looks over at him, enjoying his handsome profile and wishing I could do more than daydream about a vacation fling, but now wasn't the time to risk another scandal. He didn't seem like the type to sell a story to a tabloid, but did anyone ever appear on the surface to be a heartless sellout?

About forty-five minutes into the trip, I was impatient to arrive at the ranch. "Are we close yet?"

"About halfway."

"Halfway?" Surprise made my voice higher and shriller than I'd intended. "Really?"

"We're cutting through the Medicine Bow National Forest right now. It's gorgeous, isn't it?"

"Absolutely. I just didn't realize..." I could have sworn Tori told me the ranch was a half hour from the airport. I wanted to have a look at a map on my phone, but there was no cell reception. Zero bars. Hopefully, the ranch had reliable WiFi, so I could do a few online meetings later in the week. I felt twitchy when I thought about being away from work for too long.

"What do you do if you run out of gas out here?" I asked. "I haven't seen any service stations."

He scratched his chin. "Yeah, that's why we make sure we have a full tank when we leave home. You'd have to walk a long way to find a gas station. Or hope someone comes along and gives you a ride." He looked over at me and saw where my mind was going. "Don't worry. I have flares, blankets, and other supplies in case of car trouble. When you live out here, you come prepared or suffer the consequences."

There was something incredibly sexy about a man with survival skills who could take care of a flat tire or keep me warm in a snowstorm. Maybe that appeal dated back to our prehistoric ancestors, embedded somewhere in our genetic code? It reminded me of Paul, my college boyfriend, during my years at Middlebury College in Vermont. He introduced me to hiking and cross-country skiing, and he never went anywhere without his trusty Swiss army knife.

I still thought about Paul sometimes and wondered how different my life would have been if we'd stayed together. Then again, if I hadn't married Freddy, I wouldn't have had Julien and Serge, my sweet boys, and I might not have built Ms. Match with Tori. According to his social media, Paul was happily married with two kids up in Vermont. Things turned out the way they were supposed to, but sometimes I still couldn't help but wonder…what if?

An hour and a half after leaving the airport, we finally arrived at the gate for Silver Sage Ranch. After being on a plane for so long, my body was looking forward to a long bath, a hot meal, and maybe a walk around the property. I'd expected a fancy entrance, something like stone pillars or a fountain surrounded by a professionally manicured flower bed; instead, we drove up to a red gate, slightly rusted, with a humble sign hanging over it, the name of the ranch burned into the wood. That was a surprise. Maybe the resort was going for the earthy, minimalist vibe?

Matthew hopped out of the truck and swung open the gate like someone who had done it a million times. Then he climbed back inside the SUV.

"Welcome to Silver Sage Ranch, Mrs. Wagonblast. I sure hope you enjoy your time here."

CHAPTER 3

MATTHEW

*I*t was an understatement to say that our ranch's new guest wasn't our typical visitor. When I spotted her outside the airport terminal with her sleek hairdo and head-to-toe black outfit and designer shades, I assumed she wasn't waiting for me. She was absolutely gorgeous in a classy, expensive kind of way, and we didn't get many people dressing like her out here. From the diamond studs in her ears to the designer labels on her luggage, nothing about her said "wilderness lover" except the awe in her eyes as we drove through southeastern Wyoming, the place I called home. She clearly found the scenery beautiful, but her choice of our ranch bewildered me. There were so many guest ranches in the state, not to mention neighboring states, that offered more of a high-end experience. Why stay with us at Silver Sage?

Eventually, she mentioned her sister found our ranch, which offered an explanation. Perhaps she believed Lauren needed a more rugged experience, away from her pampered lifestyle? If that was the case, she was in for a surprise, and I needed to prepare myself for complaints, which was irritating to say the least. The ranch couldn't afford a poor review from someone who didn't do their research before taking a trip out west.

As we drove to Silver Sage, I reminded myself that I was jumping to judgment. I didn't know this woman at all and probably shouldn't be creating a personality for her based on her jewelry and luggage. That was something I had a tendency to do—size people up and try to predict who they were and how to handle them. It helped me make sure guests had a good ranch experience, but I wasn't always right. As we drove together, I discovered she had a sense of humor and wasn't raised in the lap of luxury. Maybe my initial assumptions about her were wrong.

The four-mile ride from the gate of the ranch to the main buildings was a bumpy one, and I mean that literally. Rocks and ruts pitted the dirt road, resulting in a jerky ride that tested a vehicle's shocks. As we bounced along in our seats, I glanced over at my new guest.

"You doing okay?"

She'd hidden her eyes behind dark sunglasses, but it was clear from the tension in her jawline that she was gritting her perfectly straight white teeth. "I'm glad I'm not the one driving this road. You're clearly an expert."

She was flattering me, and to be honest, it was working on me. Internally, I smacked myself for driving one-handed, showing off my dirt road navigational skills when she was probably only being kind. Was a woman like Lauren really impressed by a guy who arrived to pick her up in a filthy vehicle and an equally dirty shirt? I needed to get a grip and go take a cold shower. It wasn't professional to be thinking about a guest in that kind of way.

"I can't wait to settle in," she said. "Maybe I'll take a long walk. I hear there's some lovely hiking out here."

I tried to ignore the lines of her long legs as she stretched them out in the seat next to me. "There are lots of beautiful views. All joking aside, how do you really feel about cows?"

"Why?" She didn't sound pleased.

"We let our neighbor's cattle graze on our land so you might meet some of the herd when you're hiking. They're truly harmless, I promise."

"Oh. Good to know."

It didn't sound good with her. Was she a staunch vegetarian or allergic to cattle? The last thing I needed was a high maintenance visitor right now.

"We offer guided hikes, so if that would be more appealing, I can arrange one for you." Guided hikes. Ha! No one on staff had time for that kind of thing, but I'd have to take time out of someone's schedule if she wanted a guide. I couldn't have her running into wayward cows, then suing me for emotional trauma. "Are you a vegetarian?"

Damn, I hoped not. If I didn't tell Chef Damon ahead of time that we had a guest with special dietary needs, he had a hissy fit.

"No," she said. "I'm an omnivore."

Thank God. Also, who used words like omnivore in casual conversation?

"Speaking of food, dinner will be in the dining room at six, and you can sit wherever you'd like." I tried to think of a way to explain our current guest situation. "The ranch is a bit under-booked currently. We have a larger party coming in a few weeks, but right now there are two families here, the Jernigans and the Shahs. And you, of course."

"Wow, that's it?"

Her surprise concerned me. Our lack of bookings probably signaled to her we were a subpar establishment, and I hurried to set her straight.

"Don't worry." I smiled at her confidently. "That just means you'll get personalized service from us."

Having made that promise, I could only pray Chef Damon wouldn't choose that night to have a relapse. When he was sober, he produced amazing meals. Unfortunately, the man liked his wine, and the grapes made him unpredictable.

I parked the truck outside our main office, a small log cabin with a tiny front porch and a welcome sign on the door.

"I'll check you in here," I said. "Then my right-hand man Tyler can take you and your bags to your cabin. We don't have roads for our trucks all throughout the guest areas because you wouldn't want to hear us driving around when you're trying to rest and relax. Instead, we use golf carts to deliver things to the cabins and cottages."

We had twelve guest cabins of varying sizes and layouts, as well as two large houses, the Cottonwood Cottage and the Bluebell Cottage, that extended families or groups of friends could occupy. Unfortunately, we hadn't rented out the cottages in a while, but a large party was arriving in about three weeks to rent the entire ranch.

As we stood on the office's porch, I gestured toward the nearby buildings.

"That's the dining room over yonder." I shamefully peppered my speech with words like *howdy* and *yonder* when I was with guests to add to their Western experience. "And that's the Round Room where we have events like dancing and storytelling."

"And it's actually round," she said. "What a pretty wrap-around porch."

"Yeah, that's probably my favorite place on the property. In case you need to find me, you can look here in the office first, and if it's empty, pick up one of the walkie talkies and give me a shout."

"So the other office staff won't be here?" She looked completely perplexed that there would be no one else to answer phones and greet guests, and I wasn't about to inform her why that was the situation.

"Sometimes another staff member is in the office, but

we're often out on the property somewhere, helping guests or delivering things. You can also try my cell phone, but the walkies work better out here."

"Okay."

She was probably used to calling downstairs for room service and buckets of ice at all hours of the day and night. Unfortunately, I didn't have the money for full-time office staff or overnight employees to cater to our guests' midnight whims. I could only hope that the scenery and activities at the ranch would be enough to keep her happy. Those were the reasons people came here, not the premium service, although guests never seemed to mind. What we lacked in sparkle and shine, we made up for with warmth and personality.

We went inside the office so I could check her in using an archaic laptop whose processing speed was so slow it would have been faster to power it with a hamster on a wheel. As we waited for my screen to load, she looked at me warily.

"You do have WiFi, right?"

Well, crap.

"We do. It's not the strongest signal in the world, but we do have it. The office has the best connection, so if you need to do work while you're here, I'm happy to let you use my space." I pointed behind me. "I have a small private office back there."

"That's kind of you." She pulled off her sunglasses, and I got my first look at her eyes. Big brown peepers with thick, long lashes. Doe eyes, my mother would have called them. I stared into them, getting lost in their mahogany depths, until she spoke again. "Is it possible to get a glass of water?"

"Of course! Feel free to get a drink of your choice." I gestured over to the beverage station in the corner of the office, which was basically a water cooler and a machine that made hot drinks. When I replaced my parents' ancient Norelco automatic drip coffee maker, I thought I'd made a serious upgrade. Now, the single-serve beverage maker and basket of plastic pods that went with it, looked terribly low budget.

She crossed the room to take a closer look. "Ooh, what flavors of tea do you have?" Her face fell as she picked through our selection. "Actually, I think I'm okay right now."

"What's wrong?"

She smiled politely. "It's fine. I don't drink caffeine this late in the day and there's nothing decaf."

Well, crap on a cracker. "I can definitely order some. What do you like?"

"Decaf green tea is my favorite," she said. "But I don't want to put you to any trouble." She paused and licked her lips. "I do enjoy matcha lattes with oat milk in the morning. Do you have a coffee bar with a barista somewhere at the ranch?"

I felt my eyes widen. "A barista? Uh, no, ma'am." I still didn't understand how one squeezed milk from an oat or a nut, but I knew better than to admit that. "I'll do my best to get some matcha though, and I believe we have non-dairy milk in the kitchen."

The screen door to the office swung open with a loud creak.

"Hey, boss." Tyler sauntered into the office with our wrangler Walt close behind him. I'd radioed Tyler about taking the new guest to her cabin, but I didn't know why Walt was there, too. My first thought was that there was bad news.

"Everything okay?" I asked Walt.

"Yep." He leaned against the doorframe, kicking the heel of one boot in front of the toe of the other. "Came to tell you Sam got Doug sorted out. He gave him an injection for the swelling and said he should be fine in a day or two."

I breathed a sigh of relief. My brother Sam took care of

the ranch horses free of charge, and if he said Doug would be okay, I believed him.

"Excellent news. Please let me introduce our guest Lauren Wagonblast from New York."

They both tipped their cowboy hats and said a polite hello, not even blinking at the sound of her unusual last name, although I saw an amused twinkle in Walt's eyes.

"Tyler will take you to your cabin now," I told Lauren, "unless you need something else?" Something else I couldn't provide, like matcha lattes or a barista.

"No, I think I'll unpack and let my family know I arrived safely. I might take a little nap before dinner."

"I'll see you in the dining room at six."

We didn't have enough guests to do multiple sittings for dinner like we used to when the ranch was in its heyday. The Jernigans and Shahs were longtime visitors to the ranch, but it was tough to bring in new business when the facilities on the property were sorely outdated. If we didn't make improvements soon, even our loyal guests would stop coming.

"Yes," she said, "thank you so much. Nice meeting you, Walt." She turned and walked out of the office with Tyler, and I did my best not to assess her backside, although I couldn't say Walt showed the same restraint.

"Hey," I warned him. "Eyes up. This is a highbrow establishment."

Walt laughed and cocked his head to the side. "Is it?"

Over the years I'd known him, he hadn't changed much except for the fact that his black hair and mustache turned to a silvery gray. At sixty-four, he was still a skilled wrangler, no doubt about it, and the staff and guests adored him, but physically he was slowing down. Next summer, he'd definitely need a younger wrangler working with him.

"What's a lady like her doing out here?" Walt's voice had

grown gruff from age and the Marlboro Reds I'd been asking him to quit since I first met him.

"I guess she wanted a rugged ranch experience?" I scratched the back of my neck where I'd gotten a strip of sunburn from tending to the fence that morning. "Honestly, I have no idea."

"Give her the deluxe Silver Sage Ranch package then," he said with a wink.

"And what's that?" I waited for the punchline I knew was coming.

"The deluxe ranch package is everything you can think of selling her, from the super deluxe trail ride to the super deluxe cookout experience. That's how you keep this place afloat, dummy. Upcharge everything."

"I'm not going to fleece my guests, Walt."

"It's not fleecing if—"

There was a knock on the door, and we both spun around to see Lauren peeking her head inside. My stomach took a nosedive, and Walt swore under his breath as we braced ourselves for the dressing down we deserved.

"One more thing," she said in a cheery voice. "If either of you gentlemen head into town, I'd like to come with you. I didn't have proper hiking shoes at home, so I'd like to buy some here, as well as a few more things I might need. Oh, and I'd really like to get the deluxe ranch experience. Don't skimp on a single thing while I'm here." She let the screen door slam shut in her wake.

I dropped my head into my hands as Walt cackled. No wonder this place was about to go belly up.

CHAPTER 4

MATTHEW

*I*nstead of entering the dining room through the door used by guests, I passed through the kitchen so I could check on Damon Gansevoort, our head chef. This was my nightly ritual. When I hired him at the start of the previous summer, he'd told me he was recently sober and asked me to keep the dinner wine out of the kitchen. We both quickly learned that he needed much more distance than that from temptation.

After the first evening with a drunk cook at the stove stirring up scorched risotto, I worked harder to make sure none of the wine made its way into his hands. I did such a good job securing the wine that he moved on to the stash of liquor in the Round Room and went on another bender. When I called him into my office to fire him, he confessed he'd lost his daughter and wife in a car accident and, when those memories hit, he'd do whatever was necessary to get a drink to numb the pain. I couldn't help but empathize with the guy, especially having recently lost my own parents in a wreck. I pledged to keep him on staff and lock away all the alcohol on the premises. My efforts were successful, and we signed a contract for him to return the following summer season.

This summer, he'd only had one incident, and, fortunately, it was the night of our cookout, so he wasn't required to prepare food for guests, anyway. Now I lived in fear of him tumbling off the wagon again, so to speak. The second I walked into the kitchen and heard him barking directions at his sous chef, an unflappable young woman aptly named Serenity, I knew he was fine. Bad mood, good food was the saying around here.

"Evening, Serenity."

She glanced over her shoulder while still agitating a pan on the stove. "Hi, boss."

Every day, I was thankful that Serenity didn't take our chef's moods personally. In fact, it appeared they were developing a mentor-student relationship. One day in the staff mess hall, I even heard her gently tease him, and he'd nearly smiled. A small miracle.

Chef, which was not only Damon's job title but what we called him around the ranch, stood at a different stove, sampling a chunk of what looked like fried potato. The intense concentration on his face told me he knew more about flavors than anyone I'd ever met. In response to whatever he tasted, he added several dashes of Kosher salt to the roasting pan.

"Evening, Chef."

His silence didn't surprise me. When he was cooking, he didn't bother with the niceties like greetings or "God bless you" when someone sneezed. In fact, if you sneezed in his kitchen, he'd probably take a meat cleaver to one of your limbs. Sometimes I forgot about his germophobia, which is why I reached out to taste one of the recently washed green beans sitting in a colander.

"Are these local?" I asked.

Chef snapped a kitchen cloth in my direction. "Do not infect my vegetables with your grubby hands. And, yes, they're local."

I lifted an eyebrow at him. "Is that any way to speak to the man who pays your salary?"

"Fine, put your paws all over them." He picked up a giant roasting pan full of chopped vegetables and carried it to one of our industrial-sized ovens. "And when you pass Giardia to your guests, you can explain to the health department how it happened."

I backed away from the vegetables. "It's not like I've had my hands in cow excrement today, but okay."

Serenity looked over at me, waiting to see if I was going to push things further. I wasn't. Damon was sober, the kitchen smelled delicious, and, by the look of things, the meal would roll out on time. All this good news had me feeling downright optimistic.

"And I'm not making chicken tenders for those kids out there," Chef said. "If they want shitty food, they can go to The Marmot."

The Mangy Marmot was a bar and grill owned by a good friend of mine, and I didn't appreciate his slight on her establishment. "Fine, if anyone requests chicken tenders, Serenity will cook them because we're here to make our guests happy, even if we think it's beneath us to do so."

Chef whirled around and headed to his rack of saucepans. "Fine. Now get out of my kitchen."

I was pretty mellow when it came to his moods, but I was still his boss, and he needed to show me some basic respect. "Excuse me?"

He lit the burner, sighing deeply. "*Please* get out of my kitchen so I can focus."

"Slightly better." I plucked a bean out of the colander while his back was turned and winked at Serenity.

Out in the dining room, Gigi was already sitting at our usual table, head bent over a book. None of our guests had arrived yet, so I chomped on the green bean as I headed over to my daughter. Before taking my seat, I tipped my head so I could read the title on the cover.

"Another dystopian novel, huh?" I couldn't imagine finding it entertaining to read about the end of the world, especially when it seemed to be happening in real time, but to each their own.

"Uh huh…" She didn't look up when she spoke.

"Please put the book away now that I've joined you." I took it out of her hands and marked her place before closing it.

"You're not supposed to fold the pages!" she squealed. "Our school librarian told us that's one of the worst things you can do to a book."

I tried to undo the damage by smoothing out the crease I'd made. "Sorry."

She pulled a bookmark with a stallion on it out of her back pocket and slid it between the pages. "Seriously, Dad, you should know better at your age."

It was bad enough I made her eat in the dining room when she'd begged me to eat in the staff kitchen instead. Now I tried to fold a page down in her book? The audacity.

"Who's that lady?" she asked, pointing to Lauren who was entering the dining room. From her silver sandals to her silky black dress, all the way up to her delicate diamond earrings, she was the picture of elegance and grace. She gave me a little wave as she took a seat at a window-adjacent table, and I smiled back at her, trying to look like a professional ranch owner and not a goofy bumpkin.

"Don't point," I told Gigi. "She's a guest from New York. Lauren Wagonblast."

"What?" Gigi bugged out her eyes. "I know we're not supposed to make fun of people's names, but Wagonblast? That's awful. Poor lady. And she's here all by herself. Do you think she's alone because of her terrible name?"

"No, Gigi, I don't think that's the reason. Some people like to travel by themselves."

She had a point, though. I couldn't ever remember a woman coming to the ranch by herself.

Gigi shrugged. "Okay. She just looks like someone who would go to a big city on vacation to visit museums or something like that."

She was right again. Never in my life had I used the word "chic" but when I looked at Lauren Wagonblast (unfortunate name aside), I understood she was the definition of it.

"Maybe she wanted a change." I thought about her request for matcha lattes and hoped the change she wanted included her beverages.

"Maybe she's a fugitive from justice," Gigi suggested. "Or a government spy." She watched Lauren with the eyes of someone with a big imagination. "She could also be here to give us a review. You should treat her really well and make sure she has a good time."

The deluxe ranch treatment, I thought with a cringe. I didn't believe for one second that a magazine or website sent Mrs. Wagonblast to review the ranch. We should only be so lucky.

I tugged on Gigi's braid. "You should be a writer someday, since you're so good at making up stories about people. I need to go over and say hello to her."

As I strode over to Lauren's table, I prayed Chef was going to prepare something magnificent tonight. She looked like someone who was used to five-star meals, and I needed him to put on his best cooking performance for her first night at the ranch.

"Good evening," I said to her with a tip of my head.

"Hello, Matthew." She smiled up at me, and I was under the spell of those brown eyes again. "How are you?"

"I'm well, thank you." It was time to put on those fancy

manners my mother taught me. "I hope your accommodations are to your liking?"

"My cabin is fine," she said. "The bed is so comfortable that I slept for an hour this afternoon. I was wondering, do you have a map of the ranch?"

"I have some in the office," I said, "but, honestly, once you walk around the property tomorrow, you'll have this area figured out in no time. All the buildings are concentrated in one area. You will want a map for the hiking trails, though. If you plan to go on a long hike alone, make sure you tell us first and take enough water with you, of course."

She nodded, but her eyes told me she still had questions. "How do I make a reservation for the spa?"

"You mean the hot springs?" I was glad she'd asked about this amenity because it was something special we offered. A few years back, a Canadian named Luke Daltry moved to Three Rivers, the town nearest to the ranch, and renovated the facilities at the hot springs. The mineral waters were supposed to have healing properties, and guests had raved about their experiences over there.

"We offer trips by request," I continued. "It's prettier under the stars, so we usually go in the evening. Plus, it's nice to soak after a day of riding."

Lauren tilted her head and frowned. "No, I mean the spa here at the ranch. I'd like to look a t the menu of everything you offer."

I widened my stance, feeling like our conversation was about to hit a rut in the road. "We don't have that kind of spa at Silver Sage." Had she really booked a trip here when she knew nothing about us? The best I could offer for a facial was some locally sourced eggs and milk. Actually, that sounded more like an omelet than something a lady would put on her face.

"You don't have a spa? Are you sure?" She was looking at me like I was the one who had gotten bad information.

"Pretty darn sure." I took a deep breath and tamped down my irritation. "I'm not sure why you thought we did."

"When my sister described this place, it sounded very different from what I'm seeing here. I'm just wondering if there's been some mistake." She looked worried now, and worried wasn't good.

"We had your reservation." My chest tightened as I prepared myself for a confrontation. First, she heard us talking about the "deluxe ranch package," and now this? "You're paid in full for the week, so I don't believe there's been a mistake on our part."

"It's almost like she sent me to the wrong Silver Sage Ranch," she said with a little laugh.

"There's not another one in Wyoming," I said. "Someone did tell me about a Silvery Sage Resort and Spa that opened last summer in Montana, but that's nowhere near here. Not even the same state."

Her eyes widened. "Did you say Montana?"

Oh crap. "Yes."

"Oh, my God." She pressed her hand to her forehead. "I think I'm at the wrong ranch."

MANY THINGS CAN GO wrong for guests when they're on vacation—accidents, health conditions, family conflicts, emergencies back home. We'd dealt with our fair share of these events at the ranch, both the odd and unexpected as well as the routine. In our history, however, I couldn't remember a guest ever coming here by mistake.

After Lauren's revelation, she stepped outside to call her sister, and from what I saw through the window, it looked like quite an animated conversation. Yikes. Someone was in trouble. A few minutes later, she returned to tell me her sister asked an assistant to book Lauren a trip to Silvery Sage

Resort and Spa in Montana. That person did some half-assed Googling and booked her a stay at Silver Sage Ranch in Wyoming instead. I had many reasons not to feel bad about the situation, one of them being that this other outfit stole our name. Still, my instinct was to solve the problem for everyone's benefit.

"I promise we can make sure you have an outstanding stay at the original Silver Sage Ranch," I assured her. "Please sleep on it and consider giving us a chance."

She looked exhausted and shell-shocked, and she didn't seem at all convinced. And yes, I sounded desperate because I was. We direly needed the money she'd paid us, and although, technically, I didn't have to give her a refund, I had this annoying thing called a conscience. There was only one way to fix the situation—I needed her to stay put and have a wonderful time.

"I'll think about it over dinner," Lauren said. "I'm sorry to involve you in my mess."

"It's fine," I said, backing off. "Mistakes happen." I was glad it wasn't my mistake.

Fortunately, the dinner Chef prepared was delicious, and although our server Kyra, who was Tyler's girlfriend, wasn't the most genteel person in the world, she had a bright smile and a friendly attitude. Overall, I thought the meal went down well and might even sway Lauren toward staying a few more days. While she was having her coffee and dessert, I returned to her table.

"I'm sorry to bother you again," I said, "but I wanted to make sure everything was satisfactory with your meal and that you have everything you need for tonight?"

"The food was wonderful," she said. "Thank you for checking on me."

I could tell by the tension in her smile what she was really thinking. "But you're leaving, anyway."

"It's honestly nothing personal. I just think it's best if I go to Montana, as originally planned." She knitted her hands together on her lap, toying with the wedding ring on her slim finger. "I'm probably more of a resort and spa person, really. I insist on paying for my week here, of course. It's not your fault that a mistake was made on my end."

I'd never seen anyone look so unhappy when they were about to embark on a week at a high-dollar spa. If she'd seemed excited about her trip, I would have let it go, but I couldn't ignore the melancholy surrounding her decision, not when I knew the power of this place. I'd seen couples reignite their marriages at our ranch. I'd witnessed kids overcoming fears and building new confidence. We'd had families choose our ranch to celebrate birthdays, anniversaries and even one celebration-of-life service. What I was about to tell her about Silver Sage wasn't only in my self-interest, but in hers, too.

"May I sit down for a moment?" I asked.

She looked surprised but gestured to the seat across from her, and I took it. I measured my words carefully, as I always did with guests, but in this case, I was about to get more personal than usual.

"I don't know you well, Lauren, but I know this place. Silver Sage is pretty special. We have a lot to offer in the way of life-changing experiences. I also think you're underestimating yourself when you suggest you aren't the type to enjoy a dude ranch. You can saddle up and get out there on the trails again, and—I hope I can say this without sounding arrogant—you'll get more out of a week here than you would in two weeks at that fancy-pants spa." I wasn't sure if I'd gone too far, but she was listening intently. "And that has nothing to do with me. I've just seen some magical things happen for people at this ranch, and judging by the sadness in your eyes, I think this place could be what you need right now."

A smile flickered on the edges of her mouth. "You make a compelling case for staying."

"All I'm asking for is a couple of days. If you're not enjoying ranch life, no hard feelings. I'll drive you to the airport myself and wish you well at the resort in Montana."

"It is beautiful here." Her words unfolded slowly. "And my bed really is comfortable. Okay, I'll give it two more days and see how I feel."

"It's decided then." I clapped my hands together. "I think you're going to fall in love with Wyoming. Most people do."

CHAPTER 5

LAUREN

"Freaking Sully," Tori fumed when I called for the second time that evening about the botched booking. "What am I going to do with that girl?"

Sully, short for Sullivan, was a sweet young woman from Savannah and a recent hire who didn't have the attention to detail necessary for a fast-paced administrative job. If we wanted to avoid firing her, Tori needed to find something else for her to do at the company.

My sister's anger soothed my own. "I keep telling you it's fine. This place isn't bad. It's just kind of…empty."

"Like *Psycho* empty?" Her voice had gone up an octave, and I knew she was freaking out.

"No, like the ranch has seen better days kind of empty. It's actually got a lot of charm though, and the landscape here is absolutely gorgeous. I've never seen so much blue sky in my life. The downside is that the facilities are a bit rundown and the staff is limited, from what I can tell."

She clearly wasn't listening to me. "I'm going to call the resort in Montana right now and reserve you a room there, and then we'll figure out your flights. If they're full, we'll find you a different resort to stay at. You should be relaxing and pampering yourself."

"I told the owner I'd stay at least a few days," I said. "Let me see how it goes, and I'll update you, okay?"

"How about I reserve a room and then, if you don't want it, I'll cancel?"

I sighed, knowing two things were true—I'd never win this argument, and she had a point. "Fine, make a reservation for me."

"So what's the deal with this ranch owner who convinced you to stay? A grown son running a vacant hotel in the middle of nowhere sounds very *Psycho* to me." Her wild imagination always cracked me up.

"There are other guests here, and Matthew has a cute daughter and seems totally normal. I really don't get serial killer vibes from him. Also, I can't face packing and traveling again, so it's better if I stay put for a little while."

"How old is this Matthew guy?" Oh no, I'd piqued her interest. The matchmaker in my sister smelled testosterone, and that wasn't good.

"Probably around our age. I'm not sure."

"Is he attractive?" I knew why she was asking this question. Did his gorgeous blue eyes and perfect forearms have anything to do with why I agreed to stay at the ranch? Possibly, but I would never admit it.

"He's attractive, but I'm not interested in him that way." I was such a liar. "My life is complicated enough right now. I don't need to add sex with a ranch owner to it. Besides, it wouldn't be fair involving someone else in my drama. What if the press found out?"

"Oh, please. You're in Bumblefuck, Wyoming. No one is ever going to find out about what happens there."

For some reason, I resented her flippant assessment of this place. "It's actually magnificent out here. The air is so clean and fresh. It's delightful, really."

She paused before responding. "You sound so much calmer. No panic attacks on the flight or afterwards?"

"Not one." The panic attacks, which were a wave of impending doom that knocked me to my knees, had begun long before Freddy's full frontal moment at the party. My doctor thought they were a combination of work and personal stress, and he prescribed anxiety medication as a cure. They didn't happen as often now, but one occasionally hit, and I had to breathe and visualize my way through them.

"Thank God. I've been really worried about you, honey."

"I know." Her sisterly concern put a lump in my throat. "I'm sorry for making you worry. I should never have kept the marriage charade going for so long."

"Don't you dare apologize to me. You did nothing wrong, and we all know that. Freddy is the only villain in this story, and karma will get him, eventually. I hesitate to tell you this, but Joyce called me this morning. Do you want to hear what she said?"

Our agent, Joyce Cohen, negotiated all our deals pertaining to the show, and Tori was probably about to tell me that my marital drama had shot our chances at selling the rights to *Ms. Match* to a streaming service. This nightmare would never end.

"Hit me with it. I'm lying down right now so this is a good time in case I faint."

"Stop catastrophizing. This is good news. Direct Play isn't the only company vying for the syndication rights for our show. Two other streaming services have come forward with offers, and there's a freaking bidding war going on!"

My heart rate sped up. "Are you kidding me?"

"Nope. It's happening." She bubbled over with excitement. "This whole Freddy situation has been horrible for you personally, but it's also bringing new viewers to *Ms. Match*, and our value has skyrocketed. Sorry, I don't mean to sound so happy about profiting from your heartache."

"Hell, something good should come out of it. I just can't believe it." Although I shouldn't have been surprised. Drama sold.

"I know," she said. "Thank goodness I pushed for executive producer credits for both of us, or we would have gotten hosed in all of this. The numbers they're talking, Lolo…it's a lot." She told me the amount, and my jaw dropped.

She continued talking as my brain tried to catch up with what she was telling me. We were already living a lifestyle I never even dreamed of as a kid, but this kind of money was way beyond that. This was serious syndication money.

"If you're cool with it," she said, "Joyce will negotiate the best deal she can get us and then, once we approve it, she'll send the contracts over to our lawyers. It's going to move quickly."

"Of course, go for it." I looked around my little cabin, wondering what *Ms. Match* viewers would think of me now, huddled under a Pendleton blanket and thumbing through a magazine called *Fly Fisherman* while eating airport snacks. Not exactly the glamorous life one would expect of someone about to earn millions on a syndication deal. "Thank you for taking care of all this. I feel guilty that I'm here when this deal is going down in New York."

"Stop. I don't mind at all. There's a couple more important things to think about before we sign onto this though. If you do the deal before you finalize your divorce, this becomes a marital asset. You'd have to split it with Freddy."

"Oh, hell no!" This man had taken enough from me already. He wasn't getting my syndication money too. "That's not happening."

"Exactly. Which is why you need to get your divorce papers moving and get Freddy to sign them ASAP. I told Joyce that the deal needs to be kept completely quiet in the press because we can't have Freddy finding out about it and using it as leverage in the divorce."

"Damn it." The thought of giving him one more dime made me sick to my stomach. "I'll talk to my lawyer again and see where we're at with the settlement."

"Good. Put it on the fast track. Here's the other thing that worries me. As much as we'd both profit from this deal, you know what it means if people watch all the old episodes."

Of course I did. "It's going to turn into a game of *Where's Waldo* with everyone looking for Freddy."

Tori was the star of the show, but viewers liked seeing me, her twin sister, interacting with her. Freddy only appeared in a handful of episodes across five seasons, always because I'd paid him to film with us, but those few appearances would now be gold. Who knew what viewers would extrapolate from seeing Freddy and me on screen together? Streaming our show in its entirety would certainly keep my personal drama alive in the press and on social media.

"Just remember," Tori said, "this kind of money would make it easier to keep your private life private from now on. That kind of insulation from the world doesn't come cheap."

"Plus, I have to pay for this divorce." Bitterness crept into my tone. "He's going to get half of what we have, and I'll probably have to pay him alimony, too. We're going to ask him to take a lump sum instead. I really want to walk away from this marriage and never have to deal with Freddy again. Ever."

"I don't know how realistic that is," she said gently. "Graduations, weddings, grandkids—Serge and Julien will keep you and Freddy in each other's lives."

"I *hate* that, but you're right." We'd worked so hard to make sure our marital issues didn't affect the children, and it was hard to admit that my maneuvering resulted in more pain and embarrassment than if I'd divorced Freddy years ago.

"Julien called me today," she said, "and from the way he was talking, he wants nothing to do with Freddy ever again.

He said you told him to forgive his dad for hooking up with a bartender at a public event, which means you're a better woman than I am."

Serge and Julien both knew Freddy and I had privately separated, and Serge seemed to believe that Freddy's "mistake" at Jentori was an embarrassing error in judgment but not a betrayal of me. Julien, my fiercely loyal rule follower, saw it differently.

"My higher self prevailed," I said with a sigh. "I don't want him to hate his dad for my sake."

"You're a seriously good human. I'll hate Freddy forever, though, and you'll never convince me otherwise. If I could have him permanently exiled from the United States, I would. Hell, if I could make him disappear completely, that would even be better, but I can't go to jail, Lolo. I need my gel nails and weekly blowouts."

I laughed, but I knew she was only half kidding. "I can't believe I'm at the wrong ranch."

She clicked her tongue. "I know, right? This is something that would happen to me, not you."

It was true. Normally, I over-planned everything so that my copious lists had sub-lists. As a finance person, I rarely left anything to chance, and I'd surprised myself by not being more upset about Sully's error. Maybe being publicly humiliated had broken something inside of me. I wasn't even completely sure what clothing I'd packed in my bag until I put everything away in the cabin's closet and dresser.

"My mind hasn't been razor sharp lately. I keep thinking about what happened that night." I pinched the bridge of my nose and squeezed my eyes shut. "She had her hands in his pants, Tori. What was he thinking? We were all right on the other side of that curtain. Is he some kind of adrenaline junkie? I know people have sex in public places, but that was just so…"

"Stupid," she finished for me. "It was stupid. He was

thinking with his dick, and he's probably in a midlife crisis. I know it seems like life won't get better, honey, but it will. This too shall pass, as Mom says."

"I know. I need to think about other things and not dwell on the past." Easier said than done. "Hey, apparently, there are cows on this ranch who might join me on my hikes."

"Good God, we need to get you out of there. Do cows attack humans?"

"Pretty sure they're peaceful creatures. At least I hope so." I shook a handful of trail mix from the bag into my hand. "Someday we're going to look back on all of this and laugh. Right now I want to cry."

"Don't cry," she said. "Or do if it makes you feel better. I'm going to chew out Sully and make that reservation, just in case."

"Thanks, sis."

"No problem. I love you. And send me a picture of this Matthew guy when you get a chance. I need an image in my mind."

How did she realize he was hot when I hadn't confirmed it? Twin sister second sense was the only explanation.

"Fine, I'll try to get one when he's not looking. That won't be weird at all."

I'd have to find Matthew in the morning anyway. If I planned to hike, I was going to need something other than sandals to wear. There had to be a store somewhere in the area. Every time I thought about that wrangler telling Matthew to give me the "deluxe ranch experience," I laughed. It was only funny because Matthew had sounded so horrified by the idea of tricking me. My gut was right about him being an honest person. If only I'd gone with my gut in those days leading up to my wedding and not married Freddy. By the time I'd realized he might not be a man of integrity, we'd already invited three hundred of our closest friends and family to attend our nuptials at his cousin's villa in Provence.

Canceling a destination wedding felt catastrophic at the time, and I convinced myself that his flirtatiousness and self-centered behavior would get better.

Not so much.

"Get those divorce papers signed," she said. "I don't care if you have to offer him more now. You're going to do so well in this syndication deal that you can afford to pay him a little extra to get this thing over with. Remember that."

We hung up the phone, and I knew I should feel euphoric about the syndication deal. Money brought independence, and this was the culmination of many years of hard work. Except…sometimes it seemed like my professional life was the only place where I was winning. Yes, I had two wonderful kids, I couldn't forget about that, but they were both grown up and didn't need me much anymore. My siblings were both in serious relationships, and I'd let a lot of my friendships fizzle out. My apartment was quiet in the evenings, and for the first time in my adult life, I was lonely. Did I want a romantic relationship? A new career challenge? A trip on one of those cruise ships that sails around the world? I wasn't exactly sure, but something had become clear in my mind on that beautiful drive to the ranch. There had to be another adventure in store for the second half of my life, and I was going to find it.

CHAPTER 6

MATTHEW

*T*yler, sweaty and dirty from a morning of putting a new belt on the dryer, poked his head into the office. It brought back memories of when I was around his age, finished with college and helping my parents run the ranch. This place used to be bustling with guests from May through August, and everyone in the family was expected to pitch in and do their part. Tyler seemed to love the place as much as I did, and I wished he could have seen it in its prime.

"I'm gonna head out in a few minutes to pick up supplies in town," he said, "but I need a shower first."

"Sounds good. Take my truck. Keys are in it."

That was one of the nice things about living at the ranch —you never had to lock a car door. You might need to carry bear spray with you, but that was another story.

He nodded crisply. "You got it. Okay if Gigi comes with me?"

She was somewhere on the premises, but I wasn't exactly sure where she'd gone after grabbing a muffin from the breakfast tray in the staff mess hall. Probably to the stables.

"I think she'd love that, Ty. Thanks. You can call her on the walkie. She has it with her." Gigi looked up to Tyler and his girlfriend Kyra like the older siblings she never had. They were good kids to choose as role models—hard working, responsible and level-headed.

After he was gone, I worked on some accounting, trying not to think about my intriguing guest from Manhattan. She wasn't at breakfast, at least not when I stopped by the dining room, and I needed to find her soon so we could book some activities for the day. Why was she wearing a wedding ring but vacationing by herself? And why was her sister planning trips for her? Lauren Wagonblast was certainly a woman of mystery. It felt like she was running from something, but I couldn't understand what that could be.

As if on cue, she strode into the office wearing black shorts that exposed her tanned, shapely legs. My heartbeat quickened at the sight of her like a damn schoolboy with a crush. She'd paired her shorts with a white t-shirt that somehow looked a lot more expensive than the white t-shirt I was wearing, even though they both seemed to be made of cotton. Must have been the way she wore it, and she did wear it well.

"Good morning," she said. "I came to check if anyone is heading to town today?" She glanced toward my bluetooth speaker. "You listen to K-pop?"

"Ummm…" Dammit, I'd left Blackpink playing without realizing it. I reached over and slapped the power button. "My daughter loves this band, and I listen so I can relate. You know how it is." I shrugged and sighed, to clarify that I was doing it for my kid. "Parenting."

Why couldn't I have been listening to Willie Nelson or John Prine or something else cool for a fifty-one-year-old man working in his office? The truth was, Gigi listened to these songs so much they'd become earworms for me. If one came into my head, I had to play it or I'd be humming those stupid lyrics all day.

"It's cool you're trying to connect with her that way. I still listen to pop music from the eighties and nineties." She smiled self-consciously. "I guess that makes me old."

"I don't think anyone could see you as old." Was that the best compliment I could come up with? I'd completely lost my touch with women.

"Thank you, that's sweet. I came in to ask about a ride to the shops in town. I really need better shoes for hiking."

I looked down at her feet, clad in gold sandals that looked like something out of a gladiator movie. She'd painted her toenails the same color as her cheeks when she blushed. Dammit, even her feet were irresistible, and I wasn't even the foot fetish type.

In the hubbub of my busy day, I'd forgotten that she'd made a request for a ride to the store. Tyler was going into downtown Three Rivers, and he could take her with him. She didn't know that though, and he hadn't left yet, which gave me an idea.

"I'm heading into town in a few minutes if you want a ride." I snapped my laptop shut. "It's about a thirty-minute drive, door to door, but you'll find a store there that can supply what you need." Should I be going into town with everything I had on my plate that day? Probably not, but I was doing it, anyway.

"Really?" Her big brown eyes widened, her pretty pink lips parted slightly, and a surge of desire rushed through me like lightning in a storm. "That would be great. I can grab my purse and be back in five minutes if that works for you?"

I stood up from my seat and found I needed to readjust myself. Nothing like getting overexcited about driving a lady into town. Was I sixteen again? I needed to get it together and act like a proper ranch manager.

"Sounds fine. I'll be here."

I watched her walk back to her cabin, then sprinted to staff housing to find Tyler. The staff cabin for the men—two rooms with bunk beds separated by a communal bathroom—wasn't far away, but it was uphill and I was panting by the time I got there. I found Tyler heading toward the bathroom with his shampoo and towel in hand.

"You don't need to do the supply run," I said between gasps. "I'm gonna do it myself."

"Are you sure?" He tossed the towel over his shoulder. "I don't mind going."

"No, it's fine. I need a few things in town." I was still a dad and needed to figure out what my daughter would do while I was gone. "Maybe Gigi could take a trail ride?"

He looked slightly baffled, no doubt wondering why I'd run there like I was being chased, but he didn't question me about it. I knew I liked that boy.

"Sure," he said. "She can help Walt with today's guest ride. She loves showing off her skills."

"Perfect! Thanks, Ty."

As I sauntered back to the office, I literally smacked the smile off my face.

"Get it together, dumbass," I muttered to myself. "She's a guest, not your new girlfriend."

Who did think I was, getting excited about driving this woman anywhere? She wore a wedding ring, a clear sign she was taken, not to mention that the diamond on it was probably worth as much as this ranch. Well, maybe not that much, but it was a huge rock. There was also the issue of her preference for fancy spas over dude ranches. My eyes needed to stay focused on one thing, and that was making sure she had a wonderful time at Silver Sage and stayed for the full week. Maybe she'd even write us a nice review or tell her friends about our place.

Just be cool, Matthew Hart. Play it cool.

"Do you mind if we make a quick stop at the vet's office before we hit the store?" I asked Lauren as we drove toward town. "I need to pick something up from my brother. I've got a barn cat with worms." If ever there was a sentence that reminded me a woman like Lauren was out of my league, it was "I've got a barn cat with worms." I loved my Wyoming lifestyle, but it sure wasn't glamorous. Fortunately, Lauren didn't ask me to take her directly to the nearest airport.

"Of course, that's fine." She pulled her sunglasses out of her bag and slid them on her face. "I have no plans today except shopping for appropriate shoes and learning more about ranch life. I'm looking forward to checking out Three Rivers."

"It's a small town." I didn't want her expectations to get too high. "Population of less than two thousand people." Guests came to the ranch to spend time outdoors, away from civilization, so I rarely had to play tour guide in Three Rivers. "As far as shopping, we've got The General Store, Ranch Apparel, Feed & Grain, and a Family Dollar. Probably not the type of shopping you're accustomed to in New York."

"I'm not expecting there to be a Saks Fifth Avenue," she said dryly.

"That's good because high fashion here is a new pair of boots and a Stetson."

"See, that's perfect. Maybe I'll buy some boots. I want to sample the local flavors and see where people shop and hang out. That's the fun part of traveling to new places." She seemed more cheerful than the previous day, like maybe she'd gotten some good rest and woken up with a more positive outlook on life.

"Oh!" I snapped my fingers. "I forgot. We also have a new beauty parlor with a gift shop inside it. I've heard they sell some nice things, but I can't be sure because I get my hair cut at the ranch."

"By your wife?" Lauren asked. Was she putting feelers out to see if I was married?

"No, by Walt." I laughed at Lauren's shocked expression.

"The man I met in the office yesterday? Your head wrangler?"

I didn't realize how odd it sounded until I saw her reaction.

"Yep. He cuts Tyler's hair, too." When my brothers and I were little kids, Walt buzzed our hair every summer. Somehow, he got into the routine of cutting it for us during the school year, too, when my father allowed us to grow it out a little longer. As an adult living in Cheyenne, I went to a proper barber, but then I moved back to the ranch two years ago and Walt offered to cut my hair again.

She studied my face. "I can't tell if you're serious or not."

"I'm serious. It's an hour round trip into town, so it's easier to let him do it. Maybe you should have him give you a fresh cut while you're here."

I liked the rich, throaty sound of her laugh. "Yeah, right. I have to say, your hair looks very nice. Walt does good work."

My neck turned pink under her gaze. "Well, thank you, ma'am."

She shifted in her seat so she was no longer looking my way. "What's your brother the veterinarian like?"

"Sam's the comedian of the family," I said. "He's the knuckle-headed youngest kid who always loved making everyone laugh. He's also a damn fine vet, and an asset to this community, honestly. But don't tell him I said that. He already has a swelled head. I think you'll like him, that is, if he's around the office today."

It wasn't until I was an adult that I realized Sam used humor to defuse the tension between our father and our brother Bowie. Dad was a rather domineering figure, and Bowie reacted to that like a rattlesnake backed into a corner.

Things didn't get really bad until Bowie was in high school and truly embraced the role of teen rebel. My reaction was to be the perfect eldest son, doing everything I could to please our parents and keep the peace. My sister Faith relied on her boyfriends to rescue her from the arguments at our house, and Sam told jokes. Good times.

"What do you want to do with the rest of your day when we get back to the ranch?" I asked. "You'll have the afternoon ahead of you. Maybe a trail ride or a hike?"

She bit her bottom lip. "Maybe. I'm still nervous about getting on a horse."

I wanted to tread gently but still encourage her. "I think you'll find that it's like riding a bike. It will come back to you."

She dipped her chin and stared at me. "My older son recently had a biking accident and broke his wrist."

"Okay, maybe that was a poor example."

She looked out the window for a few minutes before saying, "I used to be adventurous in my youth, believe it or not. I always loved swimming out into the breakers in the ocean, and I even hiked on the Appalachian Trail with my college boyfriend."

"So, what happened to that girl?" I asked.

She exhaled. "I got married and had children, and it felt like someone had to stop doing all the things that could potentially get them injured or killed."

"Is your husband a daredevil?" I asked.

"He races sailboats and likes fast cars." Her expression turned grim. "I guess I kind of became a killjoy, which probably wasn't much fun for him. I've changed a lot since we first met."

There was obviously more to that relationship story, but I certainly wasn't going to pry. "We've all changed since our twenties. Parenthood will definitely do that to you. You can't avoid all risks, though." I tapped my fingers on the steering wheel. "I told you my parents died in a random car accident, and one of my friends was killed in a freak electrical accident a few years ago. He was forty years old."

She reached over and touched my arm. "That's terrible, Matthew. I can't say this conversation makes me less scared of riding a horse though."

"My point is that you're at risk simply by being alive, no matter how small you make your world. I think it's better to live a full life, using good sense about your choices, obviously. Riding can be dangerous, but we can give you a gentle horse and a helmet, and you'd be with a guide. I think that's a risk worth taking."

"Right." She turned to look out her window. "I guess you have a point. I'd like to ride again. I used to love it as a kid."

"How old are your children?" I didn't always ask my guests so many personal questions, but the more I found out about Lauren, the more I wanted to know.

"They're in their twenties. Fully grown and out in the world. So if I get thrown by a mechanical bull while I'm out here, then I guess they'll be fine."

"I wasn't planning bull riding just yet," I said through my laughter, "but it's good to know you're up for anything."

She chuckled and leaned her head on her window. "I've been so exhausted. Mostly, I'm hoping to get my energy back this week."

She might think a spa was the best way to re-energize, but in my opinion she needed some joy in her life. As the owner and manager of a guest ranch in one of the most beautiful places in America, I could definitely provide the opportunities to find that joy. It was up to her whether she let herself experience it.

"This is it." I pulled the Suburban into the parking lot at Sam's office. "You don't have to come inside if you'd rather wait here."

"Do you mind if I come in?" She smiled, looking slightly

embarrassed. "I'm a huge fan of the show *All Creatures Great and Small*, and I'd love to see a country vet's office. I know that probably sounds silly."

If Sam saw me with a beautiful guest, he was either going to flirt with her or tease me, but there was no backing out now. "It might be a disappointment, but c'mon in."

Sam had only one employee, a woman in her sixties named Cherise who was his receptionist and vet tech. Having been raised on a farm, she wasn't intimidated by any animal, including ornery ranchers who wouldn't pay their vet bills. She looked at us over the rims of her reading glasses when we walked in the door.

"Good morning!" I called out to her.

"Hey, Matthew." She was already eyeing my companion up and down.

"Cherise St. Clair, please meet one of my guests this week, Lauren Wagonblast."

Lauren shot me a surprised look, as if I'd gotten her name wrong. Was there another way to pronounce Wagonblast?

"Good afternoon, Cherise." Lauren pushed back her sunglasses on her head, so they drew the sheet of silky dark hair away from her face.

Cherise dipped her chin without smiling. "Nice to meet you."

For her that was a warm welcome. If she said nothing, that meant she didn't take a shine to you. If she really disliked you, well, you weren't coming any further than the door.

"I guess you're here for Elijah's medication?" Cherise pulled a little brown bag off a shelf. Maybe we would avoid Dr. Samuel Hart on this trip after all. "You need to bring that tomcat in here to get fixed before he impregnates other strays."

"How dare you talk that way about my faithful barn cat." I took the bag from her. "He's my mouser, not a stray, and I'll bring him in to get neutered when I can convince Walt it needs to be done. Then I have to coax Elijah into a cat carrier without getting scratched to death."

Cherise folded her arms across her chest. "Sounds like no one told Elijah he's been domesticated."

"Very funny. What do I owe you for this?"

She shook her head and waved me away. "Sam told me I'm not allowed to charge you anything." Clearly, she thought this policy of giving freebies to family members was ludicrous. I agreed with her, but Sam wouldn't let me pay him.

"You've got enough expenses," my brother told me recently when he came out to the ranch to do routine dental exams on our stable of horses. He was right about that. The bills kept on coming.

"I'm going to total it up for our records anyway," Cherise said, making notes on a receipt pad and figuring out the tax on her calculator. No fancy spreadsheets for this lady, although there was a laptop sitting on the counter that my brother had tried to get her to use so their record keeping would be easier. No luck with that one yet. Cherise kept meticulous paper records though, and she could also wrangle rowdy cats like Elijah into carrying crates, so my brother wasn't letting her go any time soon.

Just when I thought we were in the clear, Sam stepped through the front door with his mischievous dog, Jake, at his heels. As soon as Jake saw me, he tore over on his little legs, springing up for my attention. Being a Jack Russell/dachshund mix, he could only reach my ankles with his front paws, but for a little guy, he had a big presence. Today he was wearing a blue sweater vest with the word diva knitted onto the back.

I reached down to scratch his ears. "Hey, buddy. How's the most spoiled dog in Three Rivers?"

Jake looked up at me with his soulful brown eyes, as if he

were telling me that tales of his lifestyle were greatly inflated. Nonsense. I knew he got treated like a little prince.

"What a cutie pie," Lauren cooed, as Jake scurried over to demand her attention next.

"Good afternoon, big brother and guest." Sam's eyes sparkled with interest when he saw I had a lady friend with me. Damn. I was in big trouble.

CHAPTER 7

MATTHEW

"I didn't know you were coming in today." Sam's eyes traveled over to Lauren. "You usually send Tyler."

This was exactly why I didn't want to run into him. Sam was the only person I knew who could stir shit up even when he wasn't trying. And when he was trying, look out.

"I needed him to do some chores back at the ranch." As I told the lie, my neck heated, so I tried to think of cold things like sled dog races and snowmobiling. If he saw me blushing, I was dead in the water.

"Boots off!" Cherise shouted.

Lauren flinched and shot me a worried look.

"She's not talking to us," I reassured her.

Sam untied his muddy work boots and kicked them off as he spoke. "She's fussing at me because I'm filthy."

Cherise muttered, "As usual."

"Where were you this morning?" I asked.

"Calf was born out at the Taylor place, and they wanted me to check it out." He stripped off his windbreaker, which was also streaked with mud. Then he put on a disgusting pair of green Crocs that were sitting in a basket by the door. I'd never understand his choice of footwear, but he insisted they were the most comfortable thing to wear around his office. "They thought it wasn't feeding well, but it's fine. He's just a little guy. A late bloomer like you, big brother."

I was nearly six foot two, but for most of my life, I'd been battling it out to be taller than Faith and Bowie. It wasn't until late high school when I shot up and filled out, and I still ended up an inch and a half shorter than Bowie. Faith clocked in at five feet ten, and Sam was the smallest brother at six feet even.

I took a deep breath and bit the bullet. "Samuel Hart, this is Lauren Wagonblast, one of Silver Sage's new guests this week. She's from Manhattan, and she's in town looking for some hiking boots."

There. I'd stated it reasonably, even if my intro did sound a little stilted.

Sam shook her hand, tossing her the grin he used to charm the ladies. I doubted it would work on a savvy New Yorker like Lauren, and I found myself hoping it wouldn't.

"Is that right?" Sam said. "I love New York City. What part are you from?" He knew I was eager to get away and was milking this visit for all it was worth.

"Born and raised on Long Island." She elided the G and I in Long Island, so it sounded like one word. She didn't have a strong New York accent, like you hear in the movies, but it slipped out from time to time, as if she worked a little to cover it up. "But I've lived in Manhattan since graduating college, so that's really home to me now. Have you heard of Tribeca?"

"Sure, in lower Manhattan," Sam said casually, as if he were a frequent visitor to the city.

"That's right. I have a home there." She made it sound like she had many homes, which wouldn't have surprised me one bit.

Jake whined and whimpered at Lauren's feet. "Aw, can I pick him up?"

"He'd love to be picked up by a pretty lady, wouldn't you, Jake?" Sam paused as Lauren lifted the dog and cradled him in her arms. He squirmed with joy and immediately went in for a kiss, and she giggled as she let him lick her cheek. And now I was jealous of a dog.

"He's a darling," she gushed. "Look at his adorable sweater. Did you knit this for him?"

"No, Alma made that one for him. Have you met her yet? She runs the cash register over at The General."

"Not yet," I said. "We're heading over there next."

"He really is a diva," Sam said about Jake, who looked like he was in heaven. "I wasn't going to put a sweater on him this morning, but I guess he knew there was a chill in the air because he insisted on wearing one. How long are you here for, Lauren?"

"I'm booked for this week." She glanced over at me as she set Jake down on the floor. "But I'm really not sure how long I'll be here."

"I hope my brother is a good host," Sam said, "and ensures that you have an extended stay at the ranch. Right, Matthew? You'll keep her happy."

"Uh huh." I started moving toward the door, taking Lauren gently by the arm so she'd come with me. "See you later, little brother. Bye, Cherise."

"Goodbye, Jake," Lauren said, making eyes at the dog. I really didn't need this kind of adorable competition.

"I should probably stop by and check on Elijah," Sam called after us. "I'd love to visit with Miss Lauren again, too."

"Nope," I said over my shoulder. "I've got the medicine, so I'm all set. See you later."

I breathed a sigh of relief as I slammed the door behind us. Then I turned toward Lauren to see her eyes lit up with amusement.

"Little brothers," she said. "Am I right?"

I couldn't help laughing. "He's the worst."

"Yeah," she said. "Tori and I probably deserved my little brother Rocco's torment. He had twin older sisters who were constantly bossing him around."

We climbed into the Suburban, and I started it up. "I'm sure my siblings would say I was the bossy one, being the oldest." I put my arm over the back of her seat and turned to look over my shoulder so I could reverse onto the road. "What's it like having a twin?" She was good at asking questions that got people talking, but she revealed little about herself.

"For me, it was wonderful, but I can't imagine life without my other half. We're business partners and best friends, and we live about five minutes away from each other, which probably sounds a little weird and co-dependent."

"Not at all. I wish all my siblings lived that close to me." I waved out the window to folks as we cruised down the main street of town toward our destination. Ella, who ran The Mangy Marmot Bar and Grill, was walking down the street with a cup of coffee, probably purchased from The General Store where they sold the best, and only, takeout coffee in town. No matcha tea as far as I knew. My neighbor Cal was outside the store aptly called Feed & Grain, loading bags into the flatbed of his truck. No doubt they'd be asking Sam about the woman in my passenger seat. In a small town, few things escaped people's notice, especially attractive new faces.

"I'm lucky," she said. "Our younger brother Rocco lives uptown with his husband, Jamison. They're estheticians with their own business up there."

I could have pretended to know what she meant, but I was too curious. "What's an esthetician?"

"A skincare professional. They offer services like facials, hair removal, microdermabrasion."

"Oh." She chuckled at my surprised expression. "Male and female clients?"

"They serve all genders. Why? Are you looking for a good waxer, Matthew?"

I laughed and scratched my chin. "Uh, no, not at the moment, but if I am, I'll let you know."

"They're the best in Manhattan, so if you're ever in town you should come visit me, and we'll go there together and get facials."

It felt like we were flirting a little, but it had been so long for me, I wasn't quite sure.

"I've always said if I went back to New York City, the first thing would be to find a good esthetician."

She laughed and patted my arm. "Sometimes dreams do come true."

I felt a little guilty for flirting with a married woman, but she probably didn't think of what we were doing as anything more than friendly banter. Asking more about her husband was definitely prying, but I couldn't help myself.

"Is your husband off sailing his boats right now?" She didn't answer for a few seconds, and I knew I'd pushed it too far. "I'm sorry, that's none of my business."

As I pulled up to the only stoplight in town, she looked down at her rings. "No, it's fine. My marriage is a complicated situation, though, and I can't really discuss it. I know it sounds like I'm being evasive..."

"That's alright. No worries." Damn. Complicated was never good.

"How about you? I assume that was your adorable daughter eating dinner with you last night. Are you married?"

"Divorced." I wasn't interested in discussing my failed marriage. Honestly, it almost felt like another lifetime, since we'd all moved on. "My daughter, Gigi, is spending the summer at the ranch with me. You'll meet her when you're down at the stables. She likes horses more than people. If she's not riding or playing outside, she has her head stuck in a book." That last part worried my ex-wife, but I argued that if Gigi was happy, there wasn't a problem.

"She sounds delightful, and it's lovely that you get her for the entire summer."

"I know it. Gigi spends the school year with her mom and stepdad in Denver, so that's hard on us. I get to see her on some holidays and long weekends, but summer is when I get to be part of her daily life. I wish we had more time together. She's growing up too fast."

"Tell me about it. It feels like yesterday my sons were toddlers I could carry on my hip. I can't believe they're adults and out on their own."

"You seem very young to have children that age."

She smiled at me. "And here I thought your brother was the sweet talker. I had my children when I was young. Julien, my first, was a surprise. We'd planned on waiting longer."

"Gigi was a surprise, too. A honeymoon baby, but I got married later in life so I was glad to get started on father-hood. I'm sure my ex would agree that our daughter is the best thing we ever made together."

"She seems like a great kid."

I never passed up a chance to be a proud dad. "I think so. She does well in school, and she helps out around the ranch. Everyone on staff adores her. I got really lucky."

"I'm sure you're a wonderful dad," she said. "That makes a huge difference in a girl's life."

I couldn't help wondering what kind of dad her husband was. She certainly hadn't said anything complimentary about him.

"I try. I'm a little nervous about the teen years, but her mom and I co-parent pretty well, and hopefully we can navigate those waters when the time comes."

"I have no doubt you'll do just fine." She looked up at the

wooden sign on our local bar. "The Mangy Marmot. That's an interesting name."

"Weekends get a little wild, but it's a nice place to go on weeknights. Maybe we can—" I caught myself before I suggested the two of us go on what might sound like a date. After all, she was married, and it was *complicated*, not to mention she was a guest at the ranch. "Maybe we can have a little gathering in the Round Room one night to do some two-stepping." Lauren nodded, so I continued down that path. "I think the other families would like that, and I could invite a few locals. I can't let you get bored in the evenings."

I pulled into the parking lot of The General Store and shut off the engine, waiting for her response. Had she picked up on my attraction to her? Was I scaring her off?

"I don't think I'll get bored," she said, "but I'd love to learn to two-step. Sounds like I need some cowboy boots in addition to my hiking shoes."

"*Cowgirl* boots, you mean." I smiled to myself, hoping she'd pick me as a dance partner. "You've got to get a pair while you're here. When in Wyoming..."

"Exactly," she said.

We went inside the store, and I waited until she was looking at boots before I approached Alma at the register.

"Good morning, Matthew." She set aside the crossword puzzle that she'd been working on. "Can I help you?"

"I need some tea." I spoke quietly so Lauren wouldn't overhear me. "Have you ever heard of matcha?"

Her wrinkled face creased even more deeply as she thought about the question. "Is that like Machu Picchu?"

"I don't think so. It's a kind of green tea a guest requested."

"Oh, I've got boxes of green tea. Go over to the grocery section, and you'll see it."

"Has to be matcha," I said. "It's special."

Alma sighed. "People are so particular about their beverages these days. Next thing you know, we'll have a Starbucks on the corner selling pumpkin flavored coffee."

I had a feeling we were in no danger of that happening any time soon. "Can you order it for me?"

She didn't look thrilled, but she picked up her pen, nonetheless. "How many boxes do you want?"

"One would be great. I'll pay for you to put a rush on it, too."

She craned her neck to see who was at the back of the store. "Is that lady with the pretty legs the matcha drinker?"

Sometimes I wanted to live in a place where everyone minded their own business. "Yep, that's the one."

With a smirk on her lips, she winked at me. "Ah. I get it now, Matthew. Say no more. As my grandson would say, I'll hook you up with the best matcha I can find. Don't you worry, honey."

"Thank you, Alma." Lord, help me.

CHAPTER 8

LAUREN

"What do you think?" Matthew asked as we stood inside the store aptly named Ranch Apparel.

"I've never seen so many shirts in my life."

The main floor of the store housed dozens of circular racks packed full of western shirts in all colors, patterns, and sizes. Along the walls were built-in wooden shelves stocked with hundreds of pairs of jeans. I glanced over at the mannequin next to me with its bold patterned shirt, stiff Wrangler jeans, and brown leather boots. If I wasn't careful, I was going to leave this place looking like an extra from the musical "Oklahoma."

"Hey, Matthew," a young woman called out from across the store. "Need any help?"

"Hello, Kate. We're just heading upstairs to look at boots." He put his hand on the small of my back. "Right this way. Boots and hats are on the second floor."

His touch was friendly, a means of guiding me in the right direction. So why did it make me feel warm and glowing inside?

The stairs creaked as I walked up them, moving slowly so

I could take in the photographs covering the wall to our right. The framed pictures, mostly eight by tens, featured riders at rodeos and regular men and women at work on ranches. I peered at the faces of the people in them, wondering if there was a photo of Matthew up there.

"It's strange that you can live in the same country as someone," I said over my shoulder, "and your life can be so vastly different."

"Different in some ways," Matthew said from behind me. "Probably not in others."

If possible, they'd packed even more merchandise into the second floor, dividing the space into sections for hats and boots. This type of gear felt performative when worn in the city, and I was still adjusting to the idea that in Wyoming, this was their everyday business casual.

"What size and color are we looking for?" Matthew asked as we walked over to a display of women's boots.

"I guess I was thinking black or brown. I had no idea there were so many choices."

"Tons of choices. Different styles, colors and stitching. You'll want Western boots, though." He gestured to a pair of short brown leather boots. "These are work boots. You want some for fashion. Maybe something like...this." He handed me a tall turquoise boot with beige stitching. "You can't go wrong with a good pair of Justins."

His choice of a bold color surprised me. "Blue? I'm not sure."

"May I ask you a question?" He dropped his voice low and quiet, and it made my stomach dip like I'd missed a step.

"Um, I think so."

"Do you only wear black and white clothing?"

I glanced down at my white cotton tee and black linen shorts. "No, sometimes I wear gray." I looked up to see him holding back a smile. "What? I like a classic palette of neutrals. It makes it easier to dress in the morning." He was full on grinning at me now. I propped one hand on my hip. "It's called a capsule wardrobe, Matthew."

"Okay, city girl," he said. "I'm sure you know ten times more about fashion than I do, so you won't get any arguments from me." His eyes sparkled, which I already knew was a sign he was about to tease me. "How about off-white and beige? Do you wear those too?"

"Actually," I said primly, trying to look serious, "those colors wash me out."

He laughed and tugged at the brim of his cowboy hat. "I guess it's black boots today, then."

We looked around a bit more at the expansive boot collection on display before I tried on two pairs, one black and the other a light tan. They were both practical and surprisingly comfortable, but something told me to keep looking.

"Are you getting worn out?" I asked.

"Not at all," he said. "If you don't mind though, I'm going to check out the hats and then I'll be right back over."

Matthew left me to my obsessive search for the perfect pair of boots, and ten minutes later, I finally spotted the ones. Milk chocolate brown leather on the bottom and wine red leather on the uppers. Intricate flame stitching in off-white thread. They were playful but still classy, and the craftsmanship was absolute perfection.

Matthew returned, watching me as I inspected them. "They're not a neutral."

"That's okay." I smiled up at him. "I think my wardrobe needs a pop of color." When I tried them on, they molded to my feet like they were made for me. I walked back and forth, admiring how they looked in the mirror. "Am I buying my first pair of cowgirl boots?"

"You should. They look good on you."

I turned, catching him checking out not only the boots, but my legs, as well. When he looked up and our eyes connected, he knew he was busted. There was no better confirmation for how I looked in those boots than the appreciation I'd seen on his face.

I couldn't suppress a confident grin. "Sold."

~

THANKS to my morning shopping trip with Matthew, I had sturdy hiking shoes, a beautiful pair of cowgirl boots, and a secret crush on a rancher. At least I hoped it was a secret, and I hadn't been too obvious with Matthew. For the rest of the day, whether I was floating in the pool or trying to work on my laptop in my cabin, all I could think about was him. That easy smile with absolutely no pretense in it. The way he looked at me so intently, interested in who I was and what I had to say. He was sweet and genuine and...

Shit. I had to stop this nonsense. For so many reasons, this was not the time to get involved with anyone, especially a man who lived in Wyoming on a remote ranch.

Like the previous night, I ate my dinner alone. The food was delicious, but I was disappointed Matthew wasn't in the dining room. His daughter wasn't there either and, in fact, neither were the other guests.

"Where is everyone this evening?" I asked my server, Kyra.

"Tonight was the campfire cookout," she said. "Didn't Matthew tell you about it?"

"He did," I said. "I totally forgot." Matthew had invited me to the cookout when we took our trip into town that morning, but I'd declined. I wasn't ready to ride a horse into the mountains with a pack of other guests, then eat a meal and ride back in the dark. Nothing about that sounded easy or safe for my first horseback ride in thirty years.

The extra time I'd devoted to my hair and makeup before coming to dinner felt a little pathetic without

Matthew there. I decided at that moment to stop being ridiculous over a man I would never see again after this week. As a reality check, I called my divorce lawyer when I returned to my cabin to check on how the proceedings were going. Unfortunately, she didn't pick up. I knew she'd still be working because Tempest Corday-Brown never left the office before eight pm at the earliest, but I wasn't expecting her to call me back at nearly eleven-thirty New York time.

"Can you hear me?" She spoke at a volume that could probably be heard on the other side of the mountain range. "Because I'm missing every other word you say."

"We don't have the best reception out here. Hold on." After pulling on the hiking shoes I'd purchased in town, I grabbed my new can of bear spray and left my cabin. "Is this better?" I asked when I was on a path that wound through the ranch.

"It's good enough. Listen, your husband is being a prick."

My *husband*. Not for much longer, thank goodness. "That's not a surprise. How are you working this late, Tempest?"

"I'm in LA right now on a business trip. It's only eight-thirty here."

That made more sense. "What has Freddy done now?"

"He and his lawyer are playing hardball. They found out a syndication deal is in the works—don't ask me how—and they're using it as leverage. He wants alimony, not a lump sum, and he's asking for more than we offered."

"Well, we can play hardball, too." My heart rate increased as I walked up a small incline, passing by several other guest cabins. "How much alimony does he want?"

"He'll probably get seven to ten years of alimony, and he's asking for a number in the range of twenty grand a month."

I gasped as if someone had knocked the wind out of me. "We can negotiate about that, right?"

"Of course, but there's one more thing. He wants to own a percentage of Ms. Match."

"What?" I yelped like an injured dog, completely losing my composure. "Seriously? He's deranged!" A wave of nausea washed over me, and I reminded myself to take deep breaths. Nothing terrible had happened yet. This feeling of impending doom was my anxiety telling me to panic, which I would not do.

"I'd call him more of a greedy opportunist," she said. "I see those a lot in my line of work, so don't worry. We'll deal with Freddy. If you still want to get him to take a lump sum, we've got to come up with some amount you can live with. A number that will make him sign the papers and go away. I'm assuming you're a no go on giving him part ownership of the company?"

"There's no way he's getting even a tiny share of Ms. Match. I'd die first." The idea of giving him a piece of the company Tori and I built was unthinkable for so many reasons. I wanted as little to do with him as possible, and it was bad enough I'd have to see him because we shared children. Involving him in my professional life and giving him access to our company would never happen.

"We need to talk numbers, then." As if she could read my mind, she added, "You can't try to figure out what he *should* get. Divorce isn't about what's fair. It's about what's legal. He's going to get more than what you think he deserves because, let's be honest, that's just how it works. Think about it like this: what can I afford to give him without compromising my lifestyle and retirement?"

"I know he was the dependent spouse in our marriage, and he should get something, but after the way he's behaved... two hundred and forty thousand dollars a year?"

"I understand." She sighed sympathetically, as if she'd had a variation of this conversation many times before. "You probably carried the emotional load in your household, as well as being the breadwinner, and I'm guessing Freddy wasn't busting his ass cleaning the apartment and taking the kids to doctor appointments. I've met the guy, remember? Unfortunately, the court doesn't care about all that. They're going to see that you still earn a lot of money, and it's going to be hard to persuade them you can't afford to pay that much alimony."

I'd reached the first of two guest cottages, a lovely old house with shaker siding, gabled windows and a sweet wrap-around porch. Winded from the climb and the emotional conversation, I walked up the steps and took a seat on the metal glider.

"I'm not giving him a piece of the company," I said. "That's firm. If you think he won't take a lump sum, then I guess we can meet his alimony demands of twenty thousand."

"We'll offer lower," she promised. "That will give us some negotiating room. Who knows? Maybe he'll get desperate to tie things up, and he'll take eighteen."

"Maybe…"

I had no idea whether these machinations were Freddy's doing or his lawyer's. He'd never been interested in Ms. Match except as a source of money for all his extracurricular activities, so his request for a stake in the company felt like someone else's idea.

"The important thing is that he's out of your life as soon as we get this settled," she said, "and you can—"

"Dammit." My phone cut out, and I had to call her back. "Sorry, I lost you there for a minute."

"No problem. I can't imagine being somewhere that barely has cell service. How can you stand it?"

"The technology situation here isn't great," I admitted, "but the views are incredible. The sunset tonight was abso-lutely gorgeous." Heavy clouds had hung in the sky as a fiery sun sank toward the horizon. For the first time in my life, I'd wished I was a painter so I could try to capture what I was seeing.

"Nice…" She sounded distracted and ready to get on to her next task. "I'll write up a counter-offer and send it over to Freddy's lawyers, okay?"

"Sure. Tempest, thank you for calling me this evening."

"No problem. You know me, I'm always working." She said a quick goodbye before hanging up, and I couldn't help imagining that I was the woman still in her office, working late into the night, eating takeout food at her desk. It was easier to imagine that than to believe in reality—I was a guest at a dude ranch in Wyoming, with a newly purchased pair of cowgirl boots and a can of bear spray at my side.

I certainly didn't envy Tempest one bit. I'd spent many evenings working way too late, missing dinner with my kids, head bent over a spreadsheet. Back then, my career fired me up and was an important part of my identity. The money I earned meant we could provide Serge and Julien with wonderful educations and travel experiences, but those late nights weren't great for my marriage. Freddy was selfish and vain, but I had to admit that I wasn't home often and when I was there, I gave my full attention to my sons.

I missed the body I had at thirty-five—pain-free joints and tight neck skin—but I didn't long for the life I had back then. Who would miss late nights of knocking out a few more items on a to do list while gobbling down a wilted deli salad? No, thank you. I wanted more sunsets and someone wonderful by my side to enjoy them with me. It was amazing how many revelations you could have about your life and your future when you finally stood still for a few minutes and looked at the sky.

Instead of walking back to my cabin, I leaned back into the cozy cushions of the old metal glider. A little sign on the house announced it as Bluebell Cottage, which matched well with its cornflower blue shutters. What a perfect little place.

As I swung gently back and forth, I let myself relax into the waning light of the evening. When was the last time I had nothing that needed to get done and nowhere to be? I closed my eyes and let myself rock and relax, even drifting off to the place right before sleep…

At the sound of someone's boots on the dirt path that ran past the cottage, my eyes shot open and scanned the looming darkness. Approaching me was a tall person with a long stride. Probably a man. Definitely coming to the cottage. I stilled the glider, my city instincts telling me it was better to go undetected. I had that bear spray with me, just in case. My finger stayed poised on the trigger as he clomped up the porch steps in his work boots. That's when I recognized his beautiful jawline and blue eyes.

"Matthew."

He jumped backwards in surprise. "Shit!" He pressed a hand to his heart. "You scared me."

"Sorry! I didn't know it was you until you got close. I was going to douse you in bear spray if you were a rapist."

Matthew laughed. "More likely to be a bear out here at night than a rapist."

"Given the choice, I'd take the bear," I muttered.

"What are you doing out here at the cottages?"

"I was walking and needed a place to sit down and think. Do you mind?"

"Course not." He stood with his hands in his pockets, acting like he was shy about explaining his presence. "I keep my beer in the fridge here, and I was coming to get one. Care to join me?"

I wasn't sure about the drink, but I definitely wanted his company. "Sure, I can try one."

"Try one?" He unlocked the door with a key that hung on a jam-packed keychain. "You mean you've never had a beer?"

I had to smile at his look of disbelief. "Not since college, probably. I'm not even sure if I like it."

"I mean, it's no matcha…"

I pretended to be annoyed at him. "Very funny. I know you think I'm bougie."

"Ma'am, I'm not even sure what bougie means." He smiled and disappeared inside the cottage, reappearing a minute later with two bottles. Like a pro, he used the porch railing to pop off the caps before handing me one. I can't say why that turned me on, but it did. "Now this isn't microbrew beer," he said. "It's standard Budweiser."

"I wouldn't know the difference at this point."

He gestured to the glider. "May I?"

"Please do."

The glider bench was wide enough to accommodate both of us, and our legs weren't anywhere near touching, but I still felt butterflies with Matthew sitting close to me. Feeling that kind of magnetic attraction to a man was a heady experience.

"Refreshing," I said after taking a sip. "Why do you keep your beer out here? Is it so you have to burn off the calories on the way to retrieve it?"

"No." He paused before answering. "I have to hide it from someone."

"Your daughter?" I couldn't imagine that was the case unless she was a tragically young alcoholic.

"One of my employees. He has a drinking problem. If I don't lock up the alcohol, he falls off the wagon. Otherwise, he stays sober, and his job gets done."

We drank our beer in silence for at least a full minute.

"Don't you think that's a lot of trouble to go to," I said, "when he should be the one making the effort to stay sober?"

"True." He stretched his long legs out in front of him. "I know it sounds ridiculous to treat him like a child, but he's great at what he does, and I couldn't replace him, not for the same money. He's also had a rough go of it in life recently. I guess I want to help him find his way again."

Matthew was a compassionate guy, even if he did have

more to learn about co-dependence. "Your secret is safe with me."

"It's a system that works most of the time. I'm not much of a drinker myself, but we had the campfire cookout tonight, and after a long trail ride and a warm shower, a cold beer felt like the perfect way to end the evening." He sighed and stretched his arm out along the back of the glider. "It's been a long week."

"Want to talk about it?" I tried to ignore the fact that his hand was now close enough to play with my hair.

He turned toward me. "Thanks, but not really. I'd rather enjoy your company and forget my troubles for a while."

"Same," I said. "I got some crappy news from my lawyer tonight, but I'd rather not talk about it either."

He used his boots to rock the glider, and I pulled my feet up underneath me to enjoy the comforting swaying motion.

"We're a pair, huh?" he said.

"Well, it's hard to feel sorry for yourself when you see a sunset like the one tonight. Is it always that amazing?"

"Tonight was pretty, but you might get an even better one if you stay long enough." He tapped my shoulder and my heart fluttered. "See what I did there, encouraging you to stay with us longer?"

"I appreciate you encouraging me to stay. I'm still not convinced that I'm rugged enough for this place, though."

He put his hands on his knees and stood up. "You know what we should do? We should go introduce you to the horses."

"Right now?" I asked hesitantly. "In the dark?"

"Why not? Gigi is playing cards with Kyra and Tyler, and unless you have other plans…"

"Other than finishing this beer," I said, "I have no plans on my agenda tonight."

"Great. Then let's go say hello to the horse you're riding tomorrow morning."

CHAPTER 9

MATTHEW

*W*alking next to Lauren as we drank our beers felt completely easy and natural, which made no sense at all. We barely knew each other, and she was a guest, which usually meant I put on my ranch manager persona and turned into jovial, laid back Matthew Hart. Pretending to be carefree when you have the weight of the world on your shoulders is a tough act, but I had a lot of practice at it.

With Lauren, I couldn't pretend to be that guy who had everything perfectly together, or maybe I didn't want to. This was certainly the first time I'd told a guest about my alcoholic employee or my custody arrangement, so there had to be something special about her, and if I spent more time with this woman, more walls were going to come down. That was a scary and exciting thought.

Even though there was comfort in walking the ranch with Lauren, I was also hyper aware of her proximity. If our arms so much as brushed against each other, I felt a throb of longing to hold her hand in mine. I knew it wasn't appropriate to feel this way about a married guest, and yet I couldn't stop it. Attraction like that was something I hadn't experienced since my teen years, and I'd almost forgotten how good it felt.

The lights were out in the stable because Walt had long been in bed and some horses were asleep too. The one I wanted Lauren to ride was still awake and standing at the gate of her stall.

"This is Alma," I said, introducing Lauren to the brown mare I'd chosen for her. Reliable and sturdy, Alma would do the job of getting Lauren from point A to point B with no surprises.

"Alma, like the woman who works at The General Store?" she asked. "She has the same name as the horse?"

I smiled and nodded. "You picked up on that. Walt named this horse after his cousin, Alma, who you met at the store. He said it was a compliment, and I figured she'd take it as an insult, but she said it was the highest form of flattery, having a horse named after her."

"Well, hello, Alma." She stroked the bridge of Alma's nose, and the horse nickered in greeting. "She's a beauty."

That was a kind assessment. Alma didn't have unusual markings, an impressive build or a lively gait, but she had soulful eyes and was one of the best natured horses I'd ever been around.

"I'm glad you think so. She's your mount tomorrow morning. Be here at nine, and Gigi and I will take you out for a ride."

Lauren continued petting Alma as she spoke. "Are you sure you have time for that? I know you must be busy."

I shrugged and stuffed my hands in the pockets of my jeans. She was right. I had a to-do list as long as my arm. The last thing I had time for was a trail ride, and here I was promising her one. I leaned against the stall next to Alma's, trying to come up with an explanation of why I was shirking my responsibilities.

"If I wait until I'm not busy, I'll never ride in the summer.

In fact, I haven't ridden in about a month, so I'm long overdue."

"You really should enjoy these years with Gigi. Kids grow up so quickly, and before you know it, they're off to college and then out on their own." Lauren pressed her lips into a thin, taut line. "I know this is a ridiculous question, but what if I fall off? I've ridden horses before, but I'm not the most coordinated person. I once fell off my bike seat at Soul Cycle." She shot me a smile full of embarrassment and shame. "That's when I switched to Peloton. I could never go back to the gym where I crashed and burned."

"Lady," I placed a hand on her back, "you're too hard on yourself."

Lauren's sigh said it all. "You have no idea."

I had to take my hand away from the soft warmth of her blouse before I pulled her into a hug. She looked like she needed one, but that would be way too forward of me. "Listen, this is the horse I put seven-year-olds on. If you fall off, it's because you jumped."

Lauren's laughter rang through the quiet barn. "Alright, if you say so. You're gonna be sweet to me, huh?" She reached out to scratch behind Alma's ears, and the horse leaned into her hand in response.

"She won't move fast, but she'll get you there, and she'll listen to your commands even if you're feeling unsure. Believe me, she knows the trails and what's expected of her."

"I guess I have nothing to be worried about then," Lauren said.

I was the one worrying. She was a guest, and here I was spending personal time alone with her in the barn, drinking beer and thinking about how much I wanted her in my arms. There was an aching need inside me when I was around Lauren, but I had to keep this thing professional. Too much was at stake with my ranch at the moment, and I couldn't get muddled up in some improper relationship when things were falling apart around me. Literally.

"I should probably turn in for the night." I stretched my arms over my head. Every light in my brain was on, and I wasn't anywhere near sleepy, but I had to get away from Lauren before I did something stupid like ask her to have dinner with me or confess my feelings. "We've got a big day tomorrow, and I get up with the sun."

"See you tomorrow, pretty girl," she whispered, giving Alma one last pat on the head. "Thank you, Matthew. I feel much better about riding now. In fact, I'm excited about it."

She was so close and smelled so good that I felt myself being drawn closer to her. She flickered her gaze to my lips, and I knew she had the same thoughts that I did. I started to move in when one of the horses let out a rude noise, followed by an even ruder smell.

"Oh, my!" Lauren said with a laugh.

That was enough to jar me back to reality. I stepped away from her, establishing a no-kissing zone between us. I needed to get my head on straight.

"Let's get you back to your cabin," I said, "so you can get a good night's sleep."

As promised, Alma was a sweetheart on our morning ride, and Lauren looked comfortable in her Western saddle. As a kid, she'd ridden English style, which uses a smaller, lighter saddle, and I showed her how to hold the reins in one hand instead of two, as well as how to use her body, more than her hands, to guide Alma. She was a quick learner, and I could tell by her posture that she'd relaxed into her seat and was enjoying the ride. I'd given her a helmet to wear because, even though they were optional for adults at the ranch, I thought it would make her feel safer.

Gigi forged ahead of us on a Palomino gelding named Loki, blazing the trail as our guide. I stayed close to Lauren to keep a close eye on her and provide pointers. It wasn't a hardship. If anything, I was enjoying myself too much. As Lauren and I sidled side-by-side on our horses, I couldn't help but notice how natural it seemed to see her on a horse. Despite her protests that she wasn't cut out for life on a dude ranch, she seemed to fit in here just fine to me, even with those diamond studs still in her ears.

I held a loose grip on Roan Pony's reins as I walked him next to Alma. He was eager to get moving faster, but he'd read my signals and was keeping it together so far.

"You enjoying the ride?" I asked.

Lauren smiled over at me. "I'm loving it. I can't believe I almost let my anxieties keep me from riding. It's incredible out here. How did your parents come to own this wonderful place?"

"That's a complicated story." I paused, wondering if she should get the story I normally gave to guests. As usual, something made me want to tell her the whole truth and not the sanitized version. "My mother is from Minnesota. She was a middle class kid who loved horses and camping. Dad grew up on a cattle ranch in Durango, Colorado, but his mother wanted him to become a preacher, so he followed that calling, even though he was more interested in being outdoors than in a chapel. He went to a Bible college in St. Paul and met my mother at a church event. After his ordination, they came back to his hometown so he could take a position in a church there." I'd never known my dad as a minister, and it was still hard to picture him at the pulpit, although he sure did like to preach at us when he took a notion to.

"Things didn't work out in the church for him," I continued, "and around that time, my mother came into an inheritance from her grandmother, and they bought Silver Sage

Ranch. It was kind of a wild thing to do because they'd never run a guest ranch before, or done anything like it, but he grew up on a ranch and I guess he knew enough to make it work."

"Why did he leave the church? Did he ever tell you?" I looked over at her, and she blushed. "Sorry. I'm a New Yorker. We're direct, but I didn't mean to sound nosy."

I nodded briskly. "It's alright. People around here don't usually sugarcoat things either. From what I understand, he was a convincing preacher, but the senior minister felt threatened by him. Dad didn't know how to be someone's subordinate."

"You mean he was too outspoken?" she asked.

I adjusted my cowboy hat. "That's one way to put it. He really enjoyed being an authority figure, which meant he ran our household like he was the general of a small army. You didn't question your orders. Don't get me wrong, he had a lot of great attributes, and I learned so much from him. He could just be kind of domineering at times."

The path narrowed as we went downhill, and I slowed my horse to allow Alma to walk in front of Roan Pony. For several minutes, we put our conversation on hold as our horses picked their way down the rocky terrain until the path widened and leveled out again.

"Are you close to your siblings?" she asked when we were side by side.

"Definitely, although Sam is the only one who lives here, so I don't get to see Faith and Bowie very often."

"I'm lucky to have my brother and sister in New York with me."

It was another reminder her real life was far away from these mountains and valleys. I tried to picture Lauren in the big city, her fancy high heels clicking against the cement. Everything that came into my mind—like her talking on a cell phone while she hailed a cab—seemed more like a movie than reality.

"And your mom?" I asked. "Is she in the city, too?"

"Mom still lives out on Long Island, so she's not far away. I don't think she'll ever sell the house we grew up in. There are too many memories of my dad there."

"What was he like?"

A sad smile curved her lips. "He was a working class guy who had a factory job at Grumman. He mowed the lawn on Saturday and watched sports on Sunday. Salt of the earth type of guy. We adored him."

"Sounds like it," I said.

"The thing I respected most about him is that he loved us unconditionally. Dad thought that after twin girls, he was getting a boy who would play sports and work on the car with him, but he got a son who hated football and wanted to be Boy George for Halloween." She glanced over at me. "I know some gay kids love sports but my brother wasn't one of them."

"Wow. How did that go down in your house?" My father would have disowned us for a lot less than being queer, of that I was certain.

"Tori and I were the ones charged with telling him Rocco was gay. My brother was scared to come out to Dad, and my mother didn't want to be the person to break the news to him. Rocco was out of college by then, but we all thought Dad was going to flip out. Instead, he looked at us like we were idiots and said, 'You think I didn't know? Who cares? He's my son, and I love him.' I was so proud of him in that moment."

"That's amazing. You're lucky you had a dad like that. My dad couldn't even handle it when Bowie said he didn't believe in God. They fought about religion, politics, and everything else until my brother left home and never came back. Never saw my father again or spoke to him before he died." Bowie also never expressed remorse about the fact that he didn't mend fences with our father, but it must have eaten away at him. He wasn't made of stone, but he sure was stubborn and controlling sometimes, not unlike our old man.

"That's so sad," Lauren said.

Gigi turned and looked over her shoulder at us. "This is a good spot," she called out.

"She loves to stop by this creek." I pulled up Roan Pony, hopped off him, and went over to help Lauren down from Alma. She was already halfway to the ground and could have made it without my assistance, but I wanted to be there to spot her, just in case.

She looked up at me after she set her feet firmly on the dirt. "I did it. I rode a horse for the first time in almost forty years."

"You sure did. How do you feel?"

"I'm going to be sore later," she said, rubbing her legs, "but right now I feel amazing. I'm proud of myself. Thank you, Matthew. I'm not sure I would have had the courage to do this if you hadn't been so kind, introducing me to Alma and making me feel safe."

Her sweet words made me melt like butter on a biscuit. "I'm honored to be the one to get you back out here."

We walked over to the stream where Gigi had stopped to wait for us in what was just about the perfect spot. There was some shade from aspen trees and sun-warmed rocks that made excellent seats for resting by the water. I couldn't believe I'd let the whole summer slip by without a trip here.

Gigi unsnapped the chinstrap on her helmet, unleashing her sweaty hair, strands of which were stuck to her face. "I've got snacks and drinks." She slung her little backpack off her back and unzipped it. Holding out two types of Capri Sun, she looked directly at Lauren. "Fruit Punch or Grape. Pick your poison."

"Fruit punch, please." Lauren was clearly trying to hold back a smile at Gigi's choice of words.

"Grape for me," I said.

As Gigi set up our picnic area, I showed Lauren how to secure the reins so we could set the horses free to have their own snack on patches of grass nearby. Then the three of us sat down on large rocks next to the burbling creek where Gigi set out our drinks and little bags of pretzels and fruit gummies. It was the most adorable food presentation I'd ever seen, but I made sure not to say so since she clearly was feeling like quite the grown-up tour guide.

After we finished our snacks, Gigi skittered off to walk the bank of the creek in search of fish, while I moved over to the grassy meadow and leaned back on my elbows, enjoying the soft breeze against my skin and the view of the horses grazing, flicking their tails as their long necks remained bent toward the grass. Not even my looming to-do list was going to ruin this day for me. If I couldn't take some pleasure in southeastern Wyoming in the summertime, I'd never bank enough memories to make it through the long winter.

Lauren surprised me by stretching out next to me. Not only did this move put our bodies close together, it also meant her clothing might get a little dirty. I hadn't known this lady long, but I already knew she valued looking immaculate. Even today, after wearing a helmet, her hair somehow managed to appear clean and freshly brushed, unlike my own, which was mashed down by my hat. When I thought back to picking her up at the airport and taking off my sweaty shirt, then tossing it into the Suburban…she must have wondered what the hell she was getting into.

Oh well. I was Wyoming through and through and sometimes a shirt change had to happen on the fly. Life here wasn't all starched, pressed and picture perfect. So far, she seemed to be enjoying the ranch, and as long as she was with us, I wanted to show her more of the beauty of Silver Sage.

Lauren and I let the sunshine warm our faces, and I felt my sleepy eyes flicker shut. Suddenly, I realized I had no idea what time it was. When was the last time I let the day unfold before me without any kind of plan? Work had become incredibly stressful, and that wasn't how I imagined my future when I took over the ranch after my parents died. I knew it wouldn't be easy but I wasn't expecting it to be relentlessly difficult and exhausting.

"I can't believe your brother left for so long," Lauren said. "I'm not trying to pry into family drama. It's just so peaceful and perfect here. If my family owned this ranch, I'd want to visit as often as possible."

Her compliment brought a smile to my lips. "Summer is pretty magical here." I stared up at the blue sky and kicked one ankle over the other. "Wintertime is another story. It's not everyone's cup of tea."

"I hear it gets pretty cold."

I laughed quietly at her assessment of Wyoming weather. "Pretty cold is an understatement. Winters are harsh, to say the least. It can feel very isolating living out here."

I thought about how the meadow we were in would look during the winter, snow blanketing the grass and weighing down tree limbs. The animals would hibernate or burrow down in their homes through the worst of it. All extracurricular ranch activities would be at a standstill as we focused on the chores that needed to be done during the off-season.

"It gets cold in New York too, you know," she teased. "We have blizzards."

"Did you ever see the movie The Shining?" She nodded, and I raised an eyebrow at her. "Then you remember how they were snowed in at a resort? That's how it is here. The temperatures drop well below freezing. I think the coldest on record was something like negative fifty-five."

She bolted upright. "Negative fifty-five?!"

I nodded, chuckling at the sight of her wide, innocent

eyes. "My parents would drive us to the end of the ranch's driveway on a snowmobile so the bus could pick us up for school, but sometimes the conditions were too bad for even Wyoming bus drivers to get out here. We'd just stay home for days, playing cards and fighting with each other until my parents sent us all to our rooms. They seemed to forget that my brothers and I shared a room, and we would just continue the fight in there."

She smiled at me. "Sounds like Tori and me as kids."

"By the time Bowie was a young teenager, those long winters became torture for him. Being stuck in close quarters with my father wasn't easy for any of us kids, but he treated Bowie like a wild horse he was trying to break."

I got a taste of how demanding and rigid my father could be after college when I came back here to work for him at the ranch. There was no working with my father, only working *for* him, doing exactly what he said, so I moved away to Cheyenne, got my contractor's license, and built houses. I didn't think I'd ever come back here to run the ranch myself, but then you never knew what life held for you.

"I can't blame him for wanting to escape," she said, "but I'm sure you miss your brother."

"I do. Can I ask you a question about your life back in New York?" She nodded, and I sat up so I could meet her gaze. "It seems like you're here to escape from something back home. I can't help wondering what it could be."

CHAPTER 10

LAUREN

*M*atthew studied me carefully. "It's alright if you don't want to tell me."

I wasn't expecting him to confront me so bluntly about my past and why I'd come out here to a remote location by myself, leaving my normal life behind. In all fairness, we'd been having frank discussions about our families almost since I'd met him, so he certainly wasn't out of line. For two people who didn't know each other well, our conversations had been deep and vulnerable, and I felt like I could trust him to keep a secret. Could I trust everyone else around us, though? What if he told his brother Sam or a staff member my real name? Would they sell their story to the press and further jeopardize my privacy? I couldn't risk it.

"It's nothing illegal or life-threatening or anything like that," I promised. "I just needed to get away from some drama back home and clear my head. Does that make sense?"

He smiled, even though I was dodging the question. "Best it can without knowing the details. And I'm not asking for any of those. I will say, I'm sure glad that assistant sent you to the wrong place."

"Me too." Sounds of the creek filled the silence as I

thought about what to say next. I picked a few blades of grass as I formed the words in my head, wanting to make sure I got them right. "I would tell you everything if I could, Matthew, but I can't right now."

His expression was more reserved than before he asked the question. "No worries. It was too forward of me to ask. Guests deserve total privacy."

"It was fine to ask," I said quickly, "and I hope I'm more than a guest to you. I feel like we've become friends."

"I'd like to be your friend, Lauren."

The air between us crackled with what felt like way more than "friend" energy, but we were adults who understood that this was all that could exist right now, and we'd take what we could get. For a while, Matthew and I both seemed lost in our thoughts. I wished I could be someone named Lauren Wagonblast, a carefree tourist in Wyoming, not Lauren Cozzi, who was dealing with an ugly divorce and running away from a hungry media cycle. I'd been silly to think I could hide from my real life out here. No matter how far you run, even on the fastest horse in the world (which Alma most certainly was not), your past will always catch up with you.

"Let's ride some more!" Gigi called out to us. She was already pulling on her socks, having finished her wading adventure in the creek.

"I have an idea," Matthew said. "Are you up for a gallop across the field?"

My pulse rate quickened. "Maybe? I think so?"

He stood up and extended a hand toward me. "That's good enough for me."

Running Alma across an open meadow was an experience I would never forget. An awesome sense of freedom and power surged through me as horse and rider became one, the wind whipping through her mane. She might not have been the fastest horse out there, and I wasn't the best equestrian, but that didn't matter one bit. Tears streamed from my eyes and a grin stretched across my face as we pounded across the grass toward an imaginary finish line.

"And you thought it was too late for you to get back on a horse," Matthew teased as we rode back to the ranch, returning to our slower pace.

"I guess Alma and I both have a few more good years in us."

"More than a few," he said.

When we got back to the stable, we hung up our tack in a tidy room with tongue and groove paneled walls made of knotty pine, and then we brushed down the horses before putting them out in the pasture. Once we'd completed those tasks, I assumed we'd all head back to the main buildings together. Instead, Matthew handed Gigi a pitchfork.

"You go on up," he said. "We're going to muck stalls for a little while and feed and water the horses."

Gigi made a sour face. "Yuck. This is the only part of horses I don't like. The poop."

Matthew slung his arm around her thin shoulders. "Has to get done, though."

She sighed deeply, looking quite forlorn. "I know."

"I'm happy to help." I spoke up without even thinking about it first, but I meant what I said.

"No," Matthew said firmly. "I can't have a guest mucking stalls."

At the same time, Gigi cheered. "Yay! Stay and help us. We have an extra pair of barn boots you can wear."

I smiled at Matthew. "See? It's decided. I'm helping."

He shook his head at me. "I can't let you do that."

"Why not? Is it an insurance thing? Worried I'm going to slip in a pile of poo and break a leg?"

He laughed as he grabbed a wheelbarrow from a nearby wall. "No, it's not that. You're a paying guest, not staff. You shouldn't have to do any work while you're here. Especially not this kind of dirty work."

"Okay, you can pay me."

He set down the wheelbarrow and put his hands on his hips. "Pay you?"

"I'll take one of those Silver Sage Ranch caps like the one you were wearing the other day," I said. "A black one, if you have it."

He hooked his fingers in the loops of his jeans, and I could tell he was weighing whether or not to keep arguing. "Take the hat, and I'll throw in a t-shirt."

"Okay, fine," I said. "A t-shirt and a hat. Happy now?"

"You got yourself a deal." He gestured toward a nearby stall. "This way to the boots. Ladies first."

Minutes later, we were using pitchforks to sift manure out of hay, cracking jokes while we worked. I laughed harder than I had in ages.

"I can't believe Doug is a horse," I said as I cleaned his stall. "When I first got to the ranch, you and Walt were discussing his ankle, and I assumed Doug was an employee."

"He does work here," Gigi said. "So technically, he is an employee. He just gets paid in hay and oats."

"It's an unusual name for a horse," Matthew agreed. "He came to us with the name Sir Galahad, but Mom said it didn't fit him because he feared everything from garden hoses to butterflies. You'll see he has a white snip under his nose that looks kind of like a mustache, so Mom started calling him Doug after her brother. The name stuck. Walt and I are the only ones who ride him, because he spooks so easily."

"I could ride him just fine," Gigi grumbled.

"Did you ever think about selling him," I asked, "since he's not very good as a trail horse?"

Matthew frowned. "No one else would have wanted him,

and we didn't want to send him to a horse sanctuary. Doug's part of the family."

I tossed a pile of hay. "I'm learning so much about the history of this place today. I'm glad I stayed to help."

"I thought a city slicker like you would be too fancy for barn work," Matthew said with a glint in his eye.

"I'll have you know," I said haughtily, "that my first pet was a hamster, and I was the one who cleaned his cage every week, all by myself."

He whistled long and slow. "Impressive. You should have mentioned you had experience with this type of work."

"See," I said, "people aren't always what they seem on the outside. Remember that, Gigi."

"People think I'm a weirdo," she said, not sounding too sad about it. "That's what they see on the outside because I don't dress like the other girls, and I don't want to talk about boys. They have no idea how fast I can ride a horse or that I know how to take a boy down if he gives me any trouble. Right, Dad?"

"That's right, sugar. Knee him in the nuts then head butt him in the nose."

I had the cutest picture in my head of Matthew teaching Gigi self-defense. Good for her. A girl needed to be prepared.

"Can we stop now?" Gigi leaned on the handle of her pitchfork. "I'm tired."

"Fifteen more minutes," Matthew said. "Tired is good. It means you worked hard."

"That's what you always say."

I smiled as I tossed manure into the wheelbarrow, enjoying their father-daughter banter. He could not have been a more different parent than Freddy, who overindulged our kids terribly. I always had to be the strict parent because someone had to teach the boys how to save their money and show up for their commitments even when they didn't feel like it. It annoyed me to no end that he got to be the fun parent all the time.

"I bet your kids never had to muck stalls," Gigi said, as if she were reading my mind. "Right, Lauren?"

"My sons never mucked stalls," I admitted, "but I think they would have benefitted from it. Your dad is giving you a chance to develop a strong work ethic. That's the most important thing in life. If you have everything handed to you, you don't learn the value of hard work or how good it feels to accomplish something on your own steam. I made my sons get summer jobs from an early age because that was important to me, and now they tell me they're glad I did."

Freddy was furious the first time I "forced" Julien to work on his summer break from high school because he couldn't take the boys to France and Switzerland for months on end, frittering their days away the way he did. We were long past doing family vacations together by that point, so I told him he could have the first two weeks of summer to travel with the boys, and everything from there on had to be spent working at least a part-time job in the city. If they couldn't find their own work, I had plenty for them to do at my office. Freddy had called me a "jejune, workaholic American" to which I replied, "This workaholic American has been supporting your ass for twenty years" and that ended the summer job argument.

"I'm going to raise horses here at Silver Sage when I grow up," Gigi said, her voice singing with pride. "If Dad lets me, that is. I want to breed Appaloosas."

I expected Matthew to say something to support her dreams, and when he didn't, I took a guess at why that might be. Judging by how few guests they had at the ranch, maybe the place wasn't bringing in enough money to sustain another generation of the Hart family. The land here was beautiful, but the ranch buildings clearly needed modernizing. My heart hurt when I thought about Gigi possibly having to say goodbye to a place that meant so much to her. Certainly, Matthew had a plan in place to make sure that never happened?

Although I hadn't known her for long, I already felt a kinship to this girl. She appeared to have a rich internal life, with her books and horses, and I could definitely identify with that. Without Tori as my other half during our middle and high school years, I would have been a wallflower instead of a person who got invited to parties and asked to the prom. Gigi had something special that I didn't have as a young person though—somewhere she could be her horse-loving self and feel totally accepted—and that was Silver Sage Ranch.

"That sounds like a wonderful life plan," I said. "There's no reason you can't make those dreams come true."

Matthew didn't echo my sentiments, further making me question the future of this wonderful place. "Let's finish up here and get some lunch," he said. "There's plenty of other work I need to do this afternoon, and Lauren needs to get back to her vacation."

AFTER A DELICIOUS MIDDAY meal in the dining room, I took a long soak in my bathtub to ease the soreness that I knew was going to show up in my backside and legs after our trail ride. The bathtub in my cabin was nowhere near as luxurious as the one I'd had my eye on buying for a long time—a soaking tub made of hinoki wood harvested in Japan. This was a fairly standard steel tub with some age on it, along with that scratchy anti-slip material on the bottom that wasn't exactly comfortable on the buttocks. Still, the hot water felt good on my muscles and, as I relaxed, I daydreamed about Matthew astride his muscular Appaloosa gelding. No wonder the Marlboro Man was such a sex symbol back in the day.

Ridiculously, I found myself wondering what Matthew would look like with a thick mustache. Facial hair aside, there was something about a man on horseback, riding through an open expanse of land. I really thought he was going to kiss me when we were alone in the stables the previous evening. I certainly was giving him the signals that I wanted it to happen, but the stupid rings on my left hand probably made him stop.

Why was I still wearing them, anyway? I twisted the beautiful emerald-cut diamond engagement ring, the soapy water loosening it easily on my finger. Then I pulled it off and set it on the side of the tub. The diamond encrusted platinum wedding band was a little harder to get over my knuckle, but I eventually succeeded. Symbolically speaking, they represented a union that soured way too early and then lingered on way too long. Still, they'd been with me for a long time, and my finger felt naked.

"Goodbye," I whispered, feeling a little silly about talking to inanimate objects. Examining my heart for any lingering sadness about my divorce, I found nothing but regret that I'd never get to wear those beautiful rings again. It would be stupid not to sell them, but they still held sentimental value for me, representing a time in my life that wasn't all bad. I raised two wonderful boys and built a company with my sister. Maybe that's why I left them on my hand for so long, but it was time for a fresh start.

As I got dressed after my soak, I checked my phone for the first time since before my morning ride. A missed call from Tori sent me into a panic. Had something happened at Ms. Match or, more importantly, to our mom? No one had been able to contact me for more than half the day.

Thank goodness she picked up her phone when I called her back.

"Calm down," Tori said. "I just called to see how things were going there. I miss you."

We'd been apart for similar stretches of time when one of us was on vacation, but the distance between us now felt vast. Whether that was because I was in a remote location without reliable access to WiFi and cellular service or because I was having experiences I hadn't told her about... well, it was difficult to say.

"I miss you, too," I said. "I'm having fun here though. I can't believe I'm saying this, but landing at the wrong ranch might be the best mistake that's ever happened to me."

When I described my lovely morning trail ride, I didn't mention that I was the only guest with Matthew and Gigi. I also didn't tell Tori how handsome and attentive he was, or that we'd shared a beer and a visit to the stables the evening before. She would have been happy for me, I was sure of it, but she'd also encourage me to have a vacation fling with him, and even hearing that would cheapen what I felt for Matthew. He wasn't one-night stand material. Matthew was a guy you fell for, head over heels, and cherished deeply. Not that I would have minded finding out whether I could enjoy casual sex, and I'd certainly imagined what it would be like if I could spend the night with him.

"I'm so glad you're having fun," she said. "I was able to get you a reservation at Silvery Sage Resort and Spa in Montana, but they didn't have any openings until a week from Tuesday."

"I really appreciate that, but I'm very comfortable here, so I think I'll stay put. I might visit the shooting range tomorrow. There's also a horseback ride up to a campfire cookout in the mountains next week that sounds pretty great. They prepare beans and cornbread over an open fire."

"A shooting range? Camping survival tactics? Oh God, I've sent you to a doomsday cult! Do they teach you how to skin rabbits, too?"

Now it was my turn to tell her to calm down. "Chill out, Tori. This is normal Western stuff, nothing bizarre." At least it seemed normal, but what did I know? I wasn't even sure how to make a campfire, much less cook over one.

"I hate to ask you this, but have you heard anything from Tempest about whether Freddy has agreed to your terms?" she asked. "Or is he still being a greedy butthead?"

"Greedy butthead," I confirmed. "They've been negotiating all week, and I'm expecting a call from her tomorrow."

"I hope to hear good news soon then," she said. "Until then, have fun with the hot rancher."

"Wh-what?"

Tori made a tsk tsk noise at me. "Dear sister, don't think you can fool me for one second. Any time his name comes up, your voice changes. And I know what he looks like. I Googled his ranch and saw his photo."

Dammit. She was good.

"Fine, he's hot."

"Uh huh."

"And maybe I'm attracted to him, but that's it. Nothing is happening or going to happen between the two of us." Lies. All lies. Was I lying to her or myself though? That was the real question.

"Oh, sure, I believe you," she said breezily. "But keep in mind, those are some famous last words you just uttered, right before the time people start getting naked."

CHAPTER 11

LAUREN

*T*he day after riding Alma, I felt emboldened to hike alone on the trails around the ranch because maybe I was more cut out for ranch life than I'd given myself credit for. I could do this thing! Bottle of water in hand, I headed away from the cabins, trudging along the dirt paths that climbed to higher altitudes and, eventually, to a path through the aspen trees. I quickly realized two things. One, my Peloton classes were finally paying off because I was in the best shape of my adult life. Two, hiking in the west was a different experience.

In the forests of the northeast, I'd loved the sense of being tucked away in a world of fallen limbs, mossy rocks and running streams. There was usually a canopy of trees obscuring the views and offering shelter from the sun. At the ranch, the landscape was completely different. Yes, there were some groves of trees for shade, but mostly I hiked out in the open, along rugged trails of rocky soil and through open fields of grasses and sagebrush, enjoying views that went on for miles. All that openness could make one feel a little exposed and uneasy. I couldn't hide from anyone, including myself.

Frequently, my thoughts turned to my impending divorce, and although I'd promised myself on the plane to Wyoming that I wouldn't spend a lot of time ruminating on my past, I couldn't help it. Few of the years Freddy and I spent together were happy ones. When I met Frederic Arnaud Tremblay at a Manhattan networking event for young entrepreneurs, I couldn't believe this suave, pedigreed man would be interested in little old me in my Ann Taylor navy blue sheath dress and matching pumps. Not only was he gorgeous and cultured, he shared my dream of running his own company, which in his case was a wine import business.

Had we dated long enough, I would have realized that although he wore the appearance of wealth, his immediate family had piddled away what was left of their fortune by living extravagantly. More importantly, Freddy might have had plans to start a business, but he completely lacked the work ethic to execute them. Within six months of meeting, we married, I got pregnant, almost immediately got pregnant again, and soon I was the breadwinner for a family of four.

His infidelity probably started much sooner than I realized, but even when I knew for certain there were other women, I stayed with him. I wanted to spare our sons the pain of their parents splitting up and, selfishly, the thought of them spending half their time in a different house from me was unbearable. I only had them for eighteen years, and I wasn't giving up a single day with them just because their father couldn't keep his dick in his pants. Once the boys were in college, I finally asked for a legal separation. Should I have done that much sooner? Maybe. Would my life have been better or worse if I had? There was no way of knowing the answer to that question, although that didn't stop me from asking it over and over again.

By the time I was back at my cabin, sweaty and shaky with exhaustion, I'd decided what to do. I called Tempest and told her to make a deal with Freddy's lawyer. Give him anything he wanted except a piece of Ms. Match. If we made him a generous alimony offer, I was betting he'd give up his bid for part of the company. I didn't care if I had to work until I was seventy to make payments, as long as the divorce got finalized and I kept our company firmly out of his reach. After Tempest and I hung up, I felt a deep sense of peace. My relationship with Freddy should have been severed years ago, and it was time to complete the paperwork so I could fully move on with my life.

∼

"HAVE YOU MET THE COWS YET?" Matthew asked me that night in the dining room. He usually stopped by my table during dessert, but that evening he'd invited me to join Gigi and him while we ate sticky, perfectly browned pineapple upside down cake.

"Not yet," I said. "But I saw many signs of them today."

He smiled mischievously. "Should have warned you to avoid the cow patties. How are the new hiking shoes holding up?"

"Surprisingly comfortable. I have a few blisters, but nothing bandaids can't cure."

"Tell her about the dance," Gigi said, her mouth full of cake.

"I arranged a little end-of-the-week dance in the Round Room. Our neighbors, Merle and Jean Tucker, are expert two-steppers, and they love giving lessons. The party will be for guests and staff, and I think it will be a good time. I know the Shahs and the Jernigans want to come." He nodded over at the two families in the dining room. "Hope you'll be there too."

"Are you two going to dance together?" Gigi asked.

I had no idea if she was asking because I was the only

female guest with no other dance partner in sight or if she'd picked up on something between Matthew and me. Either way, I felt my cheeks warm.

"I'm sure we'll all dance with different partners," Matthew said. "That's how it usually works at these things." Finally, he met my gaze and held it. "But I'd appreciate it if Mrs. Wagonblast saved a dance for me."

My breathing felt shallower than usual as I nodded. "I can do that."

After dinner, the two of them went to the stables to check on Elijah, the barn cat, and say goodnight to Loki, Gigi's favorite horse. I wanted to ask if I could go with them, but I knew that would be horning in on father-daughter time. Still, I felt no desire to go back to my empty cabin. The more time I spent with Matthew, the more I wanted; however, a call I'd received that afternoon from my publicist made it clearer than ever I couldn't involve him in my drama.

Photographers hunted down Freddy in Paris while he was having dinner with a young woman. Although I knew her to be his cousin, the press who ran the photos made it out to be a romantic rendezvous. The same could happen to me if I wasn't careful. Photographers were still skulking around outside the Ms. Match offices, and I knew they were harassing Tori, even though she'd never admit it. Even my sons had received calls, asking for statements about their parents' marital woes. How could I involve Matthew and his daughter in that kind of mess?

No, it was better if I maintained a little distance from him, especially if we ever went off the ranch property together again. You never knew who would sell a photo for a few dollars. The disappointment I felt at not being able to pursue even a close friendship with Matthew was more motivation to get the divorce settled quickly. Once we officially signed everything, Freddy and I could leak news of our new status to the press, and I'd be truly single for the first time in decades. Now that I knew my sex drive hadn't completely gone dormant, maybe someday I'd be ready to fall in love again, or at the very least go on dates, and I had Matthew to thank for that.

I nursed my coffee for as long as I could after Matthew and Gigi left the dining room, and then I walked through the staff door to the kitchen, startling a young woman who was working on washing dishes.

"Sorry, ma'am." She wiped her wet hands on her apron. "We don't get many guests back here."

"I wanted to tell the chef that I've been enjoying his food. Would that be alright?"

"He left for the night. After he finishes cooking, he peels out of here." She blushed, realizing she'd probably said too much. "I mean, he has the rest of the evening off after preparing dinner."

"I see." Across the room, I spotted Tyler, who was constantly zipping around on a golf cart or literally running around the ranch. Currently, he was wiping down countertops. "You seem to wear a lot of hats around here, Tyler."

His grin was infectious. "That is true. I like it though. I've always had a lot of energy to burn. Got me into trouble in school. I do better when I'm busy all the time."

"It's true," the girl said. "He's always been that way." As she talked, her hands worked in the sudsy water of the deep sink, scrubbing pots.

"Seems like you're in the right job, then."

"Yeah, and Matthew is a great boss. I learn a lot from him. I want to run my own ranch someday, a place where at-risk kids can come and be around nature. I think being outside and around animals can help people. I know it helped me."

"That's a pretty awesome mission. I'd like to hear more about it someday." I meant that sincerely. People definitely didn't give Gen Z enough credit. If anyone saved the world, it would be these kids.

His eyes lit up with surprised delight. "Sure! I'd be happy to tell you more."

"I look forward to it."

"Goodnight, Mrs. Wagonblast!"

I'd never get used to that name.

With nothing left to do, I started the short walk back to my cabin. Evening had fallen, and I was enjoying the stars. As I contemplated which book to read at bedtime, a sound came out of nowhere, and it took me several seconds to process that it was getting closer. A slight tremor of the earth below my feet turned into a light drumbeat and then a pounding. But where was it coming from? I spun around and saw it, a herd of beasts bearing down on me, dust flying up around them.

I only had time to gasp before the cows were upon me. I pulled my arms close to my body, trying to make myself a smaller target, and clamped my eyes shut. The cacophony of their hooves was deafening as they hurtled past me. Time stood still and only one thought ran through my head: please, don't let me die. I'm not ready yet.

When I dared to open my eyes, the cows were running off into the distance, taking their cloud of dirt with them. I inhaled a shuddering breath and looked down to make sure everything was still there. Feet. Knees. Hands. I was intact, at least physically. As the realization of what had just happened set in, my legs shuddered, and I looked for something to grab onto for support. Fortunately, there was a low fence nearby, and I sagged against it, clutching onto a post with both hands.

"Lauren!" Matthew's voice rang out as he sprinted toward me. I'd never been so happy to see someone in my life. "You alright?"

When he was close enough, I launched myself at him, flinging my arms around his waist in a hug he clearly hadn't anticipated, as he swayed backwards on impact. I needed to hold onto something solid. Something that wasn't trying to kill me.

"Cows." His broad chest muffled my words as I clung to him with all my might.

Tenderly, he wrapped his arms around me, smoothing one hand over the back of my head. "I'm so sorry. Someone left a gate open today. They don't normally get in here, and they got spooked by something."

Sensing that he was about to let go, I pulled him closer. He smelled like fresh hay and Ivory soap, a surprisingly heady combination. "They ran straight for me."

"They weren't trying to hurt you, I promise." He caressed my back in soothing circles. "You're safe now."

A horrifying image of the cows trampling the Jernigan children ran through my head. "Don't you need to go round them up?"

"Tyler and Walt are on it. Walt is the one who radioed to say they'd gotten in."

"Oh." Even though I would have been perfectly happy to spend the rest of the evening in his arms, I reluctantly released him and stepped back. He must have thought I was a loon, latching onto him that way. "I'm alright now. Sorry for jumping at you like that."

I looked up at him, afraid that he would wear an awkward expression because of what I'd done. Female guests probably didn't violently hug him every day. Instead, what I saw in Matthew's eyes was heat, the same kind I felt when I was around him.

"You can jump at me any time."

His deep voice created an ache low in my belly. Desire pinged between us...

Cows are back in the pasture. Sorry about that. Guest left a gate open. Over.

I looked around, but it was Walt's voice blasting through the walkie attached to Matthew's belt.

Matthew sighed and brought the walkie toward his mouth. "Thanks, Walt." He attached it to his belt again, and his voice took on a more businesslike tone. "Are you sure you're okay? Can I have someone bring a cup of tea to your cabin?"

Before I could answer, Gigi ran toward us, her glasses askew on her little face. "Dad! Dad! Did you get them?"

"Everything is okay," he assured her as she arrived at his side, messy-haired and panting hard. "The herd is back where they belong, but Lauren got a little scare."

Gigi nodded. "You're not used to cows." She wasn't asking me, she was telling me. And she was right.

"No, I'm not. I bet you are, though."

She nodded. "Yeah, but I like horses a lot better."

"Me too, Gigi." I gave her a shaky smile. "Me too."

She tilted her head to one side. "What are you doing tomorrow?"

"Gigi—" Matthew started.

"I have no plans," I said, interrupting him.

"Let's go on a ride, just you and me. Dad has a full schedule."

"I'd love that." It was true. I preferred Gigi's company to riding with a group of other people.

"Cool." She was acting blasé, but I could tell she was excited. "What time?"

"I know you're an excellent rider," Matthew said to her, "but you can't take guests out alone yet. Walt can lead you two."

She looked so forlorn that I had to do something. "Maybe you can help me pick out an outfit for the dance after we ride and teach me a few steps so I don't make a fool of myself."

Gigi kicked the dirt. "Okay. I still think I'm old enough to lead a ride though."

Matthew patted her shoulder. "Give it a couple years, and you'll be leading rides, honey. I promise."

I could have stayed and chatted with them all night, but I knew he had to get her to bed, and, frankly, I needed a moment to relive the stampede and freak out in the privacy of my cabin. Then, something terrible dawned on me.

"Matthew, I think it was me. I probably left the gate open. I was taking pictures during my hike this morning, and I got distracted by this beautiful bird. I might be the one who let the cows in."

He put a hand on my shoulder, and even that small touch grounded me as I whirled with panic.

"It's okay," he said softly. "These things happen. No harm was done."

"I feel so bad, though." I was the type of person who could ride this guilt trip for hours if I let myself.

"I've done it before," Gigi said. "Don't worry, Lauren. As Dad says, shit happens."

"Gigi!" Matthew pressed his hand to his forehead, clearly mortified.

"That's one way to put it." I tried to suppress my laughter and failed. The tension in my body uncoiled. "Thanks for being so understanding. I'll be more careful next time."

"I hope you get some good rest tonight," he said.

Gigi waved to me. "See you tomorrow at breakfast."

As they walked away, Matthew put an arm around her shoulder, and a lump formed in my throat. He was a good dad. A really good dad, admirably committed to running his family's ranch. After being married to a man whose only passions were sailing, spending money and sleeping with beautiful women, it was refreshing to meet someone with values like my own. Unfortunately, I'd have to settle for being his friend, and not let it go any further than that. Then again, I couldn't help what my late night imagination would do with him, alone in my room with the curtains drawn. That was a whole different story.

CHAPTER 12

MATTHEW

*W*hile Gigi spent the morning riding and giving Lauren two-stepping lessons, I finally got caught up on some office work. It was the first uneventful day I'd had in a long time, and it occurred right when my brain kept wanting to return to the moment Lauren threw herself into my arms. I'd felt her heart pulsing against my chest as she clung to me, and I didn't want to let her go. I wasn't about to manufacture another cow stampede, but I was hoping the two-stepping party would allow me an opportunity to hold her in my arms again.

So much for distancing myself from my beautiful guest.

After his morning trail ride, Walt and I finally had a few minutes to get together in the staff mess hall to discuss the campfire cookout we were planning for the following week. Lauren said she'd ride up with us this time, so I wanted it to be extra special. More importantly, nothing could go wrong, which was a big ask at a ranch where I was putting out one fire after another.

"How about we bring your guitar and do some cowboy songs while dinner is cooking?" I suggested. During my parents' day, Walt often sang at our cookouts in his deep baritone voice, and guests loved it.

"My singing chops aren't what they used to be." He loaded up his baked potato with a huge slab of butter. "And don't tell me it's the cigarettes, cause I already know I need to quit."

"I could sing, if you'll play."

Walt gave me a grave look. "The moose might think it's mating season if you sing, son."

"Very funny. My voice isn't that bad." He raised his bushy grey eyebrows. "Alright, maybe Tyler would sing for us. Is that better?"

"Why all the fuss?" Walt asked.

"I just want to make it special for the guests. The Shahs and Jernigans are here for two weeks, and they came to one cookout already this summer, and the Mason family is back at the ranch for the first time in several years. I feel like we should do something different for this one."

"Uh huh." Walt's mouth slid into a half smile. "Nothing to do with impressing a certain New Yorker?"

My mouth hung open as I struggled to find the words to convince him otherwise. "Of course not. Although now that you mention it, I would like her to give us a rave review. She probably has a lot of wealthy friends back home who would—"

"Enjoy a no-frills ranch experience?"

I groaned and leaned my elbows on the table, letting my head fall into my hands. "Give me a break, Walt."

He laughed as he slapped my back. "No shame in admiring a beautiful woman. I once had feelings for a ranch guest." He smoothed two fingers over his mustache. "Her name was Lola. She was a showgirl."

I glared at him. "That is a Barry Manilow song."

"Fine, she was a bookkeeper from Tucson, but her name was Lola, and she came to the ranch one summer with her sisters." His eyes got a faraway look in them. "She had the prettiest smile, as well as some other lovely…assets."

This was the most Walt had ever told me about a woman he'd dated. "So what happened to her?"

"We actually met up in Telluride that winter for a little ski vacation. That was the last time I ever saw her."

"Why? What happened?"

"Turns out I don't enjoy skiing." He picked up his fork, took a bite of potato, and that was the end of his story. I knew I'd get nothing else out of him. The truth was, Walt was terrible at relationships. Everyone knew that about him. If anyone spotted him in the company of a woman—for example, leaving The Mangy Marmot on a Saturday night—he never spoke about it afterwards, at least not to me. Sometimes I thought my brother Bowie had taken on Walt as his romantic role model in life because he seemed to be cut from the same cloth.

With a loud bang and a strong breeze behind her, Gigi slammed through the mess hall's screen door. "I need two sandwiches, some apples, chips, and two drinks." She hurried past us toward the hot bar. "Potatoes? Those aren't good on a picnic."

"Sure they are," I said. "And who are you going on a picnic with?"

"Lauren. I'm taking her down to the creek again. Don't worry, we're walking this time." She reached for the bag of bread that was always present in the staff kitchen, in case someone wanted to make a sandwich. "We might bring fishing poles too."

"Wash your hands first!" I scolded.

Gigi grumbled but went over to the small sink basin on the other side of the room. The two of them on a picnic was pretty cute to envision, and I longed to go with them. Unfortunately, I had a date with a caulk gun and a new shower pan in one of the guest cottages.

"You've taken a shine to Mrs. Wagonblast, huh?" Walt asked as she dried her hands and then headed toward the bread and peanut butter.

"She's great," Gigi said as she got to work on the sandwiches. "She picked up the two-step right away. Did you know she speaks French?"

"I didn't know that," I said. "What else did you discover about her?"

Walt started to chuckle, but it turned into a coughing spell.

Gigi turned and shook a piece of whole wheat bread at him. "You need to quit smoking, Walt. It's terrible for you."

"I've cut down," he mumbled sheepishly. Being shamed by a child was humbling indeed, and I might have felt sympathetic toward him if the topic was a different one. Maybe Gigi could eventually get through to him about his smoking, because I certainly hadn't been able to.

Tyler's voice crackled through my walkie. "Come in, Boss."

"I'm here, Ty. What's up?"

"We've got a faucet in cabin three that won't shut off. I'm here now, but I believe I'm going to have to shut off the water supply to figure out the issue. Over."

Indeed, I could hear running water in the background. Wonderful. Guests who wanted a shower in the next hour or so would not be too happy, but there was nothing else to be done about it. "Copy. Do what you have to do."

"What's that saying?" Walt asked. "Heavy is the head that wears the toilet plunger?"

"Real funny. It's more of a dunce cap at this point." I was falling deep into self-pity.

"You're doing your best," he said. "Just keep on keeping on. What else can you do?"

In addition to the faucet that kept on flowing, the next few hours presented me with a tearful Kyra, who had been chewed out by Chef Damon, and a bird who flew into the dining room and refused to exit. As I finally cornered the wayward chickadee and shooed him through the back door, I asked myself what else could go wrong that day. Turns out, you should never ask yourself that question.

~

INSTEAD OF DINNER in the dining room that evening, we had what I called poolside grill grub so Chef Damon and Serenity could get a well-deserved night off. Tyler and I manned the grills and Kyra did the serving. It was nothing fancy—hamburgers, veggie burgers, corn on the cob, and a sideboard full of salads prepared by Serenity earlier in the day. Families seemed to appreciate a break from the formality of the dining room, and I did, too.

Gigi sat down to eat at a table with Lauren and, to my surprise, Walt came and joined them. He had a policy of not dining with guests, preferring to eat his meals casually with other staff members, but he was always a favorite with the people who came to stay at Silver Sage. Walt fit the western stereotype with his bushy mustache and worn Stetson, not to mention his skill with horses. People always enjoyed his sly humor and nuggets of cowboy wisdom. Why had he broken tradition by sharing a meal with a guest? As I tried to figure that out, my attention repeatedly strayed over to their table where there was lively chatter and laughter. It didn't take a genius to see that Walt had been charmed by Lauren, too, and he was thoroughly enjoying her company.

After supper, Gigi and our guests went to the Round Room to listen to a local bluegrass duo play acoustic guitar music. Hiring musicians for such a small crowd was expensive and probably foolish on my part, but it was important to me that everyone had a good time and left positive reviews. We couldn't build a business if people gave negative accounts of us on social media and travel websites. Besides, we'd always had evening entertainment in the Round Room for guests, and I wanted to keep the Silver Sage traditions alive. After making sure the performers had everything they needed, I headed back to my cabin to take a shower and rid myself of the smell of grilled meat.

When I was alone, the warm water soothing my tired muscles, I finally let myself feel the full weight of the day. It was time to acknowledge that this ranch I loved so dearly was falling apart piece by piece. The pool, the cabins and the tennis courts were all in need of major renovations or replacement. The plumbing needed updates too, and the first thing our groundskeeper had done when I took over the ranch was hand me a long list of improvements he'd been trying to get my father to make for years. We didn't have the money or the staff to stay afloat much longer, and I wasn't sure I could do a damn thing about that.

Without realizing it, I'd worked through dinner without eating, and now my stomach was painfully empty. I cured that problem by making myself a sandwich and downing a glass of milk, all accomplished while standing at the kitchen counter. The last thing I wanted to do was socialize, but I needed to check on my guests, so I slid my boots back on and headed out. Music emanated from the Round Room, windows lit with a golden glow, and when I got within twenty feet of the door, I stopped to listen. Such nights took me back to earlier times at Silver Sage, when guests filled every cabin and cottage, and evenings overflowed with laughter and camaraderie. I wanted so badly to restore our ranch to the way it once was, both for my parents' sake and my daughter's. Whether we failed or succeeded was all on my shoulders.

"Matthew?" a soft voice called out in the darkness.

I turned to see Lauren approaching. She was wearing those red boots she purchased in town, along with a pair of blue jeans and a white cotton blouse. The sight of her lifted my spirits a little.

"Hey, there. Are you headed to hear the music?" I asked.

"Yes, I'm going that way. I needed to use your office because I had to make a call and couldn't get reception anywhere else. I hope that was okay?"

My gut twisted. "Of course it's okay. I'm sorry for the inconvenience. Reception has always been an issue here." We used to encourage guests to disengage from the outside world and enjoy their time reconnecting with nature at Silver Sage, but in an era where people were addicted to their devices and had work-from-anywhere jobs, that was becoming a harder sell.

"It's fine," she said. "I was actually hoping to run into you. I saw someone racing out of here in your Suburban when I was in the office, and I was wondering if everything was okay?"

"My Suburban?" I looked over at where I'd parked it, and sure enough, the space was empty. "Did you see who was driving?"

"A man with short, curly blonde hair," she said. "That's all I could see. Why? Did you not know about it?"

"Shit. That was probably Chef Damon."

"Oh." Understanding dawned on her face. "Is he the person who isn't supposed to drink alcohol?"

"Yeah." I rubbed the tight muscles on the back of my neck. "I've got to catch up to him. How long ago did he leave?"

"About ten or fifteen minutes."

My mind started formulating a plan to get Chef back to the ranch before he wrecked himself or my vehicle. God forbid he hurt anyone before I could reach him.

"I need to ask Kyra if Gigi can sleep over in her cabin tonight because I don't know how long this is going to take me."

"I can watch her if you'd like?"

It was sweet of her to offer, but I would not let her be my babysitter. At least I could compensate Kyra for her help.

"That's alright, but I appreciate the offer." I started walking backwards toward the Round Room. "I've got to go."

"I'll go with you." She kept pace with me. "Let me help."

"Absolutely not. Get some sleep and forget I even told you about this. I'm mortified already."

She grabbed my arm, stopping me in my tracks. "Why are you embarrassed?" She looked up at me with those pretty brown eyes. "Please let me go with you. It's dark out, and you're upset. I want to help."

We had only known each other a few days and here she was, worrying about me, the guy who always took care of everyone else. My throat tightened up, making it difficult to answer, and I lowered my chin so she wouldn't see the emotion in my eyes. "I'll be fine. You're a guest—"

"I'm also your friend, right? Go talk to Gigi, and I'll meet you back at the office," she said firmly. "I'm going back to my room to grab a sweater."

Before I could argue, she was jogging away from me. Honestly, the part of me that wasn't embarrassed was glad I didn't have to go on this mission alone. Kyra was, as expected, happy to take on some babysitting hours, and Gigi was thrilled about the sleepover. I didn't bother telling either of them what was happening because I didn't need gossip spreading around the ranch. With that handled, I hurried back to the office to meet Lauren, and minutes later we were in a pickup truck, bouncing over ruts and stones on the road out of the ranch.

"Where are we going first?" she asked.

"The Mangy Marmot. If he's not there, he could be at another bar outside of town called Roy's, although I don't know how he'd hear about that place. It's all locals, and it's pretty rough."

"Like a biker bar?" Her earnest expression made me laugh.

"But less cool. A lot of guys with missing teeth and mullets." Her eyes grew round, like one of those anime characters, and despite my dire employee situation, I laughed. "Rural Wyoming is real sexy."

"Hmmm, some parts of it are sexy," she whispered, a little smile dancing on her lips.

Damn. What a waste of an evening. If Chef wasn't already dead, I might just kill him.

～

"WHAT'S OUR PLAN?" Lauren yelled into my ear to be heard above the noise that engulfed us the moment we walked into The Mangy Marmot Bar and Grill. On the weekends, everyone in a hundred-mile radius came there looking to blow off steam, get lucky, or both. I put a protective arm around Lauren's shoulder as a burly guy shoved past us on his way out the door.

"Let's head to the bar and ask my friend Ella if she's seen him."

She nodded, and I led us through the crowd to the long bar that ran along the one side of the room. Ella was pulling caps off bottles and taking orders at the same time. As we approached, she set five shot glasses up in front of her, deftly poured whiskey in them, then slid the shots down the counter to the people waiting for them. Not a drop of drink got spilled.

"Am I seeing things?" With a bit of dramatic flair, she rubbed her eyes and blinked at me. "Is that Matthew Hart at my bar? It's a miracle!"

I rolled my eyes at her. "Hey, Ella." Then I leaned in so she could hear me over the din. "I'm looking for an employee. Fifty-seven, blonde curly hair, just shy of five foot ten. Seen him tonight?"

"No," she said, "but Andy might have served him."

I glanced over at the other bartender on duty. He was as busy as she was. "Alright, thanks. We'll ask him."

She quirked an eyebrow. "I haven't met your friend yet. Are you hiding her?"

Lauren stood on her tiptoes and peered over my shoulder. "Hello!"

"This is Lauren Wagonblast," I said. "She's a ranch guest."

"Hey, there." Ella smiled politely at Lauren, then smirked at me. "Nice to meet you."

It was time to move on before Ella said something embarrassing about me to Lauren. There was a reason she and my brother Sam were best friends.

"If you see me carrying a guy out of here in a fireman's hold," I said, "just look the other way."

"That's just a typical night at The Marmot." Ella lifted her hand to wave as we left the bar area and dove into the rowdy crowd.

At first, we didn't see any sign of Chef Damon. He wasn't at the tables near the windows or in the center of the room on the Marmot's makeshift dance floor. Just as I was going to suggest we question Andy, a familiar arrogant voice rang out.

"Leaning is cheating!"

I peered over a few people's heads and spotted Chef Damon back by the pool tables, telling a guy twice his size he'd broken pool etiquette by leaning on the table.

"Follow me." I pushed my way toward Chef, and Lauren kept close behind, her hand resting on my shoulder. "Run to the front of the bar if trouble starts," I warned her.

"Seriously?" The warm tickle of her whisper on my neck made me shiver in a good way. "I'm a New Yorker, Matthew. I can handle myself."

I tried not to roll my eyes. She had no idea what this place could get like when a man accused another man of cheating at pool. Hell, I'd seen our local librarian, Melba Rooster, throw a drink in a guy's face because he insisted listening to audiobooks wasn't really reading.

"Chef!" I called out.

He spun around at the sound of his name, stumbling over his own feet. Crap. He was already drunk, which was going to make this more difficult. The only thing standing between us now was a pool table and a guy with greasy hair and pock-marked skin who looked like he'd enjoy pummeling someone tonight.

"Go away!" Chef called back to me. "I have the night off."

"Yeah, and you got here by stealing my Suburban. I thought I could trust you more than that. Now you get back in that car and come home with us." I sounded like some kind of possessive Joleen come to take back her man. My life was becoming a melodramatic mess.

Greasy guy stepped toward me, bristling for a fight. "He's not going anywhere until he pays me."

"Matthew!" A hand punched my shoulder. "What are you doing here?" I whipped my head to see the friendly grin of Luke Daltry, owner of The Eternal Springs Spa. Either he didn't notice what was going on between me and the pool players, or he was trying to diffuse the situation.

"About to get my head kicked in by"—I looked at Mr. Greaser—"what's your name, sir?"

"Dwight."

"Dwight," I repeated to Luke.

"How can I help?" He folded his arms on his chest, showing off his impressive biceps. Luke was former Canadian military, and he was ready to jump into action.

I nodded at Lauren. "Keep her safe."

"I'm fine," Lauren protested with less gusto than before.

"Okay," Luke said, moving closer to her. "You can protect me then, ma'am."

Now that I knew she'd be alright, I approached my new

friend Dwight. I wasn't about to be a hero. Black eyes and broken noses hurt worse when you were sober.

"Let's end this without violence," I said calmly. "What does he owe you?"

"Five hundred."

My mouth dropped open, and I shook my head at Chef in disbelief. "Seriously? Five hundred dollars? Are you even good at pool?"

"Yes!" Chef rapped the end of his pool stick on the floor. "He only won because he cheated!"

"That's it." Dwight spat on the floor. "You're a dead man." I expected him to run around the table to get to his opponent, but nope, he scrambled over it like Gollum going after a magical ring. I followed in hot pursuit, going around, not over. God help me, I was gonna pull a hammy trying to save this stupid man.

Chef scampered away from Dwight and, in an amateur move, tossed aside his only weapon, the pool stick. Dwight easily latched onto the back of his shirt and yanked him backwards.

"Pay up," he growled into Chef's ear as he pulled him into a headlock.

I was still moving toward them when someone grabbed my left arm and jerked me to a halt. Either Dwight had friends or other guys were itching for a fight. It didn't matter. I reflexively raised my right arm to ward off a potential blow as I rotated my left arm and backed up to slip out of his grip. Now that I was free, I had to deal with the fist he was about to throw.

CHAPTER 13

LAUREN

"Matthew! Look out!" My warning about the man approaching him from behind was drowned out by the noise in the bar. Blood pumping, I tried running to him but my chaperone shepherded me away from the melee as I strained against him.

"Stay here," he commanded, ushering me into a space against the wall. Then he hurried off toward the action. Fists were flying, and I looked on in horror with no clue how to help. I couldn't even see Matthew anymore, much less assist him. There was a pool stick on the floor near my feet, and I grabbed it because it seemed like the wise thing to do. Then I swung my head around, searching for a familiar face, finding none in sight.

Right as I was considering calling the police to stop the violence, Chef scrambled toward me with Dwight in hot pursuit. There was no time to think before I acted, letting Chef pass by then holding out the pool stick at ankle height to catch Dwight unaware. As soon as he tripped and went flying forward, I dropped the stick and scooted out of there. As I hurried toward the front of the bar, Ella, the petite bartender, appeared out of nowhere and hopped onto the pool table with a fire extinguisher in one hand and an air horn in the other. The air horn got the place silent, except for the dulcet tones of Rosanne Cash singing through the speakers, and Ella dropped it onto the pool table. Then she waved the fire extinguisher at the crowd.

"Cut it out or I'm aiming for you," she warned. "This thing will blow a man clear across the room, as you've witnessed before."

My sister's boyfriend, Nick, the retired fire captain, had told me the same thing about a blast from a fire extinguisher. He'd said to keep one under the bed "in case fires and intruders."

She aimed the nozzle at Dwight. "Clear out of here."

"He owes me money, Ella," Dwight whined.

"And you know there's no gambling in The Marmot," she shot back. "But if you leave now, I'll let you come back again to play pool and drink beer. How about that?"

She was seriously impressive, and Dwight must have thought so too, because he headed toward the door. His departure immediately ratcheted down the tension in the room since the major cause of conflict had been, for lack of a better word, extinguished.

Ella hopped off the pool table, and we both went to check on Chef, who had taken on a greenish pallor as he leaned against the wall, breathing heavily.

"You alright?" she asked.

He nodded as he swayed backwards. The tall guy, the one protecting me, moved in to catch him before he hit the ground.

"Drunk as a skunk," he pronounced as he held onto Chef around his middle. "Probably a little light-headed from the excitement, too."

"I'm fine." Chef briefly opened his eyes before shutting them and going silent.

Matthew stalked over to us, and, thank goodness, he

wasn't bleeding or limping, although there was a red area on his cheekbone that was starting to swell.

"I'll get him home, Ella," he said. "I'm sorry for disturbing the peace tonight."

"It's never peaceful here on weekends," she said briskly, tucking a wayward curl back into the bun on her head. "Seems like people are angrier and drunker lately. I think I need a new business plan."

Matthew guided Chef toward the door, and Ella and I followed behind them. The noise in the bar resumed, customers picked up chairs that had been knocked over, and life at The Mangy Marmot went on like nothing had ever happened.

"Can I get some ice?" I asked.

Her hazel eyes softened. "Are you hurt?"

"No, it's for Matthew. I think his cheek is going to bruise. I noticed some swelling."

She pressed her mouth closed as if trying to hide a smile. "Sure thing. We wouldn't want to mar that pretty face of his."

While Ella went behind the bar and filled a plastic bag with ice, I pondered whether she'd been teasing me about Matthew's good looks because she knew I had a crush on him. Was it that obvious?

"Here you go." She leaned over the bar and handed me the ice pack. That's when I noticed the animal behind her—a taxidermied furry thing about the size and color of a groundhog, posed on a stump of wood.

"What is that?" I asked, pointing to him.

"That's The Dude, our mascot. Don't worry. He died of natural causes."

"Is he a marmot?" I studied him and he stared back. "He looks disturbingly alive."

"Yeah, they're pretty adorable, honestly. You might see one around, if you stay long enough."

"Fabulous." At least they were smaller than cows.

I said goodnight to Ella and went outside to help Matthew take Chef Damon to the Suburban, which was parked in the street not far from where we'd left the pickup truck. He was compliant, but also on the verge of passing out. We managed to buckle him in before he slumped over, drunk as a skunk or, perhaps, a marmot.

"What's going on over here?" It was Sam calling to us as he crossed the street, looking freshly showered and handsome. "Are you two going to The Marmot for a drink?"

"We just left there," Matthew said grimly. "Chef got drunk and laid down a pool bet he couldn't make good on. Then a fight broke out. Now we're headed home. The end."

"I saw your truck," Sam said. "Who drove the Suburban?"

"Chef took it." Matthew didn't sound angry, only exhausted and fed up. "I drove the pickup when I came looking for him. I'm too tired to talk about it right now, Sam. I'll be back for the truck tomorrow."

"I can drive it over to the ranch. Then Tyler can take me back to town. I need to hear the long version of this story." Sam turned away, then looked back over his shoulder. "Ella is okay, right?"

"Are you kidding?" Matthew said. "She stopped the fight."

Sam grinned with admiration. "That's my girl."

"WHAT DO YOU MEAN, we can't get through the gate?" I asked.

Matthew and I were sitting in the front seat of the Suburban, facing the ranch's entry gate, which, according to him, had been padlocked by Walt.

"It's for safety," Matthew said. "It's Walt's job to lock the gate every night, and he goes to bed pretty early, so guests and employees have to tell him if they're coming home after ten. Most of our guests don't rent a car, so it's not usually an issue."

"I thought there was no one out here, so you didn't need locks. And why don't you have a key? You usually have that massive keychain with you." My voice had taken on an edge because I was tired and frustrated.

"It's back at the house. I jumped into the truck and there was a key in there already." Matthew rubbed his forehead. "I wasn't thinking."

"Let's call Walt then. Or Tyler?" It was just after midnight. We'd stopped twice on the way home—once for Chef to be sick on the side of the road and the second time because there was a pronghorn lying in our lane. Matthew could have gone around it, but he wanted to make sure the animal wasn't still alive and suffering. Fortunately, it had already passed away because I could only assume he would have had to shoot it with a gun that was hidden somewhere inside this vehicle, and I did not want to witness that.

I had traveled far, far outside of my comfort zone.

"Pull out your phone." Matthew waited for me to get it out of my purse. "No reception, right?"

He was correct. No bars. My stomach sank as reality set in. The adrenaline rush of the bar fight was gone, leaving me weary and weak-limbed, and all I wanted to do was climb into a soft bed and fall asleep.

"So, do we walk back?" We could pretty easily climb over the main gate, which was only about four feet tall.

"I don't think that's a good idea," he said. "Four miles feels longer in the dark, and you could twist an ankle in a rut."

"We also can't leave Chef here alone." He was currently snoring loudly in the backseat, dead to the world.

"Why can't we leave him?" Matthew glanced over his shoulder with a look of disgust. "He earned it."

"Because he could vomit in his sleep, and his death would be on our hands. That's how Jimi Hendrix died, you know."

Matthew raised his eyebrows at me, and something about his expression made me throw my head back and laugh at the absurdity of our situation.

"I don't want him to go all Jimi Hendrix on us," Matthew said, smiling for the first time since the bar fight. "I guess we need to spend the night out here. Do you want to sleep in the back row of the Suburban? I'm going to sleep outside."

"Outside?" He looked serious, but I laughed again anyway. "Please tell me you're joking. We don't have a tent or sleeping bags." Camping sounded fun, theoretically, like after we'd done careful planning and preparation, not because someone locked a gate and left us stranded on the roadside.

"I've got a couple sleeping bags in the back," he said, "and you can have both of them and make yourself as cozy as possible."

"So I'd sleep in here with Chef and you'd be outside?" A nasty burp resounded in the seat behind us, and I wrinkled my nose. "I think I'll sleep out there with you."

SETTING up camp hadn't taken much time at all because all we had to do was roll out two sleeping bags on the ground. I let Matthew give me his fleece jacket to use as a pillow, and then we lay down next to each other, about twenty feet from the Suburban.

"Oof." I sat up again to extricate a rock that had been poking into my right shoulder from under my sleeping bag.

"I'm so sorry about this, Lauren," Matthew said. "I feel terrible, making you sleep out here."

"It's not your fault. I forced myself on you tonight." I heard what I'd just said and blushed as I snuggled back down into my sleeping bag. "You know what I mean."

"Still, I shouldn't have let you come with me. I know The Marmot can get wild on weekends, and I should have thought about the gate being locked."

"That's a lot of shoulds." The velvety night sky above us twinkled with stars. Thousands of them. More than that. Millions of stars. It took my breath away. "Wow. Look at that."

"Yeah, it's pretty amazing out here at night. Gigi and I call it nature's show."

"I think I just saw a shooting star!" I pointed like an excited child, renewed energy surging through me. "I've never seen one in real life before."

"Really?"

"That was my first."

"Should I tell you they're actually meteoroids, not stars? They're pieces of asteroids that collided with each other. When they hit earth's atmosphere, they vaporize, and that's what you're seeing."

"Huh…I can see why they renamed it. Vaporized meteoroids don't sound as sexy as shooting stars."

Matthew chuckled and tucked his hands behind his head. "No, I guess not."

A truly chilling thought flashed through my mind. "The cows aren't out here, are they?"

"Nope," he said. "They're in for the night."

I sighed with relief before tensing again. "What about other animals like marmots and pronghorns?"

As if on cue, howling echoed in the distance.

"Oh my God," I whispered. "Werewolves."

Matthew belly laughed until I thought he was going to cry. "Those werewolves are actually regular coyotes, nothing paranormal about them. They're not looking to hurt us, I promise." I loved how patient he always was with people. Even with a bar fight brewing, he'd kept calm and tried to defuse the situation.

I wriggled my body to inch my sleeping bag a little closer to his. "They didn't sound harmless."

"Remember that pronghorn on the road? We're much more dangerous to the animals out here than they are to us. Keep out of their way and nine out of ten times they'll keep out of yours."

"Nine out of ten?" I squeaked. "What happens the tenth time?"

"I knew as soon as the words were out of my mouth that you were gonna say that."

I rolled onto my stomach and fake-screamed into my makeshift pillow. "Just keep the flashlight on tonight. Then no animals will accidentally step on us, at least."

"They'll know we're here," he said. "They have much stronger senses than we do."

"This conversation isn't very reassuring. Do you camp under the stars like this often?"

He was lying on top of his sleeping bag, looking as comfortable as could be. Meanwhile, I had my bag zipped up to my chin to ward off the chill of the evening. Unless I was hot flashing, I was always cold.

"Not as often as I'd like," he said. "I wish I could travel more, but the summer is high season here at the ranch and then there's a lot that needs to get done in the winter."

"Does the winter get lonely?"

"It gives new meaning to the word lonely. I'm not totally alone, though. Walt stays to tend the horses, and Tyler was here last winter, helping me out with projects."

"Just the dudes."

He turned his head to look at me. "Yep."

I rolled onto my side in my sleeping bag, tucked my hands under my cheek, and stared back at him. For a few moments, neither of us said anything. We just gazed into each other's eyes. I knew in that moment there was no kidding myself that this crush of mine was unreciprocated. There was as much heat in his eyes as there was in mine. Parts of me that had been dormant and gathering metaphorical dust for so long were coming back to life. I wanted something to happen. I needed it to happen.

"Do you ever get lonely for female companionship?" I asked, knowing it was a loaded question.

"Of course," he said. "Finding someone I wanted to date wasn't easy before I took over the ranch. Now it's pretty much impossible. It's not often a beautiful woman accidentally lands here instead of the fancy spa she was supposed to go to." He closed his eyes, his mouth drawing into a frown. "I'm sorry. You're married, and I shouldn't say things like that to you."

"I get lonely too," I said softly. "And I'm not married anymore." Matthew opened his eyes and waited for me to continue. "We separated a long time ago, and we're in the middle of a divorce right now. The situation is complicated for other reasons, and I didn't want to get you involved in all that." I showed him my bare left hand. "I don't know why I was still wearing my rings. Habit, I guess. Maybe protecting my heart a little, too." He narrowed his eyes like he didn't understand me. "Men leave you alone when you're wearing a wedding ring, and that means you're safe from re-entering the dating world."

He gave me a lopsided grin. "Except for this guy. I didn't leave you alone. I told myself that flirting with you was harmless, but I was kidding myself."

My heart thudded in my chest. "I flirted back, so it was only fair."

Maybe the wedding ring had been the only thing keeping us apart until now. Why hadn't that been obvious to me before? We'd both wanted this, and by removing the ring and telling him I was separated, I'd gotten rid of the only real obstacle standing in our way. Except for one more thing...

"For personal reasons that are very hard to explain, I need

to keep my private life very private. Is that okay? Can we just pretend to be ranch owner and guest in front of everyone else? I imagine that's better for you, too."

Matthew propped himself up on one elbow and leaned over me. "That's okay by me."

As I stared into his blue eyes, time seemed to stretch before us like that huge Wyoming sky, endless with possibilities. We were alone out here and had the entire night ahead of us. Anything could happen if we let it.

His fingers traced their way down my neck, where he must have felt my blood pumping. I certainly felt it. When he brought his lips to mine, my mind went as quiet as the darkness surrounding us. All I could feel were his kisses. Tender. Sweet. Delicious. As good as I'd imagined, which was such a relief I wanted to giggle. But that would have sent the wrong message.

He pulled away, looking down at me with a dazed expression. "I've been wanting to do that for days."

"Then do it some more." I reached up to draw his head down toward mine. When he kissed me this time, it was with hunger, nothing tentative about it. Our lips parted and our tongues touched. It was slow and sexy, but hot. Sensual. Suddenly, I was burning up inside my sleeping bag.

Matthew smiled against my lips. "How do you taste like strawberries?"

"It's lip balm." And it was definitely gone now, after all that kissing. Was I sweating? It was about fifty degrees outside, but my skin was on fire.

"You're edible." He brought his mouth to my neck, his facial hair scruffing against my skin.

"I'm also ticklish!" I said through my laughter.

"Good to know." He nuzzled into me, and I laughed harder. The happiness bubbling up inside of me was so pure I almost wanted to cry.

Taking his head by his ears, I redirected his mouth to

mine, and the mood shifted from playful to heated again. His kisses were intoxicating. I felt as if I'd done shots of whiskey at the bar. We kissed each other deeply, wildly, until we had to break apart for air. Then we went back in and kissed some more until, somehow, I'd rolled myself on top of him, sleeping bag and all, like a damn mummy. Whoever invented these things assumed no one would want to fool around outdoors.

"Should I unzip myself?" I tossed my hair to one side, so it wasn't hanging down in his face. "I'm getting really warm." That was an understatement. I felt like a baked potato wrapped in tinfoil.

Matthew blew out a deep breath. "As much as I want to unzip that bag and take off all your clothes and do things to you that will make you blush from the tips of your painted toes to those adorable little earlobes, I feel like maybe you aren't ready for that just yet."

"Oh." After that description, all I could feel was disappointment. Full body blushing sounded like exactly what I wanted. My body was still telling me to get naked and wild, but my heart...

In my heart, I knew he was right.

"This is the first time I've kissed a man other than my husband in about twenty-five years," I admitted. "It's a little overwhelming, but in a good way." In a way that set me ablaze and gave me hope for my sexual future.

"How long can you stay at Silver Sage?" he asked. "A few more weeks?"

"At least one more week. Maybe more."

"Then we have a little time." He pulled my head down and kissed me again. "Let me romance you, Mrs. Wagonblast."

Guilt prickled inside me, and I pulled back from him. "About that name. It's—" An animal wailed in the distance and I gripped onto Matthew's biceps, my eyes widening. "What was that?"

He laughed and gently rolled me back onto the ground, keeping one arm around me. "C'mere. I'll protect you."

And that's how I spent the rest of my first night under the stars, kissing and snuggling in the strong arms of a very sexy rancher.

CHAPTER 14

MATTHEW

I'd broken my own rule never to get involved with a guest, and I wasn't feeling too sorry about it.

"What did you say, honey?" I asked Gigi. She was sweeping the floor of the Round Room as we attempted to spruce the place up for our dance that evening.

"Do I have to dance tonight?" she said. "I want to hang out by the bar and drink Shirley Temples."

"You could dance with one of the Jernigan boys. I think the older one might be almost your height." I winked at her, knowing this suggestion would get her riled up, and she didn't disappoint.

"Ew! I'm not dancing with that kid. I saw him give his brother a wedgie yesterday. Boys are gross."

I didn't bother to mention that Tyler and I were technically boys and not gross at all because I was fine with her being repulsed by boys her age for the time being.

"At least save one dance for your old man, okay?"

"Fine," she said, "I'll dance with you, but that's it." She paused and looked at the floor. "Sweeping this place is going to take forever."

She was right. The Round Room was a large space. True

to its name, the building was a circle—or really, an octagon —matching the look of the rest of the ranch with its tongue and groove timber walls. There was a stone fireplace, also circular, at the center of the room. Seating comprised Adirondack style chairs and couches with leather seats, flanked by rustic wood side tables for holding an after-dinner drink. The floor could have used refinishing, and there was some serious age on the furniture, but I still loved this part of the ranch. Everything about it felt like home.

"Ty, is Kyra able to come and help tonight?" I called out. He was stocking the bar my father had constructed many years ago.

"Yeah, she'll be here soon to help with dinner and the party." He dumped ice into the metal cooler behind the bar, and Gigi held her ears against the clanging noise until he finished. "She's hoping we can dance together a little. Would that be okay?"

"Of course, it's okay," I said. "You two get out there. I appreciate her being here."

We could have used at least two more helpers to get everything ready in time for the start of the party, but you did the best with what you had. Thank goodness for that Hart family work ethic that Lauren had praised so highly.

"When do I need to pick up the Tuckers?" Tyler asked.

I looked down at my watch to check the time. "They're expecting you in about two hours. Hopefully, we'll be set up in time."

Merle and Jean Tucker lived down the road from our ranch, and they were old friends of my parents, as well as two-stepping dynamos, now in their seventies. I'd asked them to come and give us all a lesson tonight, but Tyler needed to chauffeur them because Merle was developing macular degeneration and Jean didn't drive well in the dark. I needed to give that boy a huge bonus at the end of the month, but where that money would come from, I had no clue.

This evening, Chef Damon would set out a light meal of sandwiches and cold salads on the pool deck for our guests, even though he considered that type of meal beneath him as a professional. I needed him to prepare a simple meal before the dance because we didn't have enough employees to staff the dining room and the Round Room. He didn't complain too much about it, not after the trouble he'd put me through the night before. We still hadn't talked in-depth about the fact that he stole the Suburban, got drunk, gambled, and had to be saved in a bar fight. He knew I was upset with him, but he was also aware I needed him to stay for the rest of the summer. Sure, I could give him an ultimatum, but then I'd have to stick to it and find a new chef, and we both knew that wasn't likely to happen.

"Is Uncle Samuel coming to the dance?" Gigi asked.

"He is." I bent down so she could sweep her pile of dirt into the dustpan I was holding. "I think he's bringing a date."

Gigi rolled her eyes as she moved the broom. "Of course he is."

She liked having her uncle all to herself, but he often had a new woman on his arm. They were always attractive and intelligent, and I had no idea where he found so many of them. Unlike Walt and Bowie, Sam could do committed relationships, and he introduced these women as his girlfriends, but no one lasted longer than a year, and he definitely never mentioned being "in love" with any of them. My sister Faith called him a serial monogamist, which seemed pretty accurate.

"Who else will be here?" Gigi asked.

"Callan Colter and his nephew are coming. You remember them?" Cal was a bachelor neighbor and an old friend of mine who went to social events even less than I did. Since his nephew, Austin, had moved to Broken Arrow

Ranch to help run the place, Cal seemed to get out more, which was a good thing.

"Yeah, I remember visiting their ranch," she said. "They had some nice horses over there." It was a cattle ranch, but of course she remembered the horses they owned.

I took the dustpan outside to the wraparound porch to toss the dirt into the garden, and who should pass by but my favorite distraction. Lauren had a book in her hand and was moving at her rapid New York pace with a long-legged stride. She'd relaxed a little since she first arrived though, smiling more easily and untense those pretty shoulders so they weren't up around her ears anymore. The memory of kissing her ran through my mind, and I couldn't help but grin when I waved to her like some lovesick fool.

"How are party preparations going?" she asked as she approached the porch steps. She was wearing a slate gray tank top that scooped low in the front and showed off her pretty collarbones.

"Going well." I took my baseball cap off to run a hand through my hair before setting it back in place. I was a sweaty mess, but she'd seen me this way before. "Still have a lot to do."

She peered inside the propped open door behind me. "Can I help you guys with getting ready?"

"I'm sure you'd rather do something else. You're on vacation." She'd already mucked the stables, for goodness' sake.

"I think I found out something about myself this week." She clenched her teeth together in a grimace. "I'm not very good at relaxing."

I laughed and shook my head. "You're only discovering this about yourself now? I could have guessed that an hour after we'd met."

"Ha ha." She playfully slugged my arm, and even that bit of contact felt good. I'd missed her, and we'd only parted a few hours earlier, when Walt unlocked the gate and we drove back to the ranch. Sleeping with her at my side had been something special. The shampoo she used made her hair smell like honeysuckle, and it was like waking up with my nose buried in sweet flowers.

"C'mon in then," I said. "I'll give you a task and then you can check it off my list."

She pressed a hand to her chest. "How did you know I love lists?"

"Lucky guess."

As we walked into the Round Room, I tried to see it through her eyes. The hand-peeled aspen log chairs matched the rustic atmosphere of the room perfectly, but their leather cushions were wearing thin. The stone fireplace was a classic feature that was also in need of a good cleaning. I hoped she could appreciate the finer details of the room despite the age on them, including the pine plank floors and the airy feeling created by the high ceiling that rose to a peak in the center. It suddenly occurred to me that maybe my nostalgia clouded my view of how this place really looked.

"This room is so interesting," she murmured after saying hello to Gigi and Tyler.

I hoped interesting was good and not a euphemism for dated and dusty.

"I've always liked it. We're trying to make it look a little festive for tonight, but I'm afraid that's not really my strong suit."

"Have you ever thought of—" she stopped herself short. "Nothing, sorry." She mimed zipping her lips.

"Go ahead," I said. "I don't mind suggestions." One of the disappointing things about running the ranch on my own, without a spouse or a sibling, was that there was no one to bounce around ideas with or share in the triumphs and struggles. Part of the joy my parents experienced in owning the ranch was building the business together. My father had been the front man and the boss, but Mom's handiwork was all over the ranch, from the choice of quilts on the beds to the website pages detailing the backstory of every horse the ranch ever owned.

"Well…" Lauren walked around the room, her hands on her hips and a pensive expression on her face. "I'm picturing little lamps on some of these tables for mood lighting. I think that would give this room a cozy glow." She looked up at the wagon wheel style chandeliers on the ceiling. "You get some light from up there, but it's still pretty dark in here."

"That's a good idea." I wondered if I could find some decent lamps at the Goodwill in Cheyenne next time I was there.

"Some cozy rugs might be nice scattered around the room to give it more warmth. It would be great if they were in a Native American pattern. Of course, you'd want to find something authentic, not a ripoff. My sister would really be the woman to help with decor. She has an amazing eye for detail."

I could see the businesswoman in her as she surveyed the room, making mental improvements. She blushed as she clocked me watching her.

"Not that you need to do anything to this room. It's charming as it is."

"No, those are good suggestions," I said. "Thank you. Would you like a drink from the bar? We just got it set up."

She waved a hand, showing off her nails, which were now stripped of paint. "No, don't be silly. Put me to work."

I tasked her with helping Gigi knock down the cobwebs that had accumulated on the ceiling of the wrap-around porch. No doubt a busy, successful woman like Lauren had a housekeeper back home, but she jumped right into the task. Meanwhile, I got the extension ladder out of the storage barn to change some of the burned out chandelier bulbs.

After finishing our clean-up of the Round Room, we parted ways so we could all get showered and dressed for dinner. I told Gigi she should eat dinner with Lauren by the pool while I tended to a few last details. The two of them got along so well that it was hard not to imagine what it would be like if I had Lauren in my life as more than a ranch guest. Obviously, that was only a dream because our lives wouldn't intersect for anything more than a vacation.

I tried to simmer down and not get too excited about seeing Lauren all gussied up, as my mother would have said. Gigi and I put on our best pairs of jeans and boots, and we both chose to wear black Western shirts that snapped down the front. Hers had roses embroidered on the front pockets. Without trying, we ended up looking like a matching pair. She found it amusing to be my mini-me, and I treasured the moment, making sure to get a photo of the two of us. In a few years, she'd probably want to look nothing like her father.

Merle and Jean Tucker were the first guests to arrive at the Round Room looking sharp, as usual, in their western wear and turquoise jewelry. Wizened with wrinkles, but still spry in spirit, they asked Tyler to start the music so they could warm up on the dance floor.

"Takes a little longer to oil the gears these days," Merle said with a wink.

Sam showed up next with a plate of homemade cookies in hand. To my surprise, Ella was with him. She must have taken a night off from The Mangy Marmot, which was out of character for her. Instead of the "bartender bun" she always wore her hair in while working, her auburn tresses hung down around her shoulders in ringlet curls. She wore pressed white jeans and an off-the-shoulder light pink blouse that showed off her shapely figure, and...was that a rosy lip gloss on her lips? The fact that Ella was dressed up all feminine and cute was unusual and a little concerning. If this was an actual date, Sam would find a way to mess up the relationship, as he always did, and in the process, he'd ruin a long-standing friendship. There was no way I was going to let that happen.

I gave Ella a brotherly hug. "I didn't know you were coming with Sam tonight. I thought you had to work?"

"I got Dakota to cover for me. You know I love to two-step." She gave me her signature extra tight squeeze before brusquely pushing me away. That hug was Ella in a nutshell. "And Sam gave me a sad story about not having a date for the evening. I didn't want him to arrive alone, looking like a loser."

"Lies." Sam handed me the plate of his delicious sea salt, chocolate chunk and caramel cookies. "She was the one without plans tonight, and I felt sorry for her."

Ella patted him on the shoulder. "Sure, you tell yourself that, Sam." She looked over at me. "I'm getting a drink before I have to attempt dancing with your brother. You know he has two left feet." Ella sauntered off to the bar where Tyler was mixing drinks. Once she was out of earshot, I stared down my brother.

"What happened to your original date?"

"Long story," Sam said. "Basically, she reconciled with her ex and couldn't make it." He sounded good natured enough about the situation, which wasn't surprising. I'd never seen Sam pining for a woman, and I longed for the day someone had him by the collar and could shake some sense into him. He needed a good humbling.

"I'm not going to ask for details," I said. "All I'm going to say is you made a good choice bringing Ella tonight. She's drama free, and you two are good friends. Right? Only friends?"

"Yes, obviously. Did you think we were on a real date? It's Ella, and you've offended me." Sam pressed a hand to his chest and gave me an indignant look. "I'm drama free too."

"Yeah, right. The anniversary party?"

There was a moment of silence during which we both

relived our parents' fortieth anniversary party, where Sam somehow ended up with two dates for the evening. It was a regrettable misunderstanding, he claimed, but that didn't stop one of the women from pushing him into the pool. Was it hilarious and well deserved? Absolutely. But it also ruined my parents' special celebration, embarrassing them in front of their family and friends.

"That was years ago," he said. "I've matured since then."

"Then how come you still break up with women before the relationship gets too serious?"

He skewered me with a look. "And how come you haven't dated anyone seriously since your divorce?"

He had a point, but I wasn't going to admit it. "I'm not avoiding it. It's just hard to date in a town this small."

"Speaking of dating..." He looked around the room. "Where's that attractive guest of yours? Miss Wagonbutt?"

If he couldn't cause his own trouble, he'd make some for me.

"Wagonblast. She's not here yet, and please be cool tonight." Instead of agreeing, he curved his lips into a villainous smile. "I'm serious, Sam. She's wealthy, and she probably has friends with money. Possibly even celebrities. I need her to have a nice evening so she'll recommend us." Sam was never going to find out that I kissed Lauren, not if I could help it.

"I'm sure that's why you want me on good behavior around her. You're hoping Jeff Bezos will forgo his yacht next summer and vacation at Silver Sage instead." He took in my ominous glare. "Fine, fine. I'll be boring and well-behaved."

"Thanks," I said, not fully believing him. "I appreciate it."

Despite Sam's dubious dating record, he wasn't a bad guy. His curious nature made him a good vet because he was forward-thinking when it came to diagnoses and treatments. In a social setting, he was always entertaining, but also somewhat unpredictable, and tonight I wanted everything to go as planned. I needed the "unexpected surprises" portion of Lauren's vacation to be limited to falling head over heels for me. No more stampeding cows or bar fights.

The Jernigans blew in like a hurricane, with their three children racing in circles around the room. The Shahs and Masons arrived shortly thereafter, their teenagers side-eyeing each other, as if they wanted to meet but weren't sure how to approach each other. I'd be sure to make introductions if they didn't do it themselves soon.

Merle called everyone over to begin the dance lesson, but Lauren still wasn't there. I hung out close to the door because she deserved to be greeted by the ranch owner like all the other guests, right? That would be the excuse I gave to Sam if he razzed me later.

Finally, Lauren floated into the Round Room in a white summer dress with short fluttery sleeves, her hair curled in waves down to her shoulders. Her tan had deepened over the last week, and it brought out the gold in her cinnamon-colored eyes. Had I ever felt my breath catch when a woman walked into a room? Not since high school when I had an unrequited crush on my history teacher, and that was a very long time ago.

Lauren sauntered over to me, and my mind went blank. Her ruby lips, painted to match her new boots, captivated my attention. There was nothing I wanted to do more than sweep her into my arms and plant a kiss on that luscious mouth.

When she reached me, she pressed a hand to her chest. "I'm so sorry I'm late. My dress wasn't ironed, and I had to let it steam in the bathroom while I showered."

I forced myself not to think about Lauren in the shower.

"No worries at all." Her boots had a heel on them, placing her closer to my height, but I still had a good four inches on her. "You look like you belong here when you wear those boots."

"Well, I figured, when in Wyoming…"

Our eyes caught, and I couldn't look away. This woman had me on a string.

"Dance lesson has started," I said. "You should jump in."

"Aren't you coming?" she asked. "I'm going to need a partner. Will you dance with me?"

CHAPTER 15

LAUREN

"I'd love to." Matthew crooked his elbow, offering me his arm like a gentleman right out of one of those romantic old movies my mother used to watch. "Shall we?"

I hooked my hand onto his bicep, my heart drumming a wild staccato beat. We joined the dance lesson as partners, and although I tried to listen to the demonstration the older couple was giving us, Matthew's presence seriously distracted me. The heat from his body seemed to warm mine, and my concentration didn't improve when we turned toward each other and he wrapped his arm around me, resting his hand on my shoulder blade.

My nerves were showing in my voice. "I hope I don't crush your toes."

Matthew's gaze connected with mine, and I mirrored his smile as we glided around the room. Slowly, my leg muscles gave up their clench, and I relaxed into the simple movements of the dance.

"You've picked it up already," Matthew said. "Last night you were camping under the stars and here you are two-stepping. Look at you, adopting a Wyoming lifestyle."

Despite my nervousness about riding and camping without a tent, I felt surprisingly at home here. There was a wild, stark beauty about southern Wyoming that was honest and raw, and although I'd come out there to hide, I'd found a piece of myself that had gone into hiding over the years. Being outdoors, riding horses, and doing physical labor made me feel alive again. The thought of going home and working at a desk all day had me wanting to leap out of my skin. I had to remind myself to stay in the moment here at this beautiful party because I wasn't going back to New York just yet.

"What are you thinking about?" Matthew asked.

"When I first arrived, you told me Silver Sage was a magical place, and you were right. I haven't felt this happy in a long time."

"I thought you were having trouble relaxing?" he said with a mischievous twinkle in his eyes.

"Maybe I didn't need to relax. Maybe I needed to do new stuff. You know what I mean? Have a new adventure."

Matthew raised his eyebrows. "How do you think I ended up running this ranch? I started asking myself questions like that, so be careful."

I threw my head back and laughed, nearly losing the rhythm with my feet. "You had an existential crisis too, huh?"

"I think it happens in middle age. Some guys buy a Ferrari. I took over a ranch. Now get ready for a spin." He twirled me in a circle, making my skirt billow out at the knees. "Not bad for a beginner."

I fluttered my eyelashes at him. "Thank you, sir."

Matthew might have been my dance partner, but he was still the ranch's owner and manager, and he had to be professional at what was ostensibly a work event for him. There would be no kissing or snuggling for us in the Round Room. That's why I'd decided to ask him to come to my cabin later that evening. I needed time alone to tell him my real name and why I had to get out of the city so quickly. I owed him the truth. Of course, I also wanted time alone with him so I could knock his boots off.

Before I extended an invitation, Tyler appeared and tapped Matthew on the shoulder. "Our new guest has arrived at the gate, boss. I'm heading that way. Be back in a few minutes, unless you want to go yourself? I know you like to make sure everything goes perfectly when first timers arrive." The boy could hardly contain his grin. I hoped he looked that way because he knew Matthew wouldn't want to leave me to greet his new guest.

"No, you can go," Matthew said. "I trust you to get him settled. Plus, we have to practice our spins some more." Without further warning, he twirled me out and then back again, leaving me breathless. It wasn't my finest dancing moment, but it was certainly the most thrilling.

"Give me more warning next time," I said as Tyler walked away. "I'm new at this."

"You seem like an old pro. You always underestimate yourself. It was the same thing with riding. You looked totally comfortable in the saddle."

"I want to get back on the trails again soon. I feel like I might be ready for a horse that's not geriatric. No offense to Alma."

Matthew laughed. "She's a good old girl, but I think you're ready for a more energetic horse next time."

"There's so much more I want to do before I leave the ranch. Aside from the blisters, courtesy of my new hiking boots, I can honestly say this has been a perfect vacation." I gazed into his blue eyes, hoping he could feel the sincerity of my words. "Silver Sage has brought me back to life in so many ways."

His gaze settled on my lips, and I was dying for him to kiss me. Maybe we could find a dark corner away from prying eyes?

"Do you want to get a drink and go out on the porch?" he asked, reading my mind.

Immediately, I stopped dancing and let my arms drop to my sides. "Please lead the way."

It might have been a while, but I knew that when a man asked you to step into a more private area, something romantic was about to happen. All that dancing had been excellent foreplay, but now I wanted Matthew to press me up against a wall and kiss me until my legs buckled.

Once again placing his hand on the small of my back, he led me toward the bar in the corner of the room where he gave Kyra our drink orders. After we got our lemonades, I wanted us to make a quick escape, but Sam, Ella and a serious-looking man around our age called us over to them, and they widened their circle to include us.

"Nice to see you again," Sam said. "I would have said hello earlier, but my brother has been monopolizing your attention all evening."

"It's the other way around," I insisted. "I've been taking up all of his time."

Sam smiled at his brother. "I'm sure he doesn't mind one bit." His good manners and angelic dimples didn't fool me. He was going to harass his older brother as much as possible for dancing with me.

"I certainly don't mind." Matthew took a sip of his drink, and I couldn't help noticing his cheeks had turned a rosy pink.

Sam gestured to the man and woman with him. "These are our friends Callan Colter and Ursula Watson."

Callan nodded politely, tipping his gray cowboy hat. "Pleasure to meet you." His frame was tall and wiry, his black hair shot through with silver. From his tanned skin, I would have guessed that he worked outdoors even if Matthew hadn't already mentioned that Callan was the rancher who grazed his herd of cattle on Silver Sage's property. His cows were the ones who nearly ended my life, but I wouldn't hold that against him. After all, I'd left the gate open.

"Nice to meet you too, Callan," I said. "Ella and I met at The Marmot the other night. Or should I call you Ursula?"

Ella raised her glass in greeting. "Hey, Lauren! Please never call me that. Sam knows I hate my given name."

"They named her after the villain in *The Little Mermaid*," Sam said. "Beware."

"Very funny." Ella fake punched him in the stomach, and he pretended to be hit, doubling over dramatically. "I was named after my German great grandmother. Why they thought a toddler could pull off a name like Ursula is beyond me."

"I never liked my name growing up either," I said. "I had two Lauras, one Lori, and another Lauren in my grade in high school. I always wanted a more original name."

"Grass is always greener," Ella said. "I wanted so badly to be a Jessica or Heather."

"Have you been enjoying your stay at Silver Sage?" Callan asked.

"It's been wonderful." I glanced up at Matthew. "In fact, if there's space for me here, I plan to stay another week."

Matthew beamed down at me. "Absolutely. I'd love to have you."

His blushed deepened as he heard his double entendre. Sam gave a strangled laugh and Ella hid her smile behind her cup. Callan pretended not to notice, but even he was fighting back a smile. Poor Matthew.

"I mean, we'd love to have you stay longer at the ranch," Matthew clarified. "All of us. Here. At the ranch."

"Thank you. I appreciate that." I squeezed his arm and tried to ease his embarrassment by changing the subject. "Ella, are you originally from here or somewhere else?"

"Born and raised in Three Rivers. My parents own a house about a mile from the bar. Like Matthew, I'm running the family business. My grandparents opened The Mangy Marmot in the late fifties. Not the German great grand-mother side, my mom's people."

"That's amazing," I said. "I'm sure your family is happy you've taken over."

"It was that or close the place. My mother has health issues, and Dad needed to retire and be home with her. I stay at their house a lot and try to help, but we also own the apartments over the bar, so I usually close up at night and go upstairs to sleep."

"I don't know how you do all those late nights." Callan shook his head. "I'd be exhausted."

"That's why I want to turn The Marmot into more of a restaurant with a bar instead of the other way around," she said. "We could change the hours and get rid of the pool tables, make it friendlier to older folks and people who want to have a fun evening that doesn't end in a brawl. People around here don't like change very much, though."

"You could close down, rebrand and reopen," I suggested. "My sister and I helped a friend of ours do that with his family's Italian restaurant on Long Island."

"Huh." Ella tapped her bottom lip with her pointer finger. "That's an interesting idea. I never thought about rebranding that way. Maybe we can brainstorm while you're here?"

"That would be fun," I said. "I'm not used to being away from work for so long, and my sister told everyone at the office not to call me with questions. I'd love to talk business with you."

"Great!" Ella looked genuinely excited. "Can you come to The Marmot for lunch one day next week?"

"I'd be happy to take you into town." Matthew tugged at his collar. "Is it warm in here or is it just me?"

I knew exactly what he was doing and played along. "It is really warm in here." I fanned myself theatrically. "I think I'm going to get some fresh air. Care to come with me, Matthew?"

He followed me toward the door, but several guests who wanted to speak with him intercepted us. Then, they pulled me into the conversation, asking me where I was from and how I was enjoying my time at the ranch. At least twenty minutes passed before we stepped outside into the darkness, the screen door closing behind us.

"Alone at last," Matthew said as we turned to face each other. "I thought they would never let us leave."

"You're a popular guy."

"Are you kidding? You're the one they're curious about. Can't say I blame them." He traced his fingers over my cheekbone and down to my chin, tilting it up to bring my mouth toward his. "I was intrigued too. I still am."

He kissed me, and the rest of the world and all its problems melted into the background. Our tongues teased, playing against each other, and any shyness we'd experienced the night before wasn't there now. The fissions of desire running through my body were all-consuming as he kissed me slowly and thoroughly. I was unaware of anything but Matthew. I was his for the taking.

A sharp voice pierced the night air, shattering our cocoon. "Lauren? Is that you?"

Recognizing the voice, but not quite believing it, I spun around.

"Oh my God." The world seemed to spin in my periphery. My almost-ex-husband Freddy stood on the steps of the Round Room. He was here at the ranch.

CHAPTER 16

LAUREN

*H*ad someone asked me before that moment what was the worst surprise of my life, it would definitely have been standing amongst a hundred and fifty people as we all watched Freddy getting a hand job from a bartender. Didn't think he could beat that, so to speak, but now he had. I pulled away from the warmth of Matthew's embrace and walked over to Freddy, my limbs jangling like a marionette on strings.

"What are you doing here?" I was still hoping this was a bad dream.

"Hello, darling," he said casually, as if he hadn't seen me kissing someone a second earlier. "A very kind assistant at your company gave me your whereabouts. I told her I needed to get in touch with you immediately, and she was quite helpful."

Sully, no doubt. I forgave her for sending me to the wrong ranch, but this mistake was unforgivable. Then again, maybe it wasn't a mistake at all. Did he pay her for this information? I'd definitely be investigating later.

"We're supposed to speak through our lawyers." I glanced

over my shoulder at Matthew, who was watching us with a dark expression on his face.

Freddy clicked his tongue. "Still an ice queen, I see."

I hated it when he called me that, probably because there was a grain of truth to it. Instead of getting emotional with Freddy and showing him my anger and pain, I'd always resorted to freezing him out. Why should I show him how badly he was hurting me? Ice queens could at least keep their dignity.

"I'm being practical." Unlike him, who flew all the way out here to have a conversation.

"Lawyers only want to take our money," he said. "I think we can settle this between the two of us, don't you? We're both reasonable adults."

Before I could ask Freddy how much he'd spent flying out here—first class, no doubt—Matthew was at my side, so close that our elbows were touching.

"Everything alright, Lauren?" he asked.

He had a few inches of height on Freddy and was brawnier, too. My ex didn't seem worried, though. Freddy slid his manicured hands into the pockets of his linen blazer and gave Matthew a quick appraisal, no doubt making judgments about his clothing and haircut. I usually smiled every time I thought about Walt trimming Matthew's hair in the barn, but nothing seemed funny at that moment.

"Matthew," I said, "this is Frederic Arnaud Tremblay, my—"

Freddy extended his hand toward Matthew. "Her husband." I wanted to smack the smile right off his face. How did I ever find him charming?

Matthew reluctantly took Freddy's hand in his and shook it. "Can someone tell me what's going on here?"

I grabbed Matthew's arm, desperate to make him understand I wasn't a creepy cheater. "We're only married in the

153

legal sense of the word. We signed separation papers over three years ago, and we haven't really had a marriage in much longer than that. Freddy doesn't live with me, and I even had the locks changed so he can't get into the apartment anymore."

"You what?" Freddy had the nerve to be offended. "Why would you do that?"

I shot him a deadly look before continuing. "We're nothing to each other except a problem to be solved. I'm sure he's here because our lawyers haven't been able to get us to come to an agreement about the divorce settlement."

"I understand," Matthew said. "It's alright." He sounded calm, but he didn't look happy.

"Ahem, excuse me." Freddy waved his hands to get our attention. "I don't know who you are, but I need to speak privately with my wife."

"I'm the owner of this property, and I can have you thrown off it if I want to." Matthew crossed his arms over his chest. "That's who I am."

"And I'm about to be your ex-wife," I reminded Freddy, "if you'd sign the damn papers instead of trying to get more money out of me."

Matthew turned toward me and placed a protective hand on my shoulder. "Do you want me to make him leave?"

"That would be my preference, but, unfortunately, I need him to stay so we can come to an agreement. I want my marriage to be officially over." I scowled at Freddy. "Go to your cabin, and I'll see you at breakfast."

"I want to talk tonight," Freddy said petulantly. "I came all the way from Europe to sort this out with you. The least you could do is make time for me now."

My eyes bugged out of my head. "The least I could do?" Realizing I'd raised my voice too loud, I grabbed Freddy's arm. "Excuse us, please."

Matthew nodded crispy. "Sure. I'll be right inside if you need me."

As the door swung closed behind Matthew, Freddy struggled free of my grip and rubbed his arm. "Ow. Nails, darling."

"You came out here uninvited and now you're demanding that I stop my lovely evening so I can talk about divorce terms with you?" I scolded. "Who do you think you are? I decide if and when I'll speak to you. And if you don't like that, you can get on a plane tomorrow and talk to my lawyers. Got it?"

"There's that Italian temper." I glared at him, and he finally caved. "Fine, we'll talk tomorrow."

I ran my hands over the skirt of my dress. "Good. I'll see you at nine."

As I turned to walk inside the Round Room, Freddy called out to me. "All these years, you acted like I was the only one running around in this marriage. Now we find out the truth." He made a scoffing noise. "Make-believe cowboy."

My hands shook, and if I weren't afraid of getting charged with assault, I would have slapped him. "I've been separated for years, and this is the first person I've met who —" I drew in a deep breath. "You know what? It's none of your business. Just make sure you treat everyone who works here with respect. Whether or not I like it, I'm associated with you, and I've had enough second-hand embarrassment to last a lifetime."

"Oh, please. What happened at the salon was more embarrassing for me than it was for you. My mother heard about it all the way in Switzerland. For you, it was free advertising. As they say, there's no such thing as bad publicity."

Just when I thought he couldn't sink any lower...

"You don't even care that you humiliated not only me but your sons, as well? Is this the role model you want to be for your children?"

Freddy reached out to pat me on the cheek, and I smacked his hand away. "Poor Lauren. You're so American. People have affairs. A lifetime of monogamy is completely unrealistic."

"I wish you'd notified me about that before we said our wedding vows." The tears were threatening again. "I meant my vows when I said them, and, silly me, I thought you did too. You knew I believed in monogamy or you wouldn't have tried to hide those first affairs."

I'd finally cracked his facade and frustration bubbled over. Spittle flew from his lips as he snapped at me. "I know you love to shame me, but you weren't the perfect wife, either. You worked all the time, and our sex life was nonexistent. What was I supposed to do?"

Mrs. Jernigan popped her head out the screen door. "Sorry to interrupt, but we're heading back to our cabin."

The look of pity she shot me turned my stomach. Freddy had succeeded in humiliating me once again. It seemed to be his entire purpose in life.

"C'mon out," I said. "I'm sorry we were so loud."

She gave me another sympathetic glance as she and her husband whisked their children past me. I could only imagine what they must have thought. There was no way I could go back inside to the dance now.

After they were gone, I moved closer to Freddy so I could speak quietly. "I know I'm not perfect, Freddy. Mistakes were made on both sides, and there's no point in rehashing the past anymore. It's time to move on."

"I agree." His anger seemed to retreat a little. "I really did come out here so we could talk like adults."

"Then I'll meet you in the dining room at nine so we can talk. Goodnight, Freddy."

I refrained from telling him not to be late. The man loved his beauty sleep, and he'd probably rest peacefully all night, while I tossed and turned, trying to predict what legal maneuvers he had in store for me. I would not let him take advantage of me. Not this time. Lauren Cozzi might have let him do it, but Lauren Wagonblast? She carried pool sticks into bar fights, and she was no man's doormat. Freddy was about to find that out.

CHAPTER 17

MATTHEW

I've never wanted so badly to kick a man off my ranch. Literally. I would have liked to launch that Freddy guy into space with the toe of my boot. I didn't know exactly what he'd done to Lauren, but from the look on her face, it wasn't good, and that filled me with a slow boiling anger that needed release. She briefly came back to the dance before saying goodnight, and although I spent the rest of the evening pretending to be fine, dancing the two-step with guests and neighbors, I was worrying about her the whole time. Once I went home, I did what any red-blooded American male would do in this situation—I did my research.

Fine, maybe research wasn't what people expected of a guy who drives a big pickup truck and can shoot a gun, but I was mature enough to know how to channel my emotions into something purposeful. Threatening Freddy or getting violent with him wasn't going to help Lauren. I needed to understand what was going on before I could assist her, and I wasn't the only one who was curious and concerned.

"What happened with Lauren?" Sam asked as I walked into my living room after putting Gigi to bed. He and Ella had come back to my house after the party.

"Her husband showed up." I set my laptop on the table and sat down between them on the couch, hoping the WiFi was going to cooperate. "He came all the way from France to see her. They're in the middle of a divorce."

Sam's eyes grew wide. "That's wild. Is he trying to win her back?"

"Nope," I said. "They're fighting over money."

Ella wrinkled her nose. "Do you think he's dangerous? A stalker type?"

I sighed and rubbed my tired eyes. "I don't think so, but I got a really bad vibe from the guy, and I'm looking into it."

"Normally, I wouldn't advise snooping." Ella scooted forward on the couch cushions. "But in this case..." She skimmed her finger across the computer's touchpad and the screen lit up.

"If it's out there on the Internet, it's public knowledge," Sam reassured me as Ella opened a Web browser.

"Plus, you're worried about her," Ella said as she typed. "I am too. Lauren seems like a sweet person."

"Drama comes to Silver Sage Ranch," Sam said as we waited for the page to load. He propped his socked feet up on the coffee table. "Who would ever have thunk it?"

Nothing came up for the search term "Lauren Wagonblast New York City." I knew her profession, and that she had a business with her sister, so we tried "twin sisters Lauren and Tori matchmakers New York City." The screen flooded with hits. I discovered her real name was Lauren Cozzi, and I quickly figured out what happened in New York earlier that summer. Her husband had humiliated her by hooking up with another woman at a party where there seemed to be a whole lot of reporters in attendance.

"I knew he had a punchable face," I said as Ella clicked a photo of Freddy leaving the scene of his crimes with a jacket held over his head to hide from the cameras. "But this is awful."

"I would chop off his weiner if he humiliated me like that." Ella cracked her knuckles. "Wait until he was asleep and—" She made a hacking motion with the side of her hand. "Off with his dick."

Sam glanced over at her, pale-faced. "Do you have to be so graphic?"

"He deserves it!" she yelped.

"Her personal life was in all the newspapers," I said. "That explains why she came out here. She probably wanted some privacy and peace. But why was her husband her date for a party if they were separated? She told me she changed the locks on her apartment so he couldn't get in."

"Sounds like they were pretending to be together," Sam said. "Or she's lying to you."

"No, he confirmed that they're divorcing," I said, "so I don't think she's lying to me. She said it was complicated, and I guess it is." I still didn't like that word.

Ella leaned in for a closer look. "She's also running in very posh circles in the big city. Why the hell did she choose this ranch to hide at? No offense."

"Hey!" Even though I was grousing at her, I understood exactly what she meant.

"She was headed to some fancy spa in Montana called Silvery Sage Resort and Spa," Sam explained. "She ended up here by mistake and then my brother seduced her."

I slammed my laptop shut. "Okay, that's enough for tonight."

"Really, Matthew?" Ella said. "You slept with a guest? I'm both shocked and proud."

"I didn't sleep with her!" I stood up, hoping they'd get the message and leave me alone. "I kissed her, that's all." And a little light fooling around, but they didn't need to know that.

Sam was delighted. "Looks like you got yourself in a pickle, Mr. Perfect."

"Don't you have a dog to get home to?" I growled.

Sam jumped up. "Right! I need to let Jake out before he pees on my bed out of spite. See you later, Romeo."

"Be her friend," Ella said as she stood up to leave. "I can tell you have feelings for her, but I'm betting she needs a friend right now more than anything."

THE MORNING AFTER THE DANCE, Lauren arrived at the poolside breakfast buffet dressed in a pretty pair of black shorts and matching short-sleeved blouse. She'd styled her hair in a sleek ponytail and her makeup was perfect, but she still couldn't hide the exhaustion shadowing her eyes. I was behind the hot bar serving pancakes because I wanted Kyra and Tyler to have a little break that morning. Most of our staff members had worked hard getting the dance set up, serving drinks and interacting with guests, and they needed some rest. Chef Damon and Serenity were in the kitchen taking care of the food. I still hadn't had the chance to have a long talk about Chef's foray into grand theft auto, or that he'd fallen off the wagon again, and I wasn't looking forward to that conversation. Still, it needed to happen.

Lauren approached me cautiously, plate in hand. "Matthew, I'm so sorry about last night. I ruined a very special evening, and I'm sure you have so many questions. I feel awful about all of this."

"Not at all." I loaded her up with flapjacks, hoping to give her a little carb energy. "Don't worry about a thing." I wanted to walk around the table and pull her into a hug, tell her I'd help her get through everything. I was way too invested in this woman's life, but I couldn't seem to help myself.

She closed her eyes for a moment and let out a deep breath. "Thank you so much. I don't know what I've done to deserve such kindness."

"You've been a delightful guest at this ranch, that's what.

You help out everywhere you can, although we shouldn't let you do any work, and you're great company." I felt myself blushing, as if I'd revealed something too personal. "Honestly, we were all worried about you last night."

She nodded and attempted to smile. "I'm okay. I want to talk to you when you have a chance, though. I feel like I need to explain more about my…situation."

"I appreciate that." I dropped my voice lower so we wouldn't be overheard. "I don't want to make your life more complicated than it already is. I'm here for you as a friend, okay?"

"Oh." Her expression stiffened, and she nodded. "I see. Thank you." Something had shifted between us, and suddenly the air felt tense. What had I said wrong? Ella had advised me to be there for her as a friend. Before I could find out what had happened, Freddy strode into the dining room looking like he was ready for a day on a yacht with his pristine chinos, button-down shirt and deck shoes.

"Please excuse me." She headed toward an open table with her plate of food.

"Good morning!" Freddy called out as he approached me. "I see we have an American-style breakfast. Eat until your pants won't button."

I would not apologize for good, hearty food. "That's right. Grab a plate, and I'll fill it. We have fruit too."

"Yum." He eyed the buffet with such a snooty look on his face that it was hard not to react, but I managed. I'd had some experience with difficult guests. "What's on tap for today, Mr. Hart? I'd love to join Lauren for whatever she has planned."

"You'll have to ask her if you're invited to join her plans," I said dully. "That's none of my business."

He stuck a fork into a slice of cantaloupe and slid it onto his plate. "You're acting quite superior for someone who was pawing my wife last night."

Trying to smile at this idiot hurt my face, but I didn't want my other guests to see my temper flare up. "From what I understand, she doesn't want to be your wife and hasn't for a long time."

His eyes sparkled with rage, but he was still smiling like an alligator. "And do you seriously think she would be with a man like you? As desperate as Lauren may be, I don't think she's ready for that kind of downgrade."

Fortunately, Chef arrived with another pan of bacon before I could leap over the buffet table and downgrade Freddy's face. No one had pushed my buttons this way since my brother Bowie and I had to share a bedroom as teenagers. Instead of storming straight back to the kitchen like he usually did, Chef stayed by my side, arms crossed over his chest.

"Is everything alright?" he asked me quietly. "I heard our new guest was giving Mrs. Wagonblast a hard time outside the Round Room last night."

I loved that even Chef was looking out for Lauren. Maybe somewhere in his alcohol addled brain the other night he comprehended her concern and care for him.

"I think she's okay," I said. "But you can burn his piece of meat tonight."

Chef's mouth twisted into the closest thing to a smile I'd ever seen from him. "I thought you were obsessed with getting us good reviews."

I glared over at the table where Freddy had taken the seat across from Lauren. "In this case, I'm willing to make an exception."

He shrugged carelessly. "I'll drop it on the floor before I cook it. He'll never know."

I pinned him down with a look. "Have you done that before, Chef?"

"Of course not." He winked at me. "But if I did, you'd never know."

~

WHEN I STOPPED by the stables after lunch, Walt was saddling up horses for a group trail ride.

He tightened the cinch on Banjo, one of our younger horses, as he looked over at me. "You coming with us today?"

"Nope." Loki nickered and swished his tail to get my attention, so I walked over to greet him. "I've got too much to do, but I wanted to check on Elijah. Has the medicine been working, you think?"

"I thought you might be out here looking for Lauren." He was right, but I certainly wouldn't admit it. Instead, I stared Walt down until he sighed. "Elijah seems fine. He left me the gift of a dead mouse on my bench this morning, which is always a fun way to start the day."

I casually leaned against the wall, crossing one leg over the other. "Since you brought her up, is Lauren riding today?"

"Oh, so you're here to check on the cat. Right…" Walt chuckled as he placed the bridle on Banjo's head. "She signed up for a ride this afternoon, and she's bringing that Freddy person with her. Says he knows how to ride. Is he really her husband?"

Gossip spread around a dude ranch like a spark in dry brush. "Technically, yes, but they're separated and in the middle of a divorce."

"Ah, I see. That sounds miserable." Walt stopped working and turned to look at me. "Are you getting yourself into trouble there, Matthew?"

I sighed and rubbed my eyes. "I hope not. I don't think so." I squinted into the distance. "Maybe?"

He laughed again and tied up Banjo so he could bring Loki out of his stall. "Okay."

"Are you giving him Loki?" I asked. "I was thinking Doug might be a better choice. Maybe you could walk them into a field of butterflies or something." Walt knew I was joking because Doug would buck if a big winged insect like a butterfly came his way.

"I take it we want this guy to suffer?" Walt asked.

"Mild suffering," I said. "Nothing deadly."

Walt's mustache twitched as he held back a smile. "I never took you for the vengeful type."

I tapped the toe of my boot against the floor. "I'm not. Put him on Banjo or Loki and make sure he has a nice ride." Sometimes being the ranch owner was a tough gig. Duty always came before vengeance.

"Oh, I'm giving him Alma today," Walt said. "Let him try to show off his riding skills on the laziest horse in southern Wyoming."

I laughed, imagining Freddy trying to urge Alma into a gallop when she was busy eating clover. "Thanks, buddy." I started to leave the barn, then stopped and looked back at him over my shoulder. "Hey, Walt? I like her a lot."

"I'm not surprised," he said. "I've spent a little time with her now, and I can see why you like her so much."

"Were you checking her out for me?" Suddenly, it made sense why he was sitting with her at dinner the other night.

"With your dad gone, I feel like I should do better looking out for you boys. Maybe I did want to make sure she was a good person. I'm a little worried about the fact she lives in New York and that her ex is here at the ranch, but I suppose a little woman trouble is more fun than none at all."

I laughed and shook my head. "That's your personal motto, huh?"

"You can't say it isn't true, can you?"

He was right. Life might be more complicated with Lauren in it, but as far as I could tell, she was worth it.

CHAPTER 18

LAUREN

*O*n the menu that evening was pan seared trout and haricot vert, which was a fancy name for green beans. Normally, I would vigorously enjoy my food, but with Freddy sitting next to me, everything lost its flavor.

"This fish isn't fresh," he said sourly after taking a tiny bite.

"Kyra said it was caught locally today," I said. "I don't think they froze and defrosted it that quickly, do you?"

Freddy shrugged one shoulder. "She lied."

In the past, I would have tried to placate him to avoid him being condescending to our server, but I wasn't going to baby Freddy anymore.

"And you're insufferable. Can we please talk about our settlement now?" Freddy had pushed off this discussion all day long, insisting that we take a trail ride together so we could relax before getting down to business. I had to hide my amusement when Walt put him on Alma. Taking off on my new mount, a glossy brown quarter horse named Banjo, and leaving Freddy in the dust was a priceless moment.

He took a sip of his wine, the only part of the meal he hadn't found a reason to criticize yet. "I know you'd like me to leave, and I'm happy to fly home tomorrow. You know what I want, and you have the power to give it to me."

"Believe me when I say that I'd love for you to leave immediately." I steadied my voice to take the waver out of it. "But you're not getting Ms. Match. I've made a very generous offer that I suggest you take because even a sliver of our company will never belong to you."

He blotted his mouth with his napkin. "You're being spiteful. You have plenty of money for your retirement. Don't you think I should, too? Having a piece of the company guarantees me a certain amount of security."

Giving him my hard-earned money was going to be a difficult pill to swallow, but giving him a piece of the company I'd built with my sister? Never.

I clenched my fists together under the table. "If you can't save some of the fortune I'll be paying you in alimony, that's on you, Freddy. Learn to live like a normal person, and you'll be fine. I accept that I was the working spouse in our marriage, and you're owed a certain amount, but you've never been a part of the company and you never will."

"I wasn't a part of it? Then why was I on your television show? Explain that to me."

"You were on three, maybe four, times in five years." I had to work hard not to snarl at him. "And, may I remind you, you were paid for those appearances."

Kyra came by our table to refill our water glasses, and we immediately stopped bickering and pasted fake smiles on our faces. We'd been playing this sick game for a long time.

"Let me know if you need anything," she said brightly, oblivious to what she'd walked into.

"Thank you." I was so tired of faking this marriage. So tired of pretending to be happy when I felt miserable inside.

Freddy's cell phone buzzed on the table. He picked it up before I could see the name on the screen, but I presumed it was his lawyer calling to find out if he'd worked me over yet.

"Hello? Hello? I can't hear you." He lowered the phone from his ear and glared at me. "The reception here is shit."

I smiled sweetly. "Try walking around the ranch. That's what I do."

To my relief, he left the table to take his call. Matthew and I were the only people left in the dining room, and both of us were sitting alone. As soon as Freddy was out the door, Matthew strode over and took the seat next to mine. My heart rate revved up at the sight of him in his chambray button down and gray chinos. The phrase "he cleans up nicely" now made perfect sense to me, although, to my surprise, I found I liked him just as well in his work clothing. Give me Matthew Hart with a summer tan, half-day of beard growth, faded t-shirt, cowboy boots and dusty jeans, and that was my idea of heaven on earth.

"Are you doing alright?" he asked quietly.

How could I answer that question? I was seriously not alright, but it wasn't in my nature to show weakness. Besides, I felt better with Matthew sitting next to me. He had a calming effect on my nervous system, even if he had suggested at breakfast that our relationship was now downgraded to friendship status.

"I'm as okay as I can be, under current circumstances."

Matthew nodded and looked down at the table. When he lifted his head and met my gaze again, his eyes told me I hadn't fooled him one bit.

"You don't have to pretend with me, Lauren. I know why you came out to the ranch. Maybe I shouldn't have done it, but I looked online and saw what happened to you in New York."

"No, it's totally fine you did." Relief flooded through me. No more secrets from Matthew. That was a good thing. "I'm so sorry I couldn't tell you everything sooner. I didn't want to get you involved in my mess, and I was afraid that if people here found out who I really was, they'd sell photos to the media."

"I hope you know I would never do that," he said. "In fact, I think everyone here at the ranch would protect you. I can at least vouch for my staff."

A lump formed in my throat, so I swallowed hard and nodded at him, trying to keep myself together. "Thank you."

"You don't have to talk about it any more if you don't want to, but I'm here if you need me. Okay?" He put his hand over mine. "I've got your back."

I still didn't trust myself to speak because the tears were too close to the surface. It had been so long since a man, besides my brother, had offered me that kind of support. At a loss for words, I nodded and turned my hand over so I could interlace my fingers with his. Maybe I shouldn't have done it, but friends could hold hands, right?

"I think I upset you this morning," he said, giving my hand a gentle squeeze. "I wanted you to know that there's no pressure from me. I'm happy to be your friend if that's all you can offer right now. Of course, I liked the direction things were headed before your..."

"Soon to be ex-husband," I supplied.

"Yeah, him," he said grimly. "Before he got here. I understand if you need to dial it back, though."

I knew Tori wouldn't advise me to put all my cards on the table so early in a relationship, but for once in my life, I wasn't going to play it safe.

"I don't want to dial it back," I said earnestly. "I want to enjoy every minute I have here with you. I'm hoping Freddy and I can settle things tonight so you and I can pick up where we left off. I totally understand if you want to steer clear of me, though. My situation is really messy, and—"

"I'd love to pick up right where we left off," he said. "I think we were mid-kiss."

His blue eyes melted me into a puddle. "You make me feel like a teenager again, Matthew. I've got butterflies." My smile faded as Freddy re-entered the dining room. "Shit. He's back."

Matthew slid his hand from mine. "Can I come by your room later tonight? Maybe we could go for a walk under the stars."

"Yes." Before I could say anything more, Freddy was taking his seat and Matthew was standing to leave.

"You might want to go check on your daughter," Freddy told him. "I just saw her poking at a snake with a stick."

"Don't worry," Matthew said calmly. "She knows the difference between a garter snake and a rattlesnake. She identified you correctly."

I tried unsuccessfully not to laugh as he walked away. "C'mon, Freddy. You have to admit you walked into that one."

"That man is incompetent and…and…"—he leaned closer to me, the fermented smell of wine on his breath—"I'm going to write a review of this place that lets everyone know how he runs his business, from the terrible WiFi to that geriatric horse I rode today. I can make sure everyone knows his ranch is a disgrace."

Panic tore through me. Freddy had connections in the world, and he could actually hurt Matthew's business if that's where he put his energy.

"Stop it, Freddy." I donned my ice queen mask. "You're acting like a child."

"I'm writing a review right now." With a flourish, he extracted his phone and tapped on the screen. Then he frowned and shoved it back in his pocket. "As soon as I have decent WiFi."

I had to act quickly and decisively. Balling my hands into fists at my sides, I tried to channel my much more confrontational twin sister. "If you do anything to hurt Matthew, I will force you to sell En Vedette in the divorce. Don't push me, or you'll find out that I can be just as vindictive as you can, and you'll have to wave goodbye to your beloved boat."

En Vedette, his racing yacht, was owned in both his name and mine, since I was the one who financed her purchase and paid the insurance. This was a trump card I'd been holding onto since our separation. Now was the time to pull it out and play it because I wasn't going to let him destroy Matthew's life. He'd already done enough damage to mine.

Sensing that he'd gone too far, Freddy's determination faltered. "Calm down. I haven't done anything yet."

I made my voice firm, using the tone I took with my sons when they were naughty little boys. "Go home. Sign the divorce papers, and we'll be done with this chapter of our lives. You want to end this as much as I do."

For a brief moment, I thought he was going to capitulate, but then his face hardened. "I'll leave the ranch, but I'm not signing anything until you agree to give me a piece of Ms. Match. You have a week to think it over, and then I go to the press with our story. I'll tell them how we faked this marriage for years because you were afraid of a divorce hurting your company. Or maybe it was really your personal reputation that you wanted to preserve?"

The thought of him exposing our charade made my stomach churn and left me grabbing at straws. "You'd rat me out to the press even if it might cost you En Vedette? That was a serious threat. I'm not bluffing. I'll make you sell your boat."

A hateful glimmer lit up his eyes. "And if I get a piece of your company, I can afford to buy a nicer one. The wonderful thing about you, Lauren, is that you're the ultimate worker bee. Your company will continue to grow and thrive, and I want a part of that success, especially the juicy syndication deal you're negotiating."

Shit. He had me in a bind, and he knew it.

"One week," I said. "Give me seven days to talk to Tori

and figure out what we're willing to give you." I wasn't giving him anything, but I needed to buy myself some time.

"Just don't wait too long to contact me with your decision. I'm leaving the ranch tomorrow morning, so you'll have to call me or my lawyer when you've come to an agreement with Tori."

"Fine."

He might have been leaving the ranch soon, but what I really needed was for Freddy to exit my life.

WHEN YOU'VE BEEN WAITING FOREVER—OR what felt like forever—to kiss someone, the minutes seemed like hours. I paced around my cabin like a caged tiger, re-brushing my teeth and obsessing about whether to apply lipstick. I looked better with a little color on my lips, but did men hate the taste of lipstick or was that a myth? Not having dated in decades, I couldn't decide.

"This is silly," I whispered to myself as I applied a light layer of scarlet to my lips, then blotted most of it away.

Maybe it was a little ridiculous to be acting head over heels for a man at my age, but that didn't stop me. The clock was ticking on my time at Silver Sage, and I wanted to make more memories before I went home. And by memories, I did mean sex.

Obviously, sex wasn't something you could forget how to do, but I was out of practice. Would I disappoint Matthew by not knowing the latest sexual tricks and trends?

No, that was silly. People had been doing it since the beginning of time, and I knew enough to get him off. The bigger question was, would I be able to climax? Even with the help of a vibrator, it didn't happen every time for me. Freddy had taken it personally when I couldn't finish, and that added pressure to the situation that only made things worse.

A knock at the door drew my attention, and I hurried to open it. Matthew was standing outside with a bouquet of purple and red wildflowers.

"Hello." He sounded shyer than usual. "Are you ready for our walk?"

Everything about him lit me up from the inside out. He was wearing a soft flannel shirt and holding flowers. Hardy wildflowers he'd plucked with those powerful hands of his that could hammer in a fence post and control a headstrong horse. What else could they do? What other beautiful, amazing, devastating things could those work-roughened hands do to me? I was going to climb him like a tree and find out.

Taking the flowers in one hand, I used the other to capture his shirt front and pull him inside my cabin. Before the door even swung shut behind him, I'd planted a kiss on his mouth. He tasted like warm sunshine and fresh air.

With a grunt of pleasure, Matthew took my face in his hands and kissed me back. His tongue teased at my lips, and I welcomed him inside, my body warming in response. Without turning my head or interrupting the kissing, I dropped the flowers onto the bed and wrapped both arms around his waist. My head spun as he moved me up against the wall. Our tongues tangling, we kissed until we were breathless. Was I someone who slid her hands onto a man's ass and squeezed those cheeks like I was sampling cantaloupes in a grocery store? In Wyoming, yes, I was that woman, and Matthew Hart's ass felt as good as it looked in his jeans.

The jut of his erection made me wild for him, and I pushed and rubbed against it with scandalous fervor. I hadn't cared about sex in years, and now I felt like I might explode if I didn't have him inside me. A tiny moan escaped my mouth, and he grabbed my right leg and hitched it up above his hip so I could have more friction. Delicious hot friction. We'd gone from zero to sixty in seconds, but I didn't want to stop. My body needed him to keep going.

Finally, our mouths broke apart so we could catch our breath, and Matthew released my leg as he drank me in with hooded eyes. "I'm bringing flowers every day."

"It's not the flowers." My hands had inched up to his waist again, and I slid them under his untucked shirt. "It's you."

He shivered in response to my touch and bent down to press his lips to the side of my neck. "Was it the waiting?" he whispered against my skin. "Because I could barely think of anything all day except kissing you."

"Me too. Oh, my God." As he nibbled a path to my earlobe, warmth spread along my inner thighs. I didn't know a man's kisses could make me feel drugged. Places on my body that had been barren wastelands were suddenly dewy with desire. Matthew ran his hand over my breast, his thumb teasing my nipple through the fabric of my dress. He gave it a little pinch and my entire body shuddered.

"Yes," I said through a moan. "That."

Our mouths found each other again, and our kisses became deep and hungry.

"Too much fabric." Matthew tugged up the flowy material of my dress. His hands skimmed over my thighs, and I trembled in response. As his fingers deftly tugged down my underwear, I shimmied until they fell to the floor. His eyes closed when he touched the cleft between my legs.

"You're so ready," he rasped.

"Take me to bed," I begged as he stroked me.

"I want you right here. Put your hands over your head." I'd never heard that deep, commanding voice from him before, but I liked it. God, I liked it. I raised my arms up, and he took hold of my slim wrists with one of his powerful hands, securing me against the wall. With his other hand, he found a new place, one that made me forget my words. My mind swirled as every nerve ending around his fingers came alive, like a cello with a virtuoso working the strings. When he asked if I was okay, all I could do was give a quick nod.

I'd always been the breadwinner, the supervisor, the one to take charge of everything during my married life, even in the bedroom. When Freddy and I were still having sex, he enjoyed me performing for him and on him, but he never took control this way. Matthew's eyes burned with a hunger that only my body could satiate.

"Matthew," I whispered. "Please." I was so close to the edge. My stomach muscles tightened as my attention focused on that one space where his fingers played.

"I don't have a condom." His voice was low and raspy. "I didn't know you wanted this so badly." He ramped up the speed of what had been slow lazy circles over my tender skin. "Just let go, beautiful girl. Let go."

The dam opened and waves of pleasure spilled forth, making me shake and cry out.

"That's good," he whispered. "So good."

Tears of joy welled in the corners of my eyes as Matthew lifted my chin and feathered a kiss on my lips.

"Thank you," I whispered against his mouth.

He smiled like he understood I was thanking him for more than that moment. "Making you happy is my pleasure."

CHAPTER 19

LAUREN

When I got out of bed the next morning, I felt like I was gliding around wearing a movie star's glow, all shimmery and youthful. I grinned at myself in the mirror, as if this new Lauren and I had a secret. Freddy had left the ranch, and Matthew and I had taken our relationship to a new and truly satisfying level. Was there a better way to begin a day than this?

My encounter with Matthew in my cabin felt like the equivalent of tectonic plates shifting. I didn't know if I could open myself up emotionally to receiving pleasure anymore, or if it was even worth the effort, not to mention the risks. It had been so damn long since a man had touched me intimately that I had no idea if I could have the kind of mind-melting orgasms that other women raved about. Not only did I know now that it could happen, I needed it to happen again. And again. And again! There would be no going back to a celibate life. No more ignoring my sensuality and physical needs. Matthew had opened that door for me, and I wasn't closing it again.

When I saw my lawyer's name on my phone, even that intrusion of reality couldn't diminish my happiness. I answered with a cheerful trill to my voice. "Hi Tempest! What's going on?"

"Freddy's lawyer contacted me late last night, but I just saw the message now." She clicked her tongue in irritation. "He always does that, like it's his power move to work later than I did. Such a dick."

I looked at the clock and realized she was calling me at a little after six in the morning New York time. "You must have just woken up."

"Exactly. I'm still in bed, but I wanted to let you know that Freddy has scheduled an interview with *Celebrity* to discuss your separation and divorce. Of course, his lawyer implied that the interview could be canceled, which means we need to agree to their terms."

I'd expected this from him, and I had a few ideas about how we could deal with it. "Doesn't our separation agreement prevent him from speaking publicly about our marital arrangement?"

"It did, but, technically speaking, he can talk about it now." I hated when she used the word technically because it always meant I was about to get screwed over. "It's complicated, but in a layperson's terms, your publicist voided that provision when she spoke with the press about the night at Jentori."

"But isn't this blackmail?" I pressed a hand to my chest, where the panic was starting to swell inside of me. "He's forcing us to give him part of the business in return for not outing me to the press!"

"It might fit the legal definition of blackmail," she said, "but if he gives the interview, the damage is already done. I think he's going to pull the trigger even if we threaten to sue him for blackmail. I can look into it, if you'd like. That's not my area, but I can talk to a colleague in my firm."

The last thing I wanted was to get tied up in a longer legal battle with Freddy. "So either I give in to his heinous demands and hand over part of my company, or I let him tank my reputation and, by association, my sister's reputation. It's a lose-lose proposition."

"There's one thing you could do," she said, "and that's beat him to the punch."

I knew exactly what she meant. "No, I'm not talking to the press."

Tempest acted like she hadn't even heard me. "You could be the first one to break the story. *Celebrity* magazine would love to have you and Tori on the cover. Tell them what happened from your point of view, and then he won't even be able to sell his side. You will effectively take out the only leverage he has right now."

Exposing my life to the tabloids didn't feel like a win.

"I can't do that," I said again. "My sons would be humiliated. Our company could lose clients and the syndication deal."

"Then you're right, you have two poor options," she said bluntly. "Pick the one you can live with. But if you want my opinion, you're assuming a lot. People might sympathize with you more than you think."

Tempest might have sounded harsh to someone else, but I'd known her a long time and understood that this was just her way. She was a straight shooter, which was why I hired her and why I liked having her as a friend. I didn't need someone blowing smoke up my butt. I needed to be surrounded by people who were honest and direct, and who had my best interests at heart.

"Give me a few more days," I said. "I need to talk to Tori, and then I'll come to a final decision."

That call would have to wait a little while though, because I was going on a date.

~

GIGI WAS HOME WITH KYRA, Freddy was out of my hair for the moment, and I was going out with a man for the first time in many years. It felt surreal and weirdly wonderful to be driving to downtown Three Rivers in a pickup truck on a Friday night. I had on my cowboy boots, blue jeans and a white blouse because Matthew said we were going somewhere casual. He'd also told me to make sure I brought my bathing suit, which made me curious.

"You're not going to make me jump into a pond at night, are you?" I asked. "You know my fear of critters."

"Don't worry," he said. "No ponds or swamps."

"Good." I took in a deep breath of sweet, crisp summer air. "Seventy-two degrees and low humidity. You have the perfect evenings here."

"You'll have to come back every summer then."

I tilted my head and smiled at him. "I just might."

Why did I feel so much lighter when I had the same problems as yesterday? Somehow, being with Matthew made me think about future possibilities instead of limitations.

"You look beautiful tonight," he said. "I like you in those boots."

"Thank you. They're breaking in perfectly."

He reached over and took my hand, running his thumb over my knuckles. "Chef Damon hasn't made his molten chocolate cake since you've been here, has he? I'll have to ask him to put it on the menu because you'd love it."

"How's he doing?" I asked.

There was a flicker of tension in Matthew's jaw. "He's still a temperamental pain in the ass, but he's not drinking at the moment."

"I know he's a great chef, but I can't help wondering why you keep him on staff if he's so unreliable? There has to be someone out there who could replace him, even if they're not quite at his level."

He sighed and waited to make the turn onto the road into

town before he answered me. "After seventeen years of sobriety, he went through a personal trauma, losing his wife and son in a car accident. That's when he went back to the booze. When I hired him, he was trying to get sober again, but it's been a challenge. I guess I feel for the guy, and I'm hoping he'll work his way through his grief. Then maybe then he can stay sober for good."

Matthew treated the people who worked for him like family, not just employees. We tried to do the same at Ms. Match, but if I'd had an employee with an issue like Chef Damon's, I probably wouldn't have given him as many chances. Matthew was possibly loyal to a fault, but I admired the way he didn't give up on people.

His phone buzzed on the seat between us.

"Would you mind reading me that text?" he asked.

A man who had nothing to hide and would let me read his messages? That was definitely new and different romantic terrain for me.

"Oh no," I said after tapping the message. "Kyra has to leave by eleven tonight. Her mom has to work the midnight shift so she has to go home and babysit her siblings."

"Darn it, I'm sorry." Matthew glanced over at me, the disappointment in his eyes mirroring my own.

"It's alright," I said. "She said we should still go out and enjoy ourselves. We just have to get you home before you turn into a pumpkin."

"Cinderella joke, huh?" he smiled at me.

"I'm the princess who's sweeping you off your feet and taking you out for the night. You work too hard and deserve a break. I've been excited about this all day."

"Me too. I've been so distracted that I poured coffee creamer in my oatmeal this morning and wore my shirt inside out."

I laughed and squeezed his hand. "I'll take that as a compliment."

"What are we going to do about this?" His tone was playful, but the mood in the truck felt heavier. "You're leaving the ranch soon and going hundreds of miles away from me. I'm going to miss you."

"Maybe we could visit each other?" I suggested tentatively, unsure if he was serious about wanting to continue our relationship after I left the ranch. "If you'd be willing to come to New York, I'd love to show you around."

"I'd like that," he said. "I'm not really sure what my plans are this winter, but I could try to arrange a visit to New York."

"It's okay if you can't," I said quickly. "I know you have Gigi to visit and the ranch to look after. You're a busy guy." Just because he was going to miss me didn't mean he wanted to fly across the country to see me. I felt silly for suggesting it.

"Hey." He waited until I looked over at him. "It's not that I don't want to visit you. I'd love to come to New York, if I can. If not, I'd love to call and write you letters."

I raised my eyebrows. "Letters?"

He laughed, looking sheepish. "Is letter writing dead? I don't know. There's something about a letter that feels more special than an email."

"You can make me a mixed tape, too," I teased.

"Got it. Mixed tapes and letter writing. Totally old school."

We were pulling into the parking lot of The Eternal Springs Spa, and to my dismay, it didn't look very impressive.

"Is this where we're swimming?" I asked as we got out of the Suburban.

"You should have seen this place before my friend Luke Daltry purchased it," he said. "I wish I could renovate Silver Sage the way he fixed up this place. He ripped down and redesigned the deck and put in a cold plunge pool and saunas. It's pretty amazing."

From the outside, the spa's main building wasn't anything more than a humble concrete house. It certainly didn't look amazing, but I tried to be diplomatic. "I had no idea what to expect."

"It's rustic," he said. "Don't expect it to be like what you'd find at a Manhattan spa."

We stepped inside the office reception area, which was nothing like its exterior. The floors were natural oak stained in a light color and the walls were a soft, pale shade of green. The sitting area contained two modern sofas covered in a white tweedy material, flanked by tree stumps fashioned into side tables. Soft lighting from several lamps cast a meditative glow around the room, enhanced by the tinkling sound of a large Japanese fountain in the corner.

I ran my finger over the smooth leaf of a jade plant. "Wow. This is lovely."

"You wouldn't believe how dark and dingy it was in here before," he said. "Luke turned the place around. Some folks in town complained that it had lost its former charm, which I guess was true if you found mold and mildew charming."

Luke poked his head out of his office behind the reception desk. I recognized him as the man who tried to shield me from the fight at The Mangy Marmot.

"Hey, buddy!" He bounded toward Matthew with Golden Retriever energy, clasping him in a bro hug. His place may have been classy, but Luke dressed Wyoming casual—blue jeans and a navy blue t-shirt advertising the hot springs. The only things setting him apart sartorially from the other men I'd seen in Three Rivers were the leather bracelet on his wrist and the Birkenstock sandals on his feet.

"Good to see you," Matthew said. "This is my friend, Lauren Wagonblast. You two met at The Marmot."

Luke smiled warmly and shook my hand, exposing a

single-line tattoo of a moose head on the inside of his arm. "Welcome to the hot springs, Lauren."

I shook his hand, which dwarfed mine. "Great to see you again under better circumstances."

"That was just a normal Friday night in Three Rivers." Luke reached for two fluffy white towels that were stacked on a shelf. "I reserved pool number seven for you. You're welcome to use the changing rooms down that hallway. Feel free to stay as long as you'd like." He pointed to a large basket with a lid. "You can drop the towels and robes in here before you go."

"Thanks," Matthew said. "We really appreciate it."

"I hope you enjoy the springs," he said. "You've got them to yourselves this evening."

Matthew and I went into separate changing stalls to put on our suits. When I'd stripped down, I looked into the mirror, trying to see myself through fresh eyes. What was I thinking, baring all this middle-aged skin?

The tiny room's fluorescent lighting revealed spider veins on my thighs and cellulite on my backside. I'd be relying on underwire and lycra to hide the effects of gravity and breast-feeding on my boobs. With a sigh of resignation, I wrestled myself into my bathing suit's one-shoulder strap. The results weren't bad if I threw my shoulders back and kept my stomach sucked in, but who wanted to walk around holding their breath? I relaxed my muscles and decided to stop trying so damn hard. It was exhausting.

Matthew, already wearing his swim trunks and t-shirt, let out an appreciative wolf whistle that did wonders for my ego. "She's got legs..." he sang, "...she knows how to use them."

It was an old ZZ Top song that probably only our generation would remember.

I blushed and slapped his arm, my cheeks heating from both embarrassment and pleasure. "Stop it."

"Why? You're gorgeous, and you don't even know it. If you must cover up perfection, they have these." He handed me one of the complimentary terry cloth robes. "But I sure was enjoying the view." He grabbed our towels and opened the door that led out to the back of the building. "After you, my lady."

With only a moment of hesitation, I threw my robe over my arm and, as I walked through the door, gave my hips a theatrical wiggle. Matthew whistled again as I laughed.

The temperature outside was dropping and darkness had fallen. We walked along the back deck that contained eight small, round pools, each one big enough to fit three to four people comfortably. They didn't look that different from hot tubs, with their steam rising into the cool night air.

"They put privacy tents around the pools during the day," Matthew explained. "Then they remove them in the evening so you can soak under the stars."

"I'm so glad we did this before I have to leave." As soon as the words were out of my mouth, I wished I hadn't mentioned my departure.

"We'll also get you to a campfire cookout before you go," Matthew said as he pulled his t-shirt over his head and set it on the ground. I attempted not to ogle him but the view was hard to ignore, just like that first day I'd seen him at the airport, when I had no idea how much my life was about to change.

"Hold on to the railing," he warned as I went down the wooden steps into our private pool. "The bottom can be a little slippery."

He wasn't kidding. They'd lined each naturally occurring pool with rocks about the size of baseballs, and the bottom was slick under my feet. I regretted the fact that I wasn't wearing water shoes of some kind, but I didn't want to say so. He already thought I was a soft city person.

"It's nice and warm." I dipped in deeper before finally

taking a seat on the slate bench built into the sides of the pool. "Do these healing waters cure plantar fasciitis? Because I think mine is flaring up again."

"You may not believe it, but there's science behind the hot springs. They can alleviate everything from muscle pain to hypertension, so yes, the water could cure your feet." He tickled my knee. "It's also good for the soul." He kept his hand on my leg, and I desperately wanted to move it about ten inches to the north.

"Another life-changing experience in Three Rivers," I said.

He sighed and bumped his shoulder against mine. "I'm sorry we can't spend the whole night together. You have no idea how disappointed I am."

"Oh, I think I do. I know what I'm missing."

"Last night was just a preview." Matthew looked over his shoulder. "We're alone for the moment. Want to fool around with me in the hot springs?"

I answered him without subtlety by climbing onto his lap so we were face to face, my legs straddling him. "Absolutely."

He wrapped his arms around me, his hands resting on my backside. "This might be the best night of my life. Definitely, top ten"

"I'm honored." I draped my arms around his neck. "But as you said, that was just a preview."

I leaned in and kissed him, and he pulled me against him with his capable hands. I was so ready, so responsive to every touch. As we kissed, little kitten noises that I'd never heard myself make before escaped my lips. This sexual tension was turning into exquisite torture. Right as I was about to suggest we rent one of the cabins at the hot springs for an hour, a voice rang out in the night air.

"Matthew Hart? Is that you?"

We sprang apart as a gaggle of older women walked towards us, all wearing white terry cloth robes, the mist from the hot springs rising in the air around them. Three of them had towels slung over their arms and the fourth had one looped over the front of her walker. They looked like a group of angels leaving work for a smoke break. I swung myself off of Matthew's lap so he could greet them without me clinging to him like Saran Wrap.

"Hey, ladies!" He secretly rearranged what was happening inside his shorts. "Going for a dip?"

When they came closer, I recognized the woman at the front of their group as Cherise, Sam's veterinary assistant. The woman with the gray pixie cut was Alma, who worked at The General Store and had a horse named after her. The other two women were strangers to me, but I had no doubt they knew Matthew.

"Luke said to tell you he was sorry," Alma said. "He wanted to give you two privacy, but he'd forgotten it was book club night." She looked over at me. "We always have a soak after our monthly book club meeting."

I glanced down to make sure my bathing suit was completely in place, covering all the vital parts. "That sounds like fun."

"It's wonderful," she said. "Patty's eczema has cleared right up since we've been coming regularly." The woman with the walker, presumably Patty, nodded vigorously in agreement.

"Lauren, you've met Cherise and Alma," Matthew said. "These other two troublemakers are Patty Watson and Raelynn Moore."

Suddenly, Raelynn looked familiar to me, too. "Have we met?"

"I work at the ranch," she said. "Head of housekeeping. You've probably seen me tearing around in a golf cart."

"That's right," I said. "You usually wear your hair up."

She looked surprised that I'd noticed and remembered.

"Only wear it down when I'm not working. I should tie it up before I get in this water, though."

"Sorry I'm late!" Another woman came rushing down the wooden deck toward us, this one much younger. I recognized her bouncy curls and petite frame immediately.

"Hi, Ella," I said. "Are you in this book club, too?"

"Oh hell, no." She put her arm around Patty. "I don't want to be in a smutty book club with my mother."

"It's not smutty, sweetheart," Patty said patiently. "It's a romance book club for senior ladies. Nothing scandalous about that."

"I'm glad you enjoy them," Ella said, "but those books are totally unrealistic. Who's going to get romanced like that in Three Rivers, Wyoming?"

After her words rang out in the night air, every single one of them looked down at us and smiled mischievously. Matthew cleared his throat and looked away, and I put my hand over my mouth to hide my delighted smile.

"What was this month's book about?" I asked, so we could change the subject.

"This week Cherise introduced us to alien romance," Alma said gaily.

Matthew made a little noise of disbelief that he twisted into a fake cough.

"Needless to say, it blew some people's minds," Cherise added. She was tall, curvaceous and, even in a white terrycloth robe and Tevas, quite formidable. "And this one was fairly tame for the genre."

"Oh, that sounds...nice," I said.

My eyes darted to Ella's as she grimaced. I had trouble imagining these women reading alien romance, but why not? It was never too late for something new and a little...out there.

Raelynn raised her eyebrows. "I don't know if I'd say nice, but it was interesting."

"And informative," Alma added. "I'd never really thought about how aliens did it."

"You realize it's fiction?" Cherise asked. "The author didn't actually go intergalactic and document these things. We still have no idea how aliens have sex, assuming they exist."

"I think it's pretty arrogant of us to think other lifeforms don't exist." Patty turned to her daughter. "See, Ella, we do talk about intellectual things at book club."

"Okay." Ella squeezed her mom's shoulder. "But I think Matthew has probably heard enough about alien intercourse for one evening. Let's leave these two alone. We didn't mean to intrude on your private time."

As they sauntered down to their pools, chattering all the way, Alma's voice traveled back to us. "I predicted they'd get together."

Apparently, Matthew heard her too, because he looked at me quizzically. "Did Alma tell you something about us?"

"You're not going to believe this," I said with a chuckle. "The day I shopped for my hiking boots at The General, she whispered to me that we made a good-looking couple. I told her I was just your guest at the ranch, and she got this odd look on her face and said, 'oh, not yet.'"

Matthew didn't laugh like I thought he would. "She actually said that?"

"Yes," I said. "Why?"

"Alma's kind of the town psychic," he explained. "She doesn't do it for money or anything, but she's known to make extremely accurate predictions. Walt says she was always like that, even as a kid. He says she has the sight." Matthew made spooky fingers in the air.

A chill passed over my bare shoulders, and I dipped deeper into the warm spring water. "Are you kidding around right now?"

Matthew smiled and shook his head. "Nope."

I'd never been a big believer in psychics or destiny, but it wouldn't surprise me if Alma had felt something brewing between Matthew and me. She must have picked up on our spark of attraction that day at The General.

He took my hand in his. "Please promise me we'll spend at least one whole night together before you leave the ranch?"

"Definitely." I leaned over and kissed him softly on the lips. "Are you okay with the book club seeing us kissing? I figured they already saw me straddling you when they came in. The jig is up."

"I don't have anything to hide," he said with a grin. "Kiss me anytime you want."

Nothing to hide. I wished I could say the same for myself.

CHAPTER 20

MATTHEW

"I have strong feelings for a woman I've only known a few weeks." I dug my shovel into the earth again. "It can't be real, right? I mean, it can't last, can it?"

Here I was, out in a field, obsessing about Lauren so badly that I was desperate enough to ask Walt for relationship advice. This was certainly a place I never thought I'd find myself. The alternative was talking to Sam or Bowie, and that wasn't going to happen. The serial monogamist and the lone wolf had nothing helpful to say, so Walt was my confidant, God help me.

"I think it can still be real." His eyes were on the dirt as he watched me dig out a rotted fence post.

"You do?" That was exactly what I wanted to hear. Maybe he was better at this advice thing than I'd given him credit for.

"My cousin Dean fell in love with his wife on a three-day trip to Reno. Sometimes love strikes hard and fast."

"Is that so?"

He nodded. "Yep, and they still can't keep their hands off each other."

I leaned on the handle of my shovel. "Walt, didn't you tell me Dean met his wife in high school?"

"That was his first wife, Edie. This is the second one I'm talking about, Geena."

"What happened to his marriage with Edie?"

Walt grimaced and rubbed his chin. "He went to Reno and met Geena."

My eyes widened in realization. "So you're comparing my relationship to your philandering cousin's?"

Walt adjusted his hat. "Well, I guess it hits different when you put it that way."

"Probably not the best example." I needed to find a better mentor for my love life.

After we'd finished replacing the post, Walt and I drove back to the office to find Sam and his dog Jake waiting for us.

"What are you two doing here?" I asked.

"Walt is babysitting Jake while I work tonight," Sam said. "I've got to make a visit out in Bitter Creek, and I might not be back until morning."

Jake pranced around my desk to paw at my work boots. I gave him a good scratch under his tiny chin, and he wagged his tail to approve of my efforts.

"So are you cooking his chicken dinner and putting him in his silk pajamas, Walt?" I asked.

Walt chuckled, and Sam took my teasing with his usual good nature. He knew it was silly to boil fresh chicken for a dog, but Jake flat-out went on a hunger strike if he smelled any type of dog food—kibble or wet—in his bowl. Years ago, Sam saved Jake from being euthanized at the shelter after his original adoptive family returned him for his bad habit of nipping people's hands and feet. To his credit, Sam trained Jake well over the years and vice versa. Jake didn't nip anymore, and Sam made fancy dog food and let him sleep on the other side of his bed. Not in silk pajamas—that part was fiction.

"He doesn't have to cook it," Sam said. "I brought Jake's food with me." He produced a plastic box and handed it to Walt. Then he turned his back to me as he quietly added, "If you can heat it up a little, that would be great. He doesn't like cold food."

I let that one go. It was nice to see Sam so invested in a loving relationship, even if it was with a spoiled little dog.

After Sam left, Walt picked up Jake and cradled him like a baby. "If your daddy doted on his girlfriends the way he dotes on you, he might be married by now."

"Maybe he knows that, so he gives all his attention to the dog." I looked at my laptop, knowing I should open it to do some accounting. My heart wasn't in it, though. I was barely going to make payroll for the rest of the summer, and every time I ran the numbers, it was more and more depressing.

Walt set Jake on the floor and rocked back on the heels of his boots. I figured he was about to head back to the stables, but he didn't go. Instead, he took his time getting a drink from the water cooler in the corner. I'd known him long enough to understand something was on his mind.

"Did you want to talk to me?" I asked.

He drained the paper cup, then tossed it in the trash. "I got a call from my nephew in Colorado. The place he's working near Fort Collins needs another wrangler."

"I see…" I sat down on my stool behind the counter, and I wanted to drop my head in my hands and weep out of pure frustration. That wouldn't be fair to Walt, though. This was a situation I should have seen coming.

"It would be a year-round position," he said. "You know I don't want to leave Silver Sage, Matthew, not to mention my feelings about living in CSU territory." I nodded, acknowledging his lifelong allegiance to University of Wyoming football. "I'm not saying I'm taking the job. This ranch has been my home for so long I can't imagine living anywhere else. And Three Rivers…I was born and raised here."

"I know that." I lifted a whining, attention hungry Jake onto my lap and stroked his back. "You've given your life to this place, and we're family. We always will be." He opened his mouth, but I cut him off. "I understand your dilemma, though. You're worried you might be out of a job soon."

He took off his sun-faded black hat and held it to his chest. "That's about the high and low of it. At my age, I can't be without work. I've saved some, but I'm still going to need a paycheck for the next six or seven years."

"Then I think you should consider taking it." I tried to ignore the lump forming in my throat. "I wish I could reassure you that things are going to turn around here, and you know I'm doing my best to make that happen, but I can't make any promises."

"You know I'll stay through the season. I can help you close up the place, too."

At this point, I wasn't sure if there would be another summer season, but he didn't need to worry about that.

"I appreciate that. Of course, I'll give you the highest recommendation possible whenever you need it."

He rubbed a weathered hand over his mouth. "I hate talking like this."

"Me too." I hated that I was in danger of losing the ranch. I also hated feeling like a failure. So many people were going to be let down unless I found a way to generate money quickly. "I'm sorry I'm not doing a better job of filling up these cabins."

Walt assessed me with his warm brown eyes, the same color as the Wyoming soil we lived on. His gaze offered me more patience and wisdom than I deserved. He was always the epitome of a cowboy to me—quiet, tough, independent. I spent a lot of time wanting to be just like him. Letting him down gutted me, and it was all I could do to hold back the emotion that was building like a tsunami inside my chest.

"If I knew how to turn this thing around—" My voice

broke, and I had to take a moment to collect myself. As if he sensed my upset, Jake put his paws on my shoulders and licked my cheek. "Hell, even if I had the magic bullet, I don't have the money to put it into action, anyway."

"You're not to blame. I feel guilty that I didn't warn you about taking over the ranch from your folks, but it wasn't my place to do so. Or at least I didn't think so at the time. I knew full well that we hadn't kept up to date on things and that the guests weren't booking like they used to. Your parents let things slip around here as they got older."

"In hindsight, I should have been more realistic about it, too." I pulled my cap off, then slid it back on again, a nervous habit of mine. "I could have inspected the books and the facilities, done my due diligence. I was thinking about what my parents would have wanted, and that was keeping the ranch going and making sure everyone got a paycheck on time."

"Losing your parents was a shock. I was hoping Bowie and Sam might help you fix things up around here. Heck, I thought even Faith might come back. Maybe if all of you took on this mountain, you could have climbed it together."

I wasn't the only dreamer around here, apparently. "And I thought I could get a bank loan big enough to renovate this place." I shook my head. "Things don't always turn out like you plan."

"I talked to Bowie last week," he said. "You need to tell him about your struggles. He doesn't seem to have a clue."

That was because I'd shared nothing about my problems with my brothers or my sister. When our parents died, Sam encouraged me to take over the ranch. Bowie didn't seem to care one way or the other and Faith tried to talk me out of it. She was the one who warned me that Mom and Dad had let it go downhill over the last ten years, but she'd always been the worrier of the family, so I'd dismissed her concerns. Shame on me.

"I don't want to burden them," I said.

"They're co-owners," Walt said. "You'd be informing, not burdening, them."

"I guess so." The thought of admitting defeat made me feel sick to my stomach.

"You've got the Titans coming at the end of the month. That will help."

I wasn't looking forward to a visit from the Order of the Titans, but they'd booked a week at the ranch for the last two years, and even when we raised the prices on them this year, they paid the increase without complaint. They billed themselves as a highly select cabal of business executives who met once a year for a week of drinking, fishing and unofficial networking. They preferred our remote location and small size because they were very secretive about their meetings, as if anyone else would actually care what they talked about. In fact, they made me sign a non-disclosure agreement so that I wouldn't spill any of their secrets.

Kyra couldn't help in the Round Room when they were on the property because once they started drinking, I couldn't trust them to be gentlemanly toward the females on staff. Nothing awful had ever happened, but they got rowdy and obnoxious in the late evening, and I wasn't taking any risks. As soon as we were on a stronger financial footing, I'd turn down their reservation requests, but we'd probably go bankrupt before then.

"They always enjoy coming out here to smoke cigars and shoot off guns." Just thinking about The Titans put a sour taste in my mouth. "They love playing cowboy."

Walt tipped his head and studied me. "I guess that's what you need to think about."

"How much I can't stand those guys?"

"What kind of place you want this to be." He leaned a shoulder against the wall, and I knew I was in for a story. Jake seemed to understand too, as he settled on my lap, curling himself into a ball. "Years ago, when your parents took over the ranch, they saw a vision for it. They wanted families to come out here for fresh air, fishing, horseback riding, and a genuine encounter with the land. Your dad might have given up the church, but this ranch became his second mission. I believe he saw communing with nature as a way to get closer to God."

I'd never heard Walt speak this way. "Dad's proselytizing finally got to you, huh?"

A slow smile spread across his face. "I did work for the man for a quarter century. At some point, his vision for this place became clear to me. Toward the end, we got away from it though. Old guests stopped coming and some of the new ones…well, they weren't here for the fishing, I can tell you that. Did your parents tell you we had some young people come out here a few years back to do ayahuasca?"

"Seriously?" Dad and Mom had definitely not mentioned that to me.

"Those idiots nearly died out there in the sagebrush in the heat of the day, tripping out of their minds and puking up their guts. We had to treat them for sunburns and dehydration. Your dad was furious."

"I can imagine." My father only talked about his triumphs, never his failures, which is why I'd never heard this story before. It was also why I didn't know that the ranch hadn't turned a profit in the last five years before I took ownership. By the time I figured it all out, I already had my heart set on reviving the place.

"So, what's your vision?" Walt asked. "Assuming you can keep it going, what would you like to see happen to the ranch?"

"I'd like to bring it back to its former glory," I said. "This place has such a beautiful history as a guest ranch. We just need to let people know we're here. With all those kids addicted to their cell phones and video games, people need Silver Sage now more than ever."

"Your parents somehow made it through the lean times. I know you will too." His words were encouraging, but Walt wasn't smiling. He doubted me, and I doubted myself. "C'mon, Jake. Time to go."

Jake jumped off my lap, and Walt opened the screen door to let him outside, then came back to grab the dog's food container. "Good luck with your lady friend. I hope that works out for you. She's real nice."

At that point, I couldn't see anything working out for me, but I nodded anyway because what else could I do? It seemed like there must be a solution to the ranch's problems, but I hadn't found it yet and time was running out for Silver Sage Ranch.

CHAPTER 21

LAUREN

*I*n any normal version of my world, Tori would have been the first person I called when I realized I had romantic feelings for someone. I'd avoided it because I knew what she would say—Matthew lived across the country; his lifestyle was the opposite of mine; and he was the first man I'd gone on a date with since my marriage imploded. She wouldn't be wrong to have reservations. I'd had concerns myself, but I wanted to figure out what to do with them before I talked to Tori about it. Even so, I owed her a call about the Freddy situation, so I left on my morning walk and crossed my fingers that the cell service would hold out for me.

"My long-lost sister from the west!" she teased. "Where have you been? Out riding and roping broncos?"

"What are you talking about?" I asked. "Do you even know what a bronco is?"

As I passed by the office, I casually turned to look through the windows, wondering if Matthew was inside. No luck. I hadn't experienced this kind of eagerness and excitement about a man since Freddy swept me off my feet. This time was different, though. I was older now and understood that fairytales didn't exist. I could see beyond good looks and charm to the real man inside, and with Matthew, I liked what I saw.

"Isn't a bronco a horse?" she asked. "Oh, do they have a mechanical bull at that bar? What's it called, The Mangy Moose?"

"The Mangy Marmot."

"Moose, marmot, whatever. I'm picturing it like something from the movie *Roadhouse*."

Obviously, she viewed my visit to the ranch as a strange and fascinating detour on the journey through my divorce, and I was afraid she'd see hooking up with Matthew as another curve in my road to single life. What I felt for him ran deeper than that though, as did my affection for this place. Since coming to the ranch, I'd finally found some answers about what I wanted to do with my future.

"No bar fights and no mechanical bull, unfortunately," I said. "I wish you could see this ranch. At every turn, there's something beautiful."

She hummed noncommittally. "It's certainly remote. We accidentally picked a good hiding spot for you. The press clearly has no idea where you are, and I can't imagine they'll ever find you there."

That was one of my worst fears—the paparazzi descending on the town or, even more horrifying, the ranch. "Unless Freddy or Sully tells them I'm here. She's out to sabotage me. She told Freddy where to find me, and I'm pretty sure she's the person who told him about the syndication deal."

Tori growled low in her throat. "He must have paid her off. Don't worry about Sully. When I fire her, I'm going to remind her she signed an NDA. If she meddles anymore, I'm going to sue her ass. As for Freddy, I still think we should consider running him over and making it look like an accident."

She was joking. Probably.

"I don't think I can live with a clear conscience if I murder the father of my children. We probably shouldn't be talking about this over the phone. I feel like a swat team is going to descend on me at any moment."

She chuckled. "Okay, fine."

"You're as disgusted as I am at the thought of giving him part of the company, right?"

She paused before responding. "Yeah, it makes me sick to my stomach."

"I don't want to do it, either." When Freddy spoke to the tabloids, it would impact her, too. We hadn't spoken about that, not really. "I'm so sorry. I hate this is going to mess up your life."

"Don't apologize to me." She sounded fierce. Fiercely protective. "Honestly, I'm just happy you're not living a lie anymore and, besides, I have Nick in my life now. He makes me feel like all this shit can't touch me. Whoever thought I'd let myself rely on a man this way?"

She said it with cheekiness, but it wasn't a joke. "It's not dependence. It's support. You finally have a guy in your life who's got your back, and I'm thrilled for you." My voice broke a little on the word thrilled. "No one deserves it more than you."

"You deserve it, too, Lolo."

"I do," I said, allowing myself to believe that fully. "And maybe someday I'll find him." Maybe I'd already found him. Even if Matthew and I never saw each other again after I left the ranch, he'd raised the bar for everyone who followed him. "For now, I'm happy that Freddy won't have ammunition to use against me anymore. At least that will be over."

"There is one other option," she said.

"What's that?"

"Get out in front of the story by telling your side to the press first." As I objected, she cut me off. "Just listen to me.

You've done nothing wrong, and we can get our publicists to help you craft every word in the best way possible. Tell the media that you and Freddy found it easier to live apart, and he agreed to come to events with you a few times a year. You weren't trying to fool anyone—"

"But we were. Or at least I was trying to fool everyone." I waved at Gigi as she rode her bike past me, up the dirt pathway that wound toward the cottages.

"That part is a little tricky." I could hear her drumming her long fingernails on her desk. "Still, I think you can phrase it so people understand you felt like there was no other choice. If society wasn't so hard on women, this wouldn't be an issue."

"No kidding," I said. "It's not enough to be great at our jobs. We have to maintain the perfect marriage and be perfect mothers to perfect children. There's never any room for mistakes."

"Try being a woman who doesn't want children," she said. "We're called self-centered, lazy or barren, or maybe all three! The patriarchy is bullshit."

I stepped off the path and into the grass, which was still wet from the rain earlier that morning. It was the first daytime rainstorm at the ranch since I'd arrived. Everything was glistening with droplets of water that reflected back tiny rainbows in the sunshine.

"You know they're going to say that I put our company first," I said, "and I neglected my husband. That I was too busy working at a company that developed other people's relationships while my own fell apart." My voice caught, and I paused to compose myself, unwilling to cry over my failed marriage yet again. "Freddy will paint himself as the victim, like he always does, and he'll tell them I made him feel ignored and unimportant, and everyone will feel sorry for him and blame the cold, ambitious wife. Maybe they're right. Maybe I was a bad wife."

"You know that's not true," Tori said sternly. "C'mon. You've done so much work on yourself to get over him and move on. Don't let him drag you down into the mud again with his gaslighting."

"You're right." I sniffled, still trying to stem the tears. "I wasn't a perfect wife, but I did my best with the tools I had at the time." Wasn't that all any of us could do?

"And," she added, "he's a total schmuck."

I laughed because my twin would never let me take part of the blame for my failed marriage, and there was no point in arguing with her. Her job was to love me and be on my side.

"If you're not going to talk to the media, can I do it?" she asked. "I want to expose that money grubbing jackass for who he really is."

"I don't know if that's a good idea, but it's tempting."

I looked up into the sky, as if it held answers. I had to think about my sons and protect them from the shrapnel of this explosion, but Freddy certainly wasn't considering them. Maybe protecting them wasn't the right way to think about it. Maybe I could help them deal with the situation instead of trying to stop it from happening? Still, my instinct was to shield them in any and every way possible.

Before I came up with an answer, I spotted something breathtaking.

"A double rainbow! Oh, wow. Look at this." I tried to turn the phone around to show her what I was seeing, but it wouldn't come across like it did in person. Even a high-quality photo couldn't capture this beauty in its truest form but that didn't stop me from taking one. "I've never seen a double rainbow. I can't believe this."

"It's beautiful," she said gently. "And you're not alone in this."

She had me tearing up again. "I know. I love you, Tori, and I appreciate all of your support."

"I love you, too," she said. "I've missed you so much, but you sound really happy out there. Maybe you should think about getting a little place in the mountains."

I couldn't believe my ears. "Seriously? You think I should get a place out here? That's exactly the idea I've been toying with for the last few days." I could certainly afford it, but what would Matthew think if I got a vacation house near his ranch? Was it way too soon? I wouldn't only be doing it for him, but it might seem that way.

"Not in Wyoming," she said, as if this was obvious. "It's way too far away. You loved Vermont, and there are beautiful towns in the Catskills. A friend of mine just got a place in Kingston."

She was missing the point. "The east coast is nothing like this. The sky out here is incredible. You feel so insignificant in this landscape but also so free. You need to come out here and see it." I looked up at the sky, disappointed she didn't understand. Even more disappointing, the rainbows were already fading. I was eager to walk back to the office and call Gigi over the walkie. What if she missed this? What if I'd missed this? I'd gone 52 years without seeing a double rainbow. If Freddy hadn't humiliated me, if I hadn't ended up at the wrong ranch, if I hadn't looked up today, I would have missed this one.

"Hold on. I have to do something." I'd circled back and was passing the office door. No one was there, so I picked up a walkie and made an announcement. "Come in, Gigi and Matthew. This is Lauren."

Two seconds later, Matthew's voice came over the speaker. "Everything okay?"

"Yes, sorry to alarm you. I wanted to make sure Gigi saw the double rainbow. Are you outside?"

I could hear the smile in his voice. "Aw, that's awesome. She's here with me at the Cottonwood Cottage looking up at it right now. Can we have lunch together today?"

I couldn't stop a smile from spreading across my face. "Absolutely."

"I'm back," I told Tori as I stepped out of the office. "I wanted to tell Matthew's daughter about the rainbow."

"Um, what's going on with you and this rancher?" As always, Tori had seen right through me. "And don't bullshit me, Lolo. I know something is going on."

"We've become a little more than friends." Friends who made out like the world was coming to an end and this was our last chance for pleasure.

"I knew it! You got laid, didn't you?"

I bit my bottom lip, regretting this conversation. "No!"

"Oh no. He couldn't get it up? Honey, that's not unusual with men our age. It happens."

"It's not that at all. He can—I don't want to talk about it over the phone, honestly."

"Okay." She didn't sound thrilled that I wasn't giving her any details, and I couldn't blame her. We usually told each other everything. "Well, I'm happy for you. You needed a vacation fling, and it sounds like you got one."

This was what I'd been afraid of. "I wouldn't call it a vacation fling. I actually like him a lot."

"What do you mean?" she asked. "You're getting emotionally involved with him?"

"Yeah, sort of." I could tell by her tone that this wasn't the time to get into it with her. "I don't know him very well yet, but we've decided to keep in touch." Why did I say we didn't know each other well? In some ways, I felt like Matthew understood me better than the man I was married to for decades.

"How can that work out? Is that why you want a vacation place out there?"

Every sentence she spoke was ruining the joy that rainbow was giving me. Without thinking, I'd already started walking toward Cottonwood Cottage, and now Matthew and Gigi were in sight. I waved to them and suddenly I didn't care what my sister thought. What was happening between Matthew and me felt right, and that was more important at the moment than anyone else's opinion.

"I have to go, Tori. I'll call you again soon."

CHAPTER 22

MATTHEW

*T*here was a picture on my phone now of Gigi and Lauren looking up at the double rainbow over the ranch. If I had questions about whether I should continue pursuing Lauren, that moment clinched it for me. Not only was I wildly attracted to her, she'd also made a genuine connection with my daughter. How could I let all of that go?

Lauren accepted my invitation to watch a movie with us after dinner, but Gigi was exhausted from another busy day at the ranch. When she went to bed around nine o'clock, Lauren and I cuddled up on my couch to watch one of my favorites, *Shawshank Redemption*. Turned out, she loved it, too. Not that it mattered because we didn't see past the first fifteen minutes of the movie.

I tried to memorize everything about her—the silky feel of her hair running through my fingers, her impossibly soft lips, the sounds she made when I touched her. Time was moving too quickly, and before I knew it, she'd be back in New York and this would all feel like a dream.

As the movie credits rolled, Lauren pulled away from me, straightening her wrinkled blouse. "Maybe I should go home. It's getting late, and you have to work tomorrow."

Lauren wore all her feelings on the outside, even though she thought she kept them hidden. Maybe other people didn't see them so easily, but I did.

"Everything okay?" I asked.

"Yeah." She twisted her fingers in her lap. "I just wanted to get something cleared up tonight. At the hot springs, you said you were going to miss me, but when I asked you to visit me in New York, you kind of gave me a maybe. It's okay if this isn't serious for you, but I'd rather know now so I don't get hurt. Let's be honest with each other, okay?"

"That wasn't about you." I took her busy hands in mine to stop her fidgeting. "I absolutely want to visit you in New York."

She smiled and exhaled. "Then why didn't you say so?"

Nothing was less appealing than telling the woman I was falling for about my failing business. Before running Silver Sage into the ground, I was a successful contractor who was so in demand that I actually had to turn away potential clients when my schedule got too full. Occasionally, I still received calls from former clients begging me to take over their renovation projects because the person they were currently working with wasn't as capable, reliable, or honest as I'd been. Moving from that level of success to being the owner of a struggling guest ranch was tough on my ego.

"Things aren't great financially with Silver Sage." Talking about it felt like poking a wound. "If they don't improve, I'll have to put the place on the market soon. I just don't know what my future holds or where I'll be living this winter. That's why I hesitated. My life is kind of complicated at the moment." We both smiled at my choice of words, which mirrored her own when I first asked about her marriage.

I waited for her reaction, knowing this might not be a huge surprise to her. Obviously, the ranch wasn't close to being fully booked, and our facilities needed updates. She heard about me doing things most resort owners would never do, like unclogging a toilet.

She squeezed my hands. "I hate that you might have to sell the ranch. I know how important it is to you and Gigi."

"I hope it won't come to that, but my parents really let things go around here. My siblings and I put money into this place, but it was like adding drops to a leaky bucket."

"Would you be willing to share what your main issues are? Maybe I can help brainstorm some solutions." She was the chief financial officer of a successful business, so I knew she wasn't asking that question casually.

I rubbed the tension in the back of my neck. "Where do I begin?"

I didn't owe her an explanation, but part of me wanted to talk about everything I'd been holding inside of me for so long. I started detailing the immediate cash flow problems, then moved on to infrastructure issues, the decline in bookings, and competition from a growing number of guest ranches in surrounding areas. At first, I was reluctant to open up, but once I got going, it was as if a pressure valve had been released. I didn't realize how badly I needed to talk to someone about my problems, someone who would truly understand and hopefully not judge me.

"Thank you," I said when I finished venting. "I have no idea why you haven't stopped me before now, but I appreciate you listening to me."

"I'm happy to listen," she said. "It sounds like you walked into a minefield of problems and issues, which was further complicated by your sentimental attachment to the ranch. I'm sure you want to keep it going for Gigi, too."

I hadn't even brought up the emotional component, but, clearly, she already understood. "It breaks my heart to think about selling, but my siblings don't feel the same connection to it I do."

"I can't believe that. I've only been here a few weeks, and I feel connected to it already."

She always seemed to say the right thing.

"Even Walt is thinking about leaving Silver Sage. I feel like I'm the only one who believes we can keep it going."

"I'm so sorry, Matthew. Please let me help in any way I can." She leaned in and kissed me, and for the first time, I didn't feel like I was in this mess alone.

Thank goodness we weren't doing anything scandalous because Gigi chose that moment to wander downstairs with drowsy eyes and messy hair. "I had a nightmare." Her voice was croaky from sleep. "Can I sit with you guys for a few minutes?"

"Of course," Lauren said before I could tell Gigi I'd take her upstairs and tuck her in. She made space for Gigi between us on the couch and patted the cushion, and my heart swelled to about twice its size with affection for her.

Gigi plopped down between us and rested against me, her little body still warm and relaxed. "I don't want to leave Loki. Can't I stay here for fifth grade and you can homeschool me? You could talk to Mom about it."

It ripped my heart out when she said things like this. Her mom and stepdad would be at the ranch in two days to take her home, and neither of us was happy about it.

"I love that idea," I said, "except for the part where I try to teach school."

"So I'll take the bus to public school," she said. "And before you say that it's too hard to get off the ranch in the winter, I've already thought that through." She paused dramatically. "We get a snowmobile."

Lauren looked over Gigi's head and raised her eyebrows, silently asking me if I was going to cave in. The choice wasn't mine to make, unfortunately, because a court agreement stated Gigi had to go back to Denver for the school year.

"I understand you want to stay longer," I said, "and I wish

you could too, but then your mom would miss you. We decided together this was best, but I know it's hard leaving Loki." She was always missing one of her parents, and one of us had to miss her, too. Divorced parenting sucked, even when the situation was amicable.

Gigi sighed and nestled against me. "I don't think it's best for me to leave Silver Sage."

I looked over at Lauren, who was watching us with soft eyes and a sad smile on her lips. The ache in my chest was nearly unbearable.

"You'll be back before you know it," I said. "I get you for Thanksgiving this year, remember?"

Gigi looked unconvinced. "I hate the end of summer."

It was Lauren's turn to sigh. "Me too."

"Me three." It was the truth. If wishes came true, Silver Sage would stay open forever, and Gigi would move here and live with me full time. Heck, if I was dreaming, Lauren would be here with us, too, wearing those red cowgirl boots and joining the smutty book club. Walt would stay on, and I'd be able to hire more staff and fill these cabins.

Wishing wouldn't make all of that happen though, and reality was quickly closing in on me. Payroll was due and my debts were mounting. Something had to give.

THE FOLLOWING EVENING, I was feeling nostalgic at the campfire cookout, knowing it was mostly likely the last one for Silver Sage. The fact that it was Lauren's first and only cookout, made it even more bittersweet. As Walt told cowboy tales to the guests, I felt tears gather in my eyes. How could something so special just go out like a candle? And how could I have let it go?

After I put Gigi to bed that night, I came across the urn in the hall closet containing my mother's ashes. Although I had nothing against cremation, it felt strange and a little creepy to have her remains sitting on a shelf between a box of flashlights and a stack of umbrellas. Long ago, Dad had purchased two plots in a Laramie cemetery where he expected one day to be buried alongside his wife, but it turned out Mom had other plans for her eternal rest. She'd secretly put it in her will to be cremated and spread around the ranch, a fun fact we discovered after their deaths. My father was one of those husbands who had the final say on everything—head of the household and all of that—and my guess was she felt it would be easier to put her final wishes in a legal document rather than try to go up against him.

The funeral home gave her ashes to me a week after we'd buried our father underground. By that time, Bowie and Faith had gone home. Was I supposed to leave our mother's remains sitting on a closet shelf for years, on the off chance all of my siblings came back here again at the same time? What if we lost the ranch and couldn't come back to the property ever again? That was a horrifying thought.

I carefully lifted her urn and carried her outside to the little garden she'd planted under the kitchen window. After looking left and right to make sure I was alone, I started talking to her.

"I'm sorry I'm not doing a great job with the ranch, Mom. It's not for lack of trying. I wish you'd told me how badly business had fallen off and how you were barely making ends meet. Then again, I imagine you wanted to tell me, and Dad wouldn't let you."

A light breeze blew across my skin, and I shivered, even though it was a warm evening. Was I crazy for thinking my mother was there with me in spirit? It sure felt that way.

"Mom, if you're here, give me a sign." An owl hooted in the distance, and I nearly jumped out of my skin. "Stop being a fool," I muttered to myself.

Then again, maybe that was Mom sending me a message.

This was her home for so many years, and she loved tending to this little patch of earth where she planted her pink-hued hollyhocks and royal purple delphinium. There were certainly more scenic spots on the property to scatter her ashes, but this was her special place next to the home where she'd raised her children. Family members could come and commune with her if they wanted to, and that felt important to me. I decided to text Sam for his opinion.

> Are you okay with me scattering Mom's ashes in her kitchen garden?

SAMUEL

> Do what you need to do, brother. Just be careful if it's windy. You don't want to end up with Mom in your hair.

I had to smile at what was a classic Sam response to my question. His irreverence was in no way a reflection on how he'd felt about her. In fact, being the youngest and having years alone with her in the house after the rest of us had flown the coop, I'd always felt like he and Mom had a special bond.

I'd already started talking aloud to her, so I might as well continue.

"You always loved this little garden, Mom, and I have wonderful memories of you tending to it with such care. This house was your home for so many years that it seems fitting to let you rest here."

I sprinkled a good bit of her ashes in the garden among her blooming flowers, but there was a lot more of her left in the urn. Should I put the remainders in some other places around the ranch? That felt a little odd. Would I want my remains scattered willy nilly all over the place?

> There's a lot in here. Should I save some?

> It's not a chocolate bar. You don't need to save some of her for later.

Aware of that. Thanks.

> Sorry. The ranch was her happy place. I think she'd want to be set free.

He was right. What was a more appropriate place for her remains than this land, even if someday it wasn't ours on paper anymore? She belonged here at Silver Sage, and I'd deal with the consequences of my decision later.

A breeze picked up, as it often did in Wyoming, and I faced in the direction it was moving to avoid blowback. Her ashes mixed with the air as I shook the urn, floating her away into the night, drifting her all over her beloved Silver Sage. She'd become one with the dirt and the sky, and that felt completely right to me.

"I promise," I whispered to her, "I'll do everything in my power to keep this place in the Hart family. I won't give up without a fight."

CHAPTER 23

LAUREN

*a*fter Matthew told me about the ranch's financial situation, an idea took shape in my mind, the pieces unfolding one at a time. Some people created with broad strokes, but for my mathematical brain, it was more like making origami. I was up most of the night working through my plans until they shaped into something real and logical. Despite lack of sleep, I was buzzing when the sun rose, and the first thing I wanted to do was get more information. I called Deborah, my financial advisor in New York, and floated my big idea past her—buying a dude ranch in Wyoming. She fell into shocked silence. Then she admitted that although I had the funds for such a purchase, she didn't support the idea.

"Why would you want all of that responsibility and stress right now?" she asked. "This is the time in life most people like you look forward to lying on a beach somewhere and enjoying the fruits of their labor. If you really want to invest in real estate, there are other options that are much more low maintenance."

The last thing I wanted to do was lie on a beach for the

next thirty years, so I thanked her for the financial information and hung up the phone.

Deborah's less than enthusiastic reaction prepared me for what could be an onslaught of well-meaning naysayers, starting with my sister. Yes, Tori was all for new business ventures, but buying a dilapidated ranch in Wyoming was going to seem like a bizarre extension of the Ms. Match brand, which was what I had planned for it. Because of our high-end client list and Tori's personal style, we were associated with exclusivity and luxury, not barn cats and bar fights. If I could get her to listen, though, I'd show her how my plan could work.

I knew one person who would be relieved by my news, and that was Matthew Hart. I couldn't wait to tell him he wouldn't have to sell his ranch to a stranger. My only concern was that he might think I was insinuating myself into his life. It was one thing to start up a relationship with a guest who lived in New York and quite another to have her buy your ranch and be a part of your life forever.

Unfortunately, the timing was never right to give Matthew my news. First, he was busy with preparations for the campfire cookout, which was as much fun as everyone said it would be with a horseback ride up to the mountains, cowboy beans and cornbread cooked over a fire, and even a few tall tales of the old west spun by Walt.

The following day was Gigi's last at Silver Sage, and she wanted to take me on another picnic down by the river. We rode Loki and Banjo out there, the late August breeze cooling our faces, and we set up our snacks on those same sunny rocks we'd visited with Matthew on my first horseback ride at the ranch. My eyes misted up when she asked if we could keep in touch by email, and I wanted to tell her that it was likely we'd meet again someday soon, but I didn't want to make promises when I wasn't sure I could keep them.

"My dad really likes you," she said as we rode back. "He's been different since you got here."

"Different in a good way?" I hoped she didn't think I'd been taking him away from her.

"Yeah," she said. "He seems happier. Last summer he didn't ride as much or go to the hot springs. He's having more fun now."

"I've been having fun too." More fun than I ever imagined when I fled to this ranch, thinking only of escape and anonymity. Who knew I'd find so much more?

Matthew and Walt took Gigi on a special moonlight ride after dinner, and although they invited me to join them, it didn't feel right to intrude. Gigi and I had done our special ride and picnic, and now she needed time with her dad and the man who was like a favorite uncle to her. While they were out on their ride, I continued making spreadsheets and planning my pitch. The property would keep its charm if we restored and renovated the current buildings, but we'd also add modernity and comfort by building new structures like a pickleball court and the wellness spa that I'd expected when I first arrived. Since there were already a plethora of dude ranches that catered to families on vacation, we'd use our ranch for other purposes. Tori called when I was finishing up my work for the evening.

"So you're still set on letting Freddy go ahead and plant his stories in the media?" Disappointment laced her tone. In all my excitement about buying the ranch, I'd almost forgotten about what was happening back home. New York felt a million miles away from here.

"I really don't want to rehash this," I said. "I've made up my mind about that situation."

"What's going on with you?" she asked. "You practically hung up on me the other day. Are you mad at me? I feel like you're keeping secrets."

"No secrets, and I'm not mad at all." Right as I spoke, an

owl screeched outside my window, as if calling me out on my lie.

"Okay." She went quiet, and I knew she didn't believe me. "How's the rancher?"

"Matthew is fine."

More uncomfortable silence ensued, which was unusual for us.

"You are coming home, aren't you?"

"Yes, of course! There's a big party arriving soon, and the ranch is completely booked so I'll be back in two or three days. I just need to buy a ticket." Matthew had said I could stay at his house when my cabin was needed for new guests, but I'd be in his way. He was so understaffed that I had no idea how he was going to get through the next few weeks.

"Then what's going on?" she demanded. "I know you, and something is off." She was losing patience with me, and although I wanted to share my ideas with Matthew first, maybe it was better if I tested out my presentation before I spoke to him?

"I've always been supportive of your business pursuits," I said. "Just remember that when I tell you what I'm about to tell you. Okay?"

"Okay, hit me with it."

I took a deep breath, clicked on the PowerPoint I'd made on my laptop for my own reference, and then dove in. "Silver Sage Ranch is in financial trouble, and Matthew might have to sell it. I've talked about it with Deborah, and I can afford to buy this place. I'm going to make an offer to him and pitch my plans for revitalizing it. It needs major updates, but it has great bones. Have you looked at the photos I've been sending you? The scenery out here is magnificent, and the property's potential is endless. Please listen before you tell me I'm nuts." I held my breath as I waited for her reaction.

"I'm just relieved you're not getting engaged. You had me worried there for a minute. Tell me more."

"If I bought the ranch, we could start doing Ms. Match couples retreats here, like we've always talked about, helping people work on their relationships. We could also do singles retreats, if we wanted to go in that direction. We've also talked about having conferences for female professionals and leaders so they could network, and this would be a great place for that too. The sticking point for starting all of that up is always the hassle and expense of finding a location. If I owned the ranch, that wouldn't be an impediment anymore."

"Interesting…what else?"

My pulse quickened because her tone was curious and engaged, like she was taking me seriously, which was almost more than I'd hoped for. "We've talked about how the show is getting stale, and we're not bringing in new viewers. It's a great time to transition to something else, a different format. I was thinking about a new version of *Ms. Match* called *Western Matchmaker*. The premise of the show would be that you come out here and match up people who live in Wyoming. Like a rancher looking for a wife to help him run his cattle ranch or a young rodeo star who's ready to settle down. Matthew's brother is a country vet who's quite a catch."

"Hate the name, but that's a fun idea," Tori said. "It's never been done before either, not that way."

"We could get footage of you doing Western things too," I said. "Like trying to ride a mechanical bull or doing some target shooting. We could film some of that at the ranch."

"And how are you going to do all this and still keep up as our CFO in New York?" she asked.

"I would spend a lot of time out here," I admitted. "We'd need to hire someone to take on a lot of my day-to-day duties in New York. I need a change, Tori. I'm stagnating at work, and I don't want to retire next year and learn Mahjong. My time here has transformed me in ways I couldn't have put into words before I got here, but it was exactly what I needed. I want this new challenge."

What I didn't need was her approval to buy the ranch, but I wanted that, too. I wanted this place to be connected to our work in New York, and for that part, I needed her onboard.

"I'm going to say to you what you said to me when I wanted to start a matchmaking company, and I asked you to quit your job and join me."

"Okay." I tried to remember back to that conversation. "What did I say?"

"You said, this isn't just about what you enjoy doing today. This is about your future. Is matchmaking what you want to spend your days and nights thinking about? Is this your passion?"

"Yes," I answered without hesitation. "I love this place. Every day I'm here, I wake up excited about what's ahead, and that's not only about Matthew or being on vacation. It's this ranch. It's so full of possibilities, and I haven't had that in my life in a long time. When my marriage fell apart, I closed the door on so many opportunities and now…I'm opening it again, but only to things I really want to let in."

"Okay, then," she said resolutely. "Buy the ranch."

THE NEXT MORNING was a hectic one at the ranch. Gigi's mom and stepdad arrived, and Tyler was busy loading the Shah family and their luggage into the Suburban for their trip to the airport. Matthew already seemed to have re-focused his energy on the large party arriving in a few days, and it felt like the right time for me to go home. I made a reservation to fly to New York in two days' time, but there was one very important conversation I needed to have before I said goodbye.

Once a bit of late afternoon calm settled on the ranch, I

was ready to pitch my offer to Matthew. I found him in the office standing behind the reservation desk as he worked on his computer.

His face lit up with a smile when he saw me. "Hey, there. I was just finishing up here and coming over to your cabin to ask if you wanted to have dinner with me."

"Can we talk in here for a few minutes?" My body was vibrating with nervous energy. "I have something on my mind."

"Sure. Let's go inside my office." He walked me into the tiny room the size of a closet where he had a desk, two chairs, and a bunch of cardboard filing boxes on the floor. I could see why he didn't want to spend much time there, since it would easily induce claustrophobia. He sat in the desk chair, and I took the other one. There was no point in beating around the bush, so I launched right in.

"Matthew, you know I adore this place, right?"

He nodded and leaned back in his chair. "I know you do, and that makes me so happy."

The tension in my chest eased a little. "Good. I haven't been here that long, but this ranch is already part of me, and so are you and the rest of the people at Silver Sage. I want to make an investment in its future." I took a deep breath. "If you're still considering selling, I would like to discuss an offer to buy the ranch."

Matthew blinked at me, speechless.

"I know this wasn't what you expected me to say today," I continued, "but believe me, I've done a lot of thinking and research before coming to this decision."

CHAPTER 24

MATTHEW

*L*auren's words swam in my head as she went through all the details of her offer. I tried to make sense of what she was saying, but it all swirled into word soup. When did she decide all of this? Did she expect me to respond with an answer right now? I thought she came over to talk about our relationship, not a business deal.

"I'm confused," I said when she finally paused. "You want to become the owner of a ranch? My ranch?"

"Yes, I do. Obviously, I don't know much about running this place, but—"

"Much?" I couldn't help emitting a rude burst of laughter. "What do you know at all about running this ranch, or any ranch for that matter?" This impolite reaction was out of character for me but, in my defense, I was in complete shock. My family had spent decades running Silver Sage, and she thought she could fly in with zero knowledge or experience and suddenly save it.

"Fine." Her cheeks reddened, but I couldn't tell if it was from anger or shame. "I'm not well versed in ranch management, but I have a lot of ideas about how to make this place profitable in the long term. I'm the chief financial officer of a highly successful business, which my sister and I built from the ground up, and we're in a very competitive market."

My ego felt like it was taking one-two punches. "And I don't have a successful business."

Owning a ranch must have seemed so simple to a businesswoman from Manhattan who had never spent a winter here. Never dealt with a horse with colic or a summer drought. Didn't know a Toolcat from a tomcat. What could she possibly understand about what I did every day?

Lauren pinched the bridge of her nose. "That's not what I meant. Can't you even listen to my ideas before you say no? I was just getting started."

I clasped my hands tightly around my coffee mug, which was uncomfortably hot.

"Go ahead." I tried to sound calmer than I felt. "Tell me the rest of your ideas."

"First, we'd use the ranch as a location to host high-end retreats for singles and couples who need relationship coaching. I have money to invest in renovations, so that's not an issue." I bristled at her breezy response, wanting to mutter something about how it must be nice to have money to throw at any project you found entertaining, but I held myself in check.

"We can make not having strong WiFi and cellular service a selling point instead of a deterrent to coming here. So many marriages can be saved, but there are constant distractions that keep us from dealing with our problems. Turn off people's phones and reconnect them with nature and each other, and I think lives can be changed for the better. I know mine has."

I wasn't going to be lured in by her sweet smile. She was giving me the hard sell because she wanted to buy the ranch from me. Her ideas weren't bad, but I hated that the ranch sounded more like a Cozzi sisters' property than one belonging to the Hart family. Then she dropped a bigger surprise on me.

"I'd also like to wrap up *Ms. Match* at the end of this season and launch a new version of our TV show. It would be a Western version of what we do as matchmakers with Tori as the star. We'd probably film some scenes at the ranch, although she'd have to travel some too. We feel like it could be an exciting spinoff series."

"You want to bring a film crew into Three Rivers and Silver Sage?" I sputtered.

"A small one. Imagine the free advertising for both the town and your ranch." Her eyes glittered with excitement. "Think of all the businesses that would benefit. Wasn't Ella saying she wanted to re-envision The Marmot as a classier place instead of a bar where fights break out every Saturday night?"

"You said this was a great place to get away and unplug, and now you want to bring in film crews?" I shook my head. "I don't think I understand your vision at all. Let me guess, you want to put in a runway for private planes so folks can swoop in and out of here with ease, right?" I'd seen this happen before, ranches building small runways for private jets so their resort would be more accessible to millionaires and billionaires. That had never sat well with me. Couldn't they fly into the regular airport like everyone else instead of contributing to global warming and destroying the peaceful atmosphere that made this place so special?

"The secluded nature of the ranch is a serious obstacle to people coming here, so we would probably need to consider that. See, these are the ideas we'd need from you, Matthew."

I closed my eyes and shook my head, horrified that she actually thought I'd suggested putting in a runway. "I can't believe this. A few days ago, you were complaining about your husband wanting a small piece of your family business, and now you want to buy mine and turn it into something that I wouldn't even recognize."

Lauren's jaw dropped, like this was news to her. "This is not the same situation at all. You said you were going to have to sell the ranch because you couldn't afford to keep it going anymore. If I bought it, you'd still be able to run the ranch and keep a connection to it. I want you to be our ranch manager."

"Oh, wow, thanks!" There was no keeping a lid on my temper now. "So if Freddy wanted to buy Ms. Match and keep you on as managing director, you'd be cool with it? Is that what you're saying? He'd call all the shots, and you'd just carry out his orders?"

"Of course not. If Freddy bought Ms. Match, I'd have to leave, but that's because I don't trust him, and I certainly don't want to be around him. If we were going out of business and you wanted to buy our company..." She had the decency to stop and think about what that would actually feel like. "I don't know what I'd do, but I certainly hope I wouldn't let my pride get in the way when I made my decision."

Everything was crumbling apart. "It's not just my pride that's hurt, Lauren. I grew up here, and this place is part of my identity. I thought you understood that." Sure, my pride was taking a hit, but it was my heart she was breaking.

Tears swam in her eyes. "And I thought you'd appreciate my interest in keeping your family's ranch alive, so I guess we were both wrong."

I pulled off my cap and tugged at my hair. "Do you care about me at all, or did you come here looking for a business opportunity?"

"Don't be ridiculous, Matthew. I didn't come out here to buy a ranch, and of course I care about you. You're part of this. We can rebuild this place together. Can't you see that?"

"And what if the relationship doesn't work out?" I asked. "What happens to your new business venture, then? What happens to me?"

"I know we'd be taking a risk here, both of us, but I think it's worth it. There are still details to work out—"

"That's just it. You figured out all the details on your own. I'd just be here to help you smooth the way to a totally different Silver Sage Ranch that looks nothing like the wonderful place my parents put their blood, sweat and tears into."

"Matthew." She was crying now, and I was choking back emotion myself. "I'm not trying to destroy your parents' hard work. I'm sorry if I caught you off guard with all of this." Her voice dropped to a whisper. "I didn't expect it to upset you this much."

I set my jaw and nodded tightly. "I guess I need to get used to fielding offers on the ranch. I sure didn't expect one coming from you today, that's all." A few hours ago, I'd been thinking about telling Lauren I was falling in love with her, and now I wasn't even sure who she was.

She pulled back her shoulders and swiped away her tears. "I think we should put a pin in this conversation. Let's take some time apart, and we'll talk again later."

I nodded slowly, feeling like a deflated balloon. "Alright. I think some time and space is definitely in order."

"Okay." She smiled through her tears. "I guess I'll see you around the ranch then."

"Yeah, I'll see you around."

I felt numb as I listened to the front door of the office shut behind her, and I let my head drop into my hands. All I could think about was what a fool I'd been. How could things get any worse?

Less than two minutes later, the front door creaked open again, and I craned my head to see who had entered. Was it

Lauren? Instead, Tyler shot toward me like a firecracker going off.

"We have a problem, boss."

CHAPTER 25

MATTHEW

"*I* found Damon." Tyler was out of breath and wild-eyed. "Drunk. In a hammock."

My stomach plummeted. "How drunk?"

"Passed out cold."

This was bad. Cataclysmically bad. We could prop up a slightly intoxicated chef for the dinner service by infusing him with black coffee and putting a few extra hands in the kitchen, but if he was unconscious? Hell, there was no way around that.

"Shit, shit, shit." I ripped off my baseball hat and slapped it repeatedly against the desk. Then I stared at it before shoving it back on my head. "Well, that didn't help."

Realizing that it was okay to laugh now, Tyler chuckled. "Looked like it helped, at least a little bit."

Feeling like the patriarch of a dysfunctional family, I placed my hand on his shoulder. "Guess the two of us are cooking, my friend."

Tyler started walking backwards, ready to move on my plan. "Got it. I'll meet you in the kitchen right after I get Chef to his cabin."

"No," I said firmly. "Leave Chef Damon where he is for

now. We'll deal with him later, after we've made our guests a meal." Lauren's voice came into my head, reminding me about Jimi Hendrix, but I refused to listen. "Let Kyra know what's going on, okay?"

So much for looking like the capable ranch owner in front of Lauren for the remainder of her stay at Silver Sage. Who knew what kind of random meal she'd be eating for dinner? As I hurried to the kitchen, I cursed Damon for picking today to go on a bender. Serenity was already there, prepping for a menu of lamb chops with a reduction of cabernet and black pepper, alongside roasted mushroom risotto and blistered cherry tomatoes. There was no way I could prepare such complicated dishes on my own, especially within a limited amount of time.

Wait a minute—cabernet?

Dammit. I'd given Serenity access to the wine for this recipe. Had Chef stolen the key from her? This was no way to run a kitchen.

She and I went through the contents of the walk-in refrigerator until we had devised a plan. The dinner entrée would be chicken, because the meat was available, and I knew how to prepare it. As sides, we'd serve baked potatoes and salad. Serenity would take care of the homemade salad dressing, then crisp up some bacon and chop fresh parsley to top off the potatoes. There was nothing exciting or gourmet about the menu but, if no other calamities occurred, it would be edible.

I tied on my apron and thanked the heavens that Chef hadn't pulled this shit during the Titans' week, with forty alpha males on the ranch. There was no way I could handle a dining room crowd of that magnitude without him. If I could get us both through the summer without another relapse, it would be a miracle.

As I grabbed the ingredients to marinate the chicken, I spun around to see Raelynn standing behind me.

"Tyler told us about Chef," she said. "I'm finished with laundry for the day, and I'm here to help you."

She should have been leaving the ranch to head home, and I didn't have the money to pay anyone overtime. From the sympathetic look on her face, she knew that already.

"It's alright." I reached for an industrial-sized container of garlic salt. "Serenity and I have got it under control."

"Cut the horse crap, Matthew," Raelynn barked in a voice I'd never heard from her before. "You've got guests and staff to feed tonight, and you need my help."

"We can handle it." I was being a stubborn mule, and we all knew it, but I couldn't seem to stop. Meanwhile, a vein was throbbing so hard in my head that I feared a stroke was coming on.

"Take the help, Matthew." Serenity said softly. "Please?"

It was the kindness in her tone that did me in. Something inside me snapped, and I grabbed hold of the counter and bowed my head. That's when I felt Raelynn come up behind me and put her arm around my waist. For a small woman, she had an iron grip. When your mom is gone and a woman her age gives you a side hug, it's enough to make you weep, and I would have shed a tear or two if there had been time for it.

"It's not your fault, honey," she whispered. "You're in a tough spot."

I nodded because if I spoke, my voice would crack. I'd pay Raelynn overtime for cooking with us because it no longer mattered if I kept to a budget. If I had to sell off equipment or even one of the horses to make payroll, I'd do it. The ranch was going to be sold either way, so it didn't really matter anymore. It was over.

I wanted to sit down, lay my head on a table and cry, but there was certainly no time for self-pity. I would channel my pain into work, like I always did. There was no other option.

THE KITCHEN BUSTLED that evening with more staff in the room than ever, creating a strangely festive atmosphere. We were all pulling together, doing tasks that were foreign to us, to achieve a common goal. Tyler put on some music, and he and Kyra got to work rolling silverware in napkins. Raelynn washed and chopped vegetables for the salads while Serenity scrubbed potatoes. Even Walt showed up to see what he could do, and I didn't even attempt to turn him away. Raelynn was right—I needed everyone's help. I'd needed help for a while now, but hadn't wanted to ask. As a result, I was beyond exhausted, ankle deep in horseshit, and finally ready to admit I wasn't getting out of this mess on my own.

The kitchen rose in temperature with the flurry of activity, and over the next few hours, we put out a main course that was tasty to eat and served on time. No, it wasn't up to our usual standards, but it had to suffice. Raelynn pulled a couple of cheesecakes out of the freezer and thawed them for dessert. With cut strawberries sliced on top, they tasted and looked pretty darn good, even if they were slightly icy in the center.

Tyler raced back into the kitchen with clean plates and a smile on his face. "Chicken is a hit, boss!" He gave his dirty dishes to Walt and Serenity, my clean-up crew, and refilled his tray with plates of cheesecake. "They're going to love this dessert."

His positivity brought a damn tear to my eye. To have someone believe in me as much as that kid did was overwhelming. If I'd had a son, I would have wanted him to be just like Tyler, and I probably needed to tell him that sooner rather than later. Serenity and Raelynn finally agreed to go home around nine o'clock, and I forced Walt out of the kitchen because he was dead on his feet and didn't need to be mopping floors. Tyler and Kyra hung around with me for the final cleanup.

"We pulled it off," Tyler said, sounding impressed with our efforts as he sanitized the counters at the end of the night.

The poor kid thought he was getting an education in running a guest ranch but all he was learning was damage control. Meanwhile, I felt like a failure as a mentor, just like I'd failed at everything else at Silver Sage. He'd be devastated when I told him the ranch was going to be sold. Tyler's father was killed in the war in Afghanistan, and he'd kind of adopted me as a male authority figure in his life. I hated to let him down, but maybe the new owners would give him a job. Thoughts of Lauren sitting in my office and offering to buy the ranch popped into my head, but I pushed them out again, not ready to deal with that problem.

"That was wild," Kyra said, pulling me from my thoughts. She leaned up against a counter, eating a piece of cheesecake without using a fork or a plate. "Are you gonna fire Chef Damon?"

"I've certainly thought about it," I said. "If you know any skilled chefs looking for a job in a remote ranch from now until the end of the summer, please let me know. Otherwise, I think we're stuck with him for the rest of the season."

The only positive thing about Chef being too drunk to work was that it kept me busy in the kitchen, meaning I couldn't make my usual rounds in the dining room. I had a legitimate reason, other than my stupid pride, to stay away from Lauren. That was a small consolation on what was an embarrassment of a night.

After we cleaned up the kitchen, it was time to pay Damon a visit. Tyler insisted on coming with me.

"Meet me at the hammocks in case he's still there," I told him grimly. "I need to get something first."

Amazingly, Chef was in the same place Tyler had found

him earlier, curled up on his side and snoring peacefully under a tree near Cottonwood Cottage. That only lasted until I took my bucket of water and doused him with it. He sputtered into consciousness like a rodeo bull whose flank strap had been tightened and then cussed at me with some colorful language. It took a few more seconds for reality to set in.

"Oh my God," he muttered. "What time is it?"

"It's eleven at night. You missed dinner service, and I'll fire your ass before the end of the season if you ever do this to me again, Damon. I'm serious. Get sober for good or get gone."

I wasn't bluffing. I should have canned him right then and there, but who would I find to cook for the Titans on such short notice? I had no choice but to pray he would stay on the straight and narrow until the end of the season.

"I'm sorry. I fell asleep." He rubbed his trembling hands over his face, and a twinge of guilt fluttered in my gut. The guy had problems, and if I lost Gigi, I'd probably try to smother my pain in some less than ideal way too. Then again, I had a business to run, and I needed a sober chef to do it.

"Sorry is nice, but it doesn't change the fact that everyone had to pitch in to help me tonight because you weren't there."

"I'm not surprised it took that many people." He looked up at me with bloodshot eyes. "Have you ever wondered how I pull off meals with so little help? I prep the food, cook it, plate it—you have no idea."

"I have no idea?" I snapped. "I'm plunging toilets and patching fences, so don't talk to me about doing things that are below your pay grade."

"And you don't think that's a problem?" he said sourly.

I stuck my hands in my pockets and nodded. "I absolutely think it's a problem. It's a problem that weighs on me night and day. Do you have more booze in your possession?"

"No."

I wasn't even going to ask him where he got it. That didn't really matter. Lauren had been right. I couldn't control Chef Damon. He had to want to stay sober on his own.

"Then go to bed and don't screw up again. You owe it to me and everyone else on staff to stay clean for a few weeks until we can wrap up the season. If you want any kind of good reference from me, you better get it together."

He seemed surprised by my harsh words, which was understandable. Typically, I handled his bouts of drunkenness with more disappointment than anger, but tonight he'd hit a nerve. He was right about us being understaffed. Trying to keep this ranch going wasn't only foolish, it was selfish. Lauren had tried to tell me that things needed to radically change around here, and she'd made a plan to do it. And how had I responded to her? I was ashamed to think about that now...

CHAPTER 26

LAUREN

*W*hen Tyler brought out dessert, he mentioned a storm was coming in from the west.

"It's gonna be a gully washer," he said. "You probably want to stay indoors."

I'd waited all evening to ask him the question on my mind, and I couldn't hold it back any longer. "Is Matthew okay? He isn't at dinner."

"Yes." Tyler looked around, shifty-eyed. "He's in the kitchen tonight."

I'd suspected that much based on the simple meal we'd eaten. "He cooked, didn't he?" Tyler resisted giving me an answer so I told a small lie. "The food was excellent. Tell him I enjoyed it."

Dinner had been fine, but certainly not excellent. It was the type of comfort food you'd cook for yourself at home, not what you'd expect from a resort, even one with the word ranch in its name. The chicken was bland and the cheesecake on the plate in front of me looked solid and a little bit frosty, as if it had recently been taken out of a freezer.

Tyler lit up with his usual happy glow. "Great! I'll let him know."

As he slipped back into the kitchen, the dining room went completely silent. All of the other guests had gone back to their cabins for the evening, and there was no reason for me to stick around except for the slim hope that Matthew might come out and speak to me. I hated that things were unresolved between us, especially when I had a divorce and a syndication deal in a similar state of limbo. Maybe in his mind we'd come to a resolution, but I didn't know what it was. Were we going to keep in touch or was our relationship ruined by my offer to purchase the ranch?

Now that I'd had time to reflect, I understood that selling his family business to a stranger might be less painful than selling it to me and staying on as manager. The worst part was that he seemed to feel betrayed, like my feelings for him were a sham. Nothing could have been further from the truth. I wanted at least one more chance to speak with Matthew to make peace with him and leave on decent terms. I'd had enough of unresolved relationships to last a lifetime. This one would get closure, even if it wasn't the ending I wanted.

LATER THAT NIGHT, alone in my cabin, sleep wouldn't come. I tossed and turned in my bed, replaying my argument with Matthew, resentful that he hadn't sought me out to apologize or talk things through. These feelings were familiar. In the earlier years of my marriage to Freddy, when our troubles first began, I waited for him to come to me with apologies and explanations. Many nights, I went to bed angry or upset, refusing to be the one to start the hard conversations.

And look how that turned out.

Impetuously, I grabbed my phone and texted Matthew, asking him to meet me in the Round Room. Before I could regret my decision, I pulled my raincoat over my pajamas, shoved my feet into my hiking shoes, and hurried out of my cabin. The storm had begun an hour earlier, and rain pelted my jacket as I squelched down the muddy pathway. I could hear Matthew's voice in my head telling me I shouldn't be outside when there was lightning. Why was I suddenly taking risks when I'd been so careful until now?

Once I made it to the steps of the Round Room's covered porch, I knew I was safe. The door to the building was unlocked, and I scurried inside, shaking water droplets from my jacket before removing it, along with my boots. Despite my best efforts, my pajama pants were damp from the rain, making me shiver with the chills.

I flipped on the lights, but the brightness of the chandeliers made me squint, so I flicked the switch again and opted for darkness. Thunder rumbled in the distance and after about twenty minutes of sitting and waiting, I closed my eyes and let my mind drift.

Matthew wasn't coming.

Why had life brought me here, to this ranch at this time, if Matthew and I weren't going to continue our relationship? Coming here, when I was supposed to be sent somewhere else, felt like destiny. Was there a different reason I'd come to Silver Sage Ranch? Certainly, it was time well spent reclaiming my joy, but I couldn't deny that Matthew was a huge part of that reawakening, especially as the one who rekindled my physical desires. I tried to imagine myself back in New York on a date with a man in finance, or even one in the arts, and it all felt wrong because I knew what I wanted for my future and it wasn't the hustle and striving of city life. I wanted time to look up at the stars. To notice the changing colors of the cottonwood and aspen trees. To saddle up and take long trail rides, even on days when there are other tasks that need to get done.

"Lauren?" Matthew stood in the doorway, lightning flashing dramatically behind him, outlining his form.

I stood up, my damp socks cold against the wood floor and hands shaking with nervous energy. "Did I wake you?"

He looked at me questioningly as he walked over. "What do you mean? I came here looking for you. You didn't answer the door to your cabin, so I thought you were asleep, and then I saw the door to the Round Room was ajar."

"Oh." So he'd come to find me. "I sent you a text."

"Sorry. I haven't checked my messages in a few hours." He pulled his phone from deep in his coat pocket but didn't bother looking at the screen. "I had to work late in the dining room, and then I had some staff issues to deal with."

"Let's sit down and talk," I suggested.

"I'll make a fire first. It's chilly in here and you're in your pajamas."

I looked down and remembered he was right, I was in my night clothes and wasn't even wearing a bra. The last time I'd left the house this underdressed was…never?

I sat down and curled my legs under me, snuggling into the chair's worn cushions. "I love a fire on a rainy night."

He shucked off his dripping jacket and hung it on the back of a chair, and then systematically stacked logs, kindling and paper in the fireplace. Next, he lit a long match and held it to the pyramid he'd built until the flame caught and traced itself along the edges of the paper. Even before he lit the fire, the general aroma of the Round Room was ashes and wood, combined with the leather of the Adirondack furniture and a lingering smell of tobacco. It wasn't unpleasant. In fact, I found it to be masculine, warm and comforting, just like Matthew.

He sat down on the loveseat next to my chair and clasped his hands together on his lap. "Didn't expect the weather to get this bad."

"Tyler warned me it would be a gully washer." We smiled gently at each other. "I guess I found out what that term means."

"I'm glad I got to see you tonight. I wanted to apologize for how I spoke to you earlier today. I was rude to you, and I'm really sorry."

I studied the lines of his face in the shadows of the room. There was no "but" or "because." His was the most direct apology I'd ever gotten from a man. I'd played out this conversation many times in my head, and in none of those scenarios had I pictured him apologizing to me from the jump.

"I forgive you," I said earnestly. "And I owe you an apology too. You were right. I wouldn't want to sell Ms. Match to someone and then stay on and work for them. I was naïve to think that scenario was going to work out. All I could see was my exciting vision for this place and all the numbers I'd crunched, and I didn't consider your feelings."

"I think my love of Silver Sage's past might hold you back from creating your new vision," Matthew said, "and I don't want to be that person. I realized after our argument that I've been running around here, trying to keep everything the same, while you were the brave one, trying to plan a future for the ranch. I admire that."

I wanted to tell him I wasn't interested in destroying the past and changing everything that made this ranch so special, but that wasn't our only obstacle. The thought of owning Silver Sage, hiring him to work under me while trying to be his girlfriend, was going to be way too uncomfortable for both of us. It wouldn't be an equal partnership, and I'd already had a marriage with a messed-up power dynamic. I didn't need to go down that road again. There was, however, one important misconception I wanted to straighten out with him.

"I need you to understand that I only started thinking about buying the ranch when you told me about your financial problems. This wasn't some grand scheme of mine when I came here."

"I know that," he said. "I was upset in the moment, but it was silly of me to think that way. If you're still interested in buying the property, I'd be happy to consider your offer among any others we receive. I'll have to go with the best one, but...you'd certainly have my attention." The pain in his voice made my heart ache.

"I have to admit, the idea of doing this with you was a huge part of the appeal." He looked up at me, and I grimaced, my cheeks heating. "Maybe I read too much into how you felt about me."

"Of course you didn't." He reached over and placed his hand on my arm. "Having such strong feelings for you is what makes this situation complicated. I'm falling in love with you, Lauren."

My heart pounded in my chest, hope rising inside me again. "Me too. I wish we could rebuild this place together because it's one of the most beautiful places left in this country." I swallowed to control my emotions. "We haven't known each other very long, but I think we'd make a good team."

"I know we would. But even after you go home, please know I'm rooting for you. I'm on your side, and I always will be. Team Lauren Cozzi aka Mrs. Wagonblast."

"I'm on your team, too." I went to him, curling up on his lap and pressing myself against his chest. His strong heartbeat drummed against my cheek. "I'm not going to stop caring about you when I leave here. You and Silver Sage are coming with me, in my heart and in all my beautiful memories from my time here."

"It doesn't seem real," he whispered into my hair. "I say the words about selling the ranch and leaving here forever, and I know what our bank account looks like, but it still doesn't feel real. I can't believe I'm going to lose this place."

"Maybe that means you haven't given up yet."

"Maybe."

He pulled me closer to him, his arms wrapped snugly

around me, and we stayed that way without speaking for a long time. The fire was blazing now, the flames radiating warmth. Matthew's skin smelled like rain and wood smoke, and I wanted to stay in the safety of his arms forever. There was a real chance we'd never see each other again after I left the ranch, depending on where life took us next, and I could hardly bear the thought of that.

Mathew's words rumbled low in his chest, his voice full of emotion. "When you get back to the city and have to deal with that ex-husband and his lawyers, don't forget what a badass you are. You wear those cowgirl boots when you need a little Wyoming courage."

I nodded, struggling to keep my tears at bay. "I'll do that." Maybe I hadn't given up yet, either. If he could fight for his family's home, I could certainly fight for what was mine—the company I'd worked so hard to build. My privacy. My dignity.

"I want you to do something for me. Call your siblings and talk to them about the ranch." I looked up into those denim blue eyes of his. "See if they can help you. Maybe they'll have ideas about how to keep this place in your family."

"Alright, I promise. Now how do you feel about going back to my house? Because this couch isn't the most comfortable place in the world, and we still have a few hours together."

"Absolutely, yes."

"C'mon then." He playfully smacked my backside, lifting the heavy mood. "It's getting late, and we don't have much time left before the sun rises."

Scented candles flickered in the darkness on Matthew's

night tables as we stood facing each other, still clothed but hopefully not for long.

The flowery framed prints on the wall stood out to me as something you wouldn't normally see in a Wyoming man's bedroom. "Was this your parents' room?"

"Yes." His tone was apologetic. "But they didn't die in here or anything."

I laughed because it was a morbidly funny, yet accurate, thing to say. "They slept in this bed though."

"Not on these sheets," he said quickly. "I brought my favorite flannel sheets with me when I moved here, and that plant over there?" He pointed to a snake plant on the dresser. "That's mine."

"That plant is yours?" I nodded sagely. "Then it's not weird at all."

He smiled as he cupped my chin in his hand. "Is this *too* weird for you? We can go upstairs to my old bedroom. You want to see my 4-H ribbons and my Heather Locklear poster? The poster is in the closet because Mom didn't want to look at it."

I slid one finger into the waistband of his jeans and pulled him closer. "I kind of do want to see that stuff, but later."

"That's good because we have bunk beds and a twin bed in there, and it's not a comfortable situation."

"You shared a room with both brothers?" His house was modest in size, and the upstairs rooms couldn't have been very spacious.

"Yep. Can we talk about something else?" He deftly undid the top button of my pajama top. "I don't want them in my head space right now."

He undid another button, and I decided not to help him with the rest since he was doing such a good job. Once again, it was nice having someone else put in the work.

"What do you want in your headspace?" I asked.

He finished the buttons and slid my pajama top off my shoulders and down my arms. "Just this."

I didn't follow his gaze downward because I was nervous, not about what we were doing, but how my breasts looked naked, without nylon and underwire to perk them up. What if he didn't like what he saw?

Matthew smiled, a heated glint shimmering in his eyes. "This is going to be fun." His thumbs made little circles over my peaked nipples, and my head fell back a few inches, my insecurities melting away.

He tugged loose the tie on my pajama pants, and together we pulled them to the floor so I could step out of them. Once I was down to my underpants, he said drank me in. "You're so beautiful."

It wasn't a line. He spoke with such earnestness that I fell even deeper in love with him.

"Now you." I started with his shirt, luxuriating in the feel of each button sliding open. Before I moved on to his pants, I ran my hands over his warm skin, reveling in the light patch of hair in the center of his chest. Too many men waxed their chest hair nowadays, and I missed seeing that hair. It was primal and sexy. If he expected me to be waxed bare down below, he was about to get a surprise.

I moved on to the button and zipper of his jeans, moving slowly because he was already straining against the fabric. Feeling his excitement made me wet, which was a relief. My body still knew what to do. If I had to tell Matthew to stop at any point during sex because my middle-aged anatomy wasn't cooperating, I was going to be supremely pissed off.

Speeding up my movements, I helped him shed his pants to the floor. He removed his boxer briefs, too, so now I was one piece of clothing in the lead. Or behind, depending on how you looked at it.

He took my face in his hands. "What's going on in that head of yours? I can tell you're overthinking." Before I could answer, he kissed me softly on the lips, as if to reassure me that whatever I was worrying about would be fine.

I decided to be honest with him and lay it all out there. "Do I look okay naked? Should I have shaved or waxed? Did the medicine I take to keep me supple down there really work?" What was the point of lying to him? At our age, there was no time for that. "In other words, I'm overthinking."

"You look totally gorgeous, and I have lube if we need it. I want you to just relax and enjoy yourself—make that your job for tonight."

I slid my arms around his bare waist, thinking how well he knew me already. "You are so…"

"Prepared?"

"Wonderful." I kissed him, and my mind finally quieted.

He walked me backwards to the bed and before I knew it, we were tangled up together on his soft flannel sheets, kissing and exploring each other's bodies. Matthew braced himself on his forearm over me, looking deeply into my eyes. What if this was your real life, my treacherous brain asked me.

It wasn't real life though. It was vacation life, and it was about to end. I told my brain to shut up and enjoy the moment.

As we lay together, he touched the dewy place between my thighs, his fingers sliding over my tender skin, building me up until my back arched involuntarily, urging him on. My hands curled into fists around the sheets as my breath stilled, the sensations at my core building to a crescendo. Unable to hold on much longer, I needed to take him with me. I reached out and stroked his hard length.

"I want you to come first," he whispered, stilling my hand.

I shook my head. "This time I want us to come together. Please? Let's try?"

He smiled down at me. "I can't say no to you."

Quickly, without finesse, I moved on top of him, straddling his body. Encouraged by his sounds of approval, I guided him inside me. There were things I wanted to do to him and with him, but this first time might not last long. We were both ramped up and needy. I grabbed the headboard behind him and began to move my hips.

"Is this good for you?" I asked as I rocked.

Matthew's eyes shuttered as he grasped onto my ass. "Perfect. You?"

"Perfect," I echoed.

Our position gave him access to places that made me whimper with pent-up pleasure. There was no pain. I sent a silent thank you to my doctor for that gift. My body was primed and ready, and it didn't take much for me to get to my climax. Delicious waves broke over me, coming again and again. Matthew must have been waiting for me to let go first, because he came quickly then, pumping wildly into me with a cry of relief. I loved watching his face as he spent himself, the pull of tension followed by divine relaxation. Absolute bliss.

Afterwards, we slept for a few hours before I woke him up so we could make love again, slower this time, luxuriating in each other's bodies. When we finished, Matthew got out of bed and lit the small wood burning stove in the bedroom. It wasn't even cold outside, but he knew I loved the comfort of a fire. As the flames danced behind the stove's glass door, we cuddled and talked softly in the darkness, our legs intertwined, my head on his chest. Once again, my mind wandered to what could have been. What if I could experience a Wyoming winter, working hard during the day then sleeping, curled up together, in this bed every night? We could spend some time in Manhattan, too, enjoying the city, and I could show Matthew and Gigi the wonders of Rockefeller Center at the holidays. My family would love him, and he'd fit in so well, bantering with Tori and Rocco, impressing

Mom with his gentlemanly manners. We could have the best of both our worlds.

I had to let go of those dreams because I was leaving in the morning, returning to New York where I'd be dealing with the fallout from Freddy's interview in *Celebrity* and finally getting him to sign a divorce settlement. Matthew would be here in Wyoming, talking to his siblings and trying to save his ranch. I had to be realistic. Unless we made a Herculean effort, this beautiful relationship was going to end. As the fire crackled, he wrapped his arms around me, spooning me from behind, as he drifted off to sleep. I forced myself to stay awake to listen to him breathe deeply, enjoying the feel of his body tucked around mine. When you know it's probably the last night you have with the man you love, you don't want to miss a second of it.

CHAPTER 27

MATTHEW

I wanted to take Lauren to the airport, but she insisted I let Tyler drive her.

"I want to say goodbye to you here at the ranch," she said as I cradled her in my arms in the early hours of the morning. Her words whispered across my skin. "I don't want to picture you at an airport. I want to see you here, surrounded by all this beauty."

When she said things like that, it was hard not to beg her to stay. Somehow, I held myself together as we said our goodbyes, and then Tyler drove her away, off of my ranch, but hopefully not out of my life forever. I wanted to take the day off and mope but, for better or worse, my job didn't allow me time to wallow. Not only did I have to prepare for the Titans, I had to call my siblings like I'd promised Lauren I would. Instead of putting it off, I bit the bullet and sent out an invitation for a video call for the following afternoon. I'd delayed this moment long enough.

Predictably, Bowie grumbled about having to download another app onto his phone because the guy who flew charter planes for a living also mistrusted most forms of modern technology. Don't anyone get him started on the evils of social media and artificial intelligence or you'd get an earful. Also predictably, my sister Faith was the first one to log onto the call. In fact, we were both ten minutes early, which gave us a few minutes to catch up with each other before the guys arrived. No doubt, at least one of my brothers would be late.

Faith gazed into the camera, her smile tired and careworn even though it was only three o'clock in the afternoon. There were mauve-colored shadows underneath her eyes and lines drawn around her mouth that could have been from age but leaned more toward melancholy. Maybe it was the bad lighting in her kitchen making her look ten years older than her forty-seven years.

"How are you?" I asked.

"I'm alright. It's great to see you, Matty." At least her voice sounded the same as always, warm and sweet, like her personality. Our mother had called me Matty, and hearing Faith say it somehow made me feel loved and bereft at the same time. "You have me curious about why you want to talk to all of us together," she continued. "I hope everything is okay? You're not sick, are you?"

"No, I'm fine."

I didn't want to get into a conversation about my problems at the ranch before our brothers joined us. In fact, I wished I could put it off indefinitely. I dreaded telling Faith more than anyone else because she'd predicted the folly of trying to save this place, and I didn't listen to her.

"How are things going down there?" I asked. "You look a little rundown."

She touched her hair, which was pulled back in a soft headband, and I could tell she was judging her appearance on her screen. "I guess I am. I've had a lot going on lately."

Her two daughters were grown and flown, as they say, with careers and social lives that kept them busy. Faith didn't work outside the home and never had. She left college in the middle of her senior year to marry Palmer, and their daughter Vesper was born a year later. She and Palmer divorced several years back, and she refused to start dating again. Taking all of that into account, I wasn't sure what "a lot going on" could mean.

"Tell me how I can help," I said.

"I'm fine. You don't need to worry about me."

I snorted. "That's never stopped either of us."

Faith laughed, and her face transformed into someone more recognizable. "That's so true. We're the worriers of the family, especially me."

Sam showed up on the call. "Hey there! Am I late?"

"Not as late as Bowie." I considered texting our wayward brother, but he rarely kept his phone on him.

"What did you want to talk to all of us about?" Sam asked.

"I'd like to wait for Bowie." I didn't want to have to tell the story twice. "Do you think he forgot?"

As if he'd heard me, Bowie logged onto the call, still pushing buttons on his keyboard. "Can you see me?" He leaned forward and squinted into his camera, his hairy face crowding the screen. "Is this on?"

"Yes, we can see you." Sam rolled his eyes. "And you're even later than I was for this call."

"There is a two-hour time difference, Samuel," Bowie said gruffly. "Plus, I had a late run last night, so I needed to sleep in a little."

"Did you go to sleep as the prince and wake up as the beast?" Sam asked, mocking Bowie's voluminous beard and wild hair. He got a laugh from almost everyone.

"He's right, you've gone feral," Faith teased. "But you're still cute."

"Yeah, yeah," Bowie said. "I'm a hairy mess. Let's move on. Why are we all on here today? Not that I don't want to see you all, but this isn't my favorite hour of the day for chatting."

"Right." I drew in a deep breath and tried to look like someone who wasn't dying inside. "I need to talk to you about the ranch. The bottom line is we aren't pulling in enough money. We've only had a handful more guests this summer than last, and I'm burning the staff out because we're always short-handed. To keep this place going, we'd need an influx of cash to hire people and renovate the property, and we don't have any money left. Faith, I should have listened to you. I'm sorry. I took on too much here." Their silence made me feel worse, but I forged ahead. "I think we should put the property on the market, so we need to talk about pricing and how and when we want to proceed with the sale. You're obviously co-owners of the property, and we need to think this through together."

Maybe the money from the sale would help Faith feel more independent from Palmer. For some reason, she still felt like she had to run all her major purchases past him. Sam had been wanting to expand his practice, and he could use this money toward that end. Bowie...well, I honestly had no idea how he'd spend some extra cash because he already owned his own plane and he certainly wasn't spending money on grooming these days. Those eyebrows were out of control.

"Think this through together?" Bowie repeated with a scowl. "Seems like you did all the thinking, and you're telling us how it's gonna be."

I was speechless. The sibling who had been back to the ranch once since he was eighteen years old was the one pushing back at me?

"Go easy on him, please," Faith said to him. "Can't you see this is hard for Matthew?"

Bowie shook his head in disbelief. "It's hard for me to hear that he's selling our family's ranch without even getting our input!"

"You haven't been down here since the funeral," I

reminded him sharply. "You don't know what I'm dealing with here, and you've shown zero interest until now. In fact, none of you have, except for Sam, who gives us free vet services. I do appreciate that, Sam. Without you, we wouldn't even be open at this point."

"What exactly did you want me to do?" Bowie snapped back at me. "I don't remember you calling on me for anything. You always said everything was fine, and you had it all under control. When have you ever asked for or accepted anyone's help?"

"I think what Bowie is trying to say," Faith said carefully, "is that we're here for you now. Maybe we can figure out a solution together?"

"There's no solution," I said. "Believe me, I've tried to find one."

"Hear me out," Sam said. "We turn the ranch into a home for aging fashion models, thirty and up. A place they can roam free and stretch those long legs."

Faith rolled her eyes. "This isn't the time for jokes, Samuel."

"I'm sorry I couldn't save this place." I gripped the handles of my chair, trying to contain my emotions. "It tears me up, thinking about losing Silver Sage."

"Then let us help," Bowie said, "and stop trying to be the lone hero who saves the day."

I bristled at his accusations. "That's not fair. I was here alone! And I'm not trying to be a hero. I'm just trying to hold things together."

"Let's talk about this calmly," Faith said. "What could we do to keep the ranch going for the time being until we can make a long-term financial plan?"

"Unfortunately, I don't have a lot of time to give," Sam said. "My practice keeps me busy, but I have some savings I could contribute."

"Savings you were going to use to expand your practice," I

said. "I don't want you to pour that money in here when I can't guarantee a return on your investment."

"Maybe it's not an investment," Sam said, finally getting serious. "Maybe it's just a way to keep our land in the family."

"I could come up there and do some cleaning and decorating," Faith said. "Those old curtains on the cabin windows are probably threadbare by now. I can sew new ones right here at home. My machine still works."

She was right. The curtains and so many other things were in poor condition. This was the first time I'd tried looking at the situation from their point of view. Maybe I did like the idea of being the one who swooped in and saved the ranch, but I couldn't do this on my own anymore.

"I'll take some time off and help with renovation projects this fall," Bowie said. "You know I love demolition."

"I'm sorry I kept you in the dark," I said, "and I do appreciate your willingness to help. We're still going to need a large infusion of cash to make major changes here, well beyond what Sam has in the bank. I don't know how we'd get our hands on that kind of money."

"What about a bank loan?" Faith asked.

"I don't think we can get another one," I said, "not when the business isn't doing well."

"We need to think of another option," Bowie said. "Could we sell off some of the land?"

I'd already considered that. "Then we can't get money from Cal for letting his cattle graze here. That income has been keeping us afloat. But I guess if we have to sell off land, we could."

"What if we found an investor?" Faith asked. I hoped she wasn't talking about Palmer. There was no way I was going into business with that asshole. It would be like Lauren selling part of her business to Freddy. Lauren...

"Someone was interested in buying the ranch," I said. "A guest who was here recently."

"Mrs. Wagonblast?" Sam said immediately.

"How did you guess?" I asked.

"Duh. Lauren Cozzi is a wealthy woman, and she loved the place. Besides, who else would it be? It's not like you've had a lot of guests lately."

He had a point there.

"Sam told me there was someone at the ranch who you'd taken a shine to," Faith said in an irritating sing-song voice. "He said he'd never seen you so smitten with anyone."

"That's Lauren." Sam smiled brightly, happy as a pig in shit.

"Enough about Matthew's crush on her," Bowie grumbled. "What did she offer for the ranch?"

"We didn't get into specific numbers." I told them about Lauren's interest in the ranch as a place for retreats. I expected them to balk when I mentioned filming a reality show on our property. Quite the opposite happened.

"You can usually get a tax break for stuff like that," Sam said.

Faith's face lit up with excitement, making her look like a different woman than the one who'd logged onto our call. "I know *Ms. Match*! Lauren and Tori seem like amazing business women. It would be like we'd partnered up with one of the people from *Shark Tank* if we go into business with them."

"I'm fine with shifting our focus," Bowie said, "as long as we get to keep our land and retain a say in what happens to it."

"Lauren was talking about buying the ranch outright," I explained. "That wouldn't give us any control over what happens here."

"How about she can have fifty percent ownership of the ranch if she makes a sizable monetary investment?" Bowie said. "Our family would keep fifty percent ownership, and we can make business decisions together."

His idea appealed to me, but I wasn't sure how Lauren would feel. "We'd need to find out the value of the ranch first, and work on our offer from there. I could bring it to her."

"Matthew needs more support from the rest of us, though," Faith said, "even if we decide to work with Lauren Cozzi. What can we do about that from now on?"

Bowie was not the person I thought would speak up first. "I could come there to the lower forty-eight and help you run the place."

The way he was talking completely baffled me. "You have your own life in Alaska. What about your charter business?"

"I'm ready for a change," Bowie said. "You know what they say, with great risk comes great reward. Let's see what we can build this ranch into."

We all stared at him. Bowie had been refusing to come back to the ranch for decades.

"Are you serious?" Faith asked. Clearly, I wasn't the only one who found his change of heart surprising.

"Totally serious," he said. "Silver Sage is my home too. I know I've been gone a long time, but that wasn't because I didn't care about you all or the ranch. You know I had to get away from Dad and make my own life. I like the idea of coming back now. I'm ready."

I wasn't sure whether I should agree to run the ranch with Bowie, whose personality had all the subtlety of a stampede. Working side by side with him every day would be the real challenge. Then again, no one worked harder than Bowie, and he had experience managing his own business. We'd have to work out our personality differences and make the best of it.

"Alright," I told him. "Let's do it."

"Keep your plane," Sam said. "We can use it to shuttle guests in and out. We'll call it Yeti Air, and you can be your own mascot."

"Hilarious," Bowie said, "but also, not a bad idea about keeping the plane."

I finally felt like I could breathe again. "Okay, we have a plan.

Sam grinned and pumped his fist. "We're gonna save Silver Sage."

CHAPTER 28

LAUREN

*O*n the flight back to New York, I cried quietly into a tissue while trying to ignore the critical gaze of the Pomeranian across the aisle. The woman holding the tiny dog on her lap ignored my weeping like everyone else in first class. Only the dog was judgmental.

"Boo hoo," I whispered to myself. "Stop with the self-pity."

There were wonderful things waiting at home. Family and friends. My beautiful apartment. A successful company and a hefty bank account that would allow me to donate to causes and candidates that were working to make a better world. On top of all that goodness, I now had a renewed love of horseback riding, and the knowledge that, yes, my body still enjoyed sex! These were huge wins.

Matthew's face drifted through my mind and melancholy crept in again, along with a flood of guilt. How could I be anything but grateful for my life? If Matthew and I didn't end up together, there were still thousands of single men to date in New York. I couldn't imagine anyone would measure up to him, but I needed to stay optimistic, just like we told our clients to do after a breakup. Had we broken up? Were we ever really a couple? There hadn't been enough time to figure all of that out.

While I was at the airport, I received a text from Freddy saying that in the morning he was meeting with a reporter to tell his side of our story. It was his last ditch grab for a piece of Ms. Match, and I didn't even bother responding to his message. Tempest and I were sending our final offer to his lawyer. If he didn't take it, we would go to court.

When Freddy's story was published, reporters would hunt me down again, and I'd face them head on this time. There was no more running away. According to Matthew, I was a badass, so I could handle the paparazzi. But if I was such a badass, why was I letting Freddy and the media publicly define who I was? I thought of Ella standing on the pool table with her fire extinguisher. Gigi galloping across the meadow on Loki. The older ladies of the smutty book club, laughing as they took a moonlight dip in the hot springs. What would they do in my situation?

With a rather loud, undignified honk, I blew my nose, opened my laptop and started typing. My fingers flew over the keyboard as my personal story flowed out of me. I wrote about spending years in an unhappy marriage for the good of everyone else; finally separating when my children were out of the house; and deciding to pretend Freddy and I were still a couple to protect my company and my pride. Because that's what it came down to—I didn't want to tell people I'd failed at marriage. Sure, I'd blamed societal expectations and protecting our brand, but ultimately I didn't want to admit that my love story, which began so beautifully, didn't have a happy ending. The last lines of my essay were the most bittersweet and exhilarating to compose—

With all of this talk about relationships coming to their natural (or way past due) conclusions, please don't misconstrue my meaning—I still believe in romantic love. I'm quite a fan of monogamous sex, and I believe matchmaking is a fantastic way to meet someone you'd never otherwise come across. Deep human connection is crucial to our wellbeing—to our very souls. I'm back out there myself, dipping my nervous toes into the dating pool, knowing that I'm perfectly imperfect, and that's (finally) good enough for me.

As I reread my essay, I made a decision. The next morning, probably around the time of Freddy's interview, I'd offer my personal essay to *Celebrity* magazine as an exclusive. I couldn't help but delight that these two events would coincide. *Celebrity* didn't have to pay me a cent for my story, but if they wanted to run it, they'd have to agree not to publish Freddy's interview. If they rejected my offer, which I doubted they would, I'd publish my story somewhere else.

"Excuse me," I said to a passing flight attendant, "may I have a glass of champagne? I have something to celebrate."

He grinned at me. "Congratulations! I'll bring some right over." Everyone was always so nice in first class.

As we flew over western Pennsylvania, I sipped my champagne from a flute, wondering why anyone would order beer when bubbly was available. Yes, I'd fallen for Matthew Hart and his ranch, but I still had a whole lot of Manhattan in me, too.

MY AIRPLANE CELEBRATION was only the first of several that week. The second victory occurred when Freddy and I finally signed divorce papers that did *not* include giving him a portion of my company. He still won a sizable alimony settlement, but some things could not be helped. The following morning, he received a call from his contact at *Celebrity* saying they'd decided not to run his interview. They were going with my personal essay instead. I wish I could have listened in on that call and seen his face, but knowing it happened would have to suffice.

With my divorce finally settled, Tori and I were free to sign our syndication deal. It turned out that streaming companies got nervous when you made them wait, and then they increased their offers. Even with my alimony payments, I was financially set for life. My divorce also made it possible for me to date publicly, and I'd already been flirted with by a man I met at my brother's dinner party. Life was going well, except for one thing. I had received zero phone calls from Matthew. We'd exchanged text messages, and he'd sent me some beautiful flowers and a pretty postcard from the ranch telling me how much he missed me, but I wanted to hear his voice and invite him to New York for a visit. Tori told me to give it another day or two, but I feared this was the beginning of the end. The distance would be too much.

By Friday afternoon, I was exhausted and ready to spend my evening with a glass of red wine and Netflix. My assistant, Jaden, had different ideas. We were having our end-of-week meeting in my office, curled up at opposite ends of my couch with our laptops balanced on our legs.

"You need to return a call to Tempest," he said, "and then you have a dinner appointment with someone who wants to discuss a possible business venture. Your sister set that up."

"Who's the dinner meeting with?" Tori hadn't mentioned this to me.

Jaden splayed out his palms. "I don't know. She told me to put it on your calendar. Seven o'clock at The River Cafe."

I dipped my chin and stared at him. "Jaden. The River Cafe? This sounds like a date situation."

"She called it a dinner meeting."

I sighed, my skin itching with irritation at my sister's deception. Conveniently, she was offsite for the day, with meetings in the morning and "working from home" scheduled in the afternoon. More likely, she was hiding from me so I couldn't accuse her of meddling in my love life. She was definitely sending me on a blind date with some guy she thought would get my mind off of Matthew.

"I hope this guy knows there's a dress code." The River Cafe, which was on the East River with stunning views of Manhattan, required a collared shirt and a jacket for men. "How did she even get a reservation? They're usually booked out for weeks or months."

"Must have used her star power," Jaden said. "It could be a real business meeting. You never know."

"I hope so."

"Although she said to tell you to wear something sexy."

I glared at him and got a cheeky grin in return. "You left that little detail out until the end, huh? You're in on this."

"I recommend that dress you wore the night of the infamous Jentori party," he said. "Reclaim it. You ate in that dress." This was Gen Z slang for looking hot, which I appreciated because Jaden was not one to hold back his honest opinions on my fashion choices. Maybe that dress did need a new story, even if it turned out to be a humorous one.

"I don't love surprises."

He cocked his head and gave me side-eye. "What else do you have going on tonight?"

He had a point. I wasn't about to admit that I'd planned on ordering some new underwear online. Getting naked with Matthew had taught me several things, including that I needed newer, sexier undergarments. Part of me was still hoping I got to put on that underwear for him.

"Fine, I'll go, but only because it's rude to stand someone up and also because I'm curious now. Please schedule a meeting with my sister for tomorrow morning. I have a few choice words I'd like to say to her."

Jaden's eyes grew wide. "Oh, I'm sure you will."

CHAPTER 29

LAUREN

I waited while the couple in front of me gave their name to the hostess of The River Cafe. As she ushered them to their table, I looked around the foyer to see if my "date" had arrived. I was early, as always, wearing what Jaden suggested, the infamous black dress and a pair of black three-inch Jimmy Choo heels. The shoes weren't nearly as comfortable as my cowgirl boots, but they fit the occasion better.

A new idea occurred to me. What if this wasn't a blind date? What if there was a surprise party waiting for me? I'd heard of women having divorce parties to celebrate the official end of their marriages, and throwing one for me was totally something Tori would do.

"I'm Lauren Cozzi," I told the hostess, who was back behind her reception desk. "Is there a reservation under my name? I'm meeting someone here."

While she scanned her screen, a voice rang out behind me.

"It's under Wagonblast." At the sound of his voice, I spun around and my breath caught in my chest.

Matthew Hart stood in front of me, but instead of

wearing dusty jeans and a t-shirt, he had on a navy blue suit, crisp white shirt and sage green tie. He'd cut his hair and styled it with products, shaved his face smooth, and carried a leather messenger-style bag on his shoulder. The man could have walked into any midtown office building and fit right in. Then I looked down at his feet and smiled. Worn-in brown leather cowboy boots.

When I looked up again, his eyes caught mine. "Hello." He took a step toward me. "Thank you for meeting me this evening."

With no consideration for where we were, I threw my arms around him, hugging him for all I was worth. He wrapped me up tightly, and tears of happiness gathered in the corners of my eyes as we held each other in the foyer of The River Cafe. I never wanted to let him go.

"I missed you," he whispered into my hair as he held me.

"Me too," I said. "I missed you so much."

Reluctantly, we separated, ignoring any eyes that were on us, and the hostess led us to our seats at a small table with a beautiful view of the river. Lights sparkled outside in the darkness, twinkling against the water. Matthew immediately reached for my hand across the table, and I knew deep down in my soul that I was exactly where I was meant to be.

"I can't really believe I'm here," he said. "Or that you agreed to see me on such short notice." As he smoothed his thumb over my palm, I got tingles in all the right places. This was real. He was here, and the sparks came with him, all the way across the country. It was strange to see Matthew in my natural environment, but it felt right to be together, just as it had at the ranch.

"I didn't agree to anything," I said with a laugh. "I didn't know who I was meeting tonight."

"That was part of my plan. I made Tori help me, so don't be mad at her."

"I can't promise that," I said with a teasing look. "Let's see how the evening goes. Why didn't you call to let me know you were on the way?"

"I wanted to surprise you. It was my turn to land on your turf and have to figure everything out for myself. Did you notice anything different about me?"

"You mean the suit? You look very handsome." That was the understatement of a lifetime. He looked good enough to eat. In fact, who needed dinner?

"I meant my haircut." He pulled his hand from mine and ran it through his closely shorn hair. "I figured a grown man should get his hair cut by someone other than his wrangler, so I took myself to a fancy salon I'd heard good things about, and they gave me an excellent shampoo and cut. I had no idea you could get a scalp massage."

My jaw dropped. This man was full of surprises. "You went to Jentori?"

"I made an appointment through your sister." He looked a little smug at having outwitted me, but what was truly amazing was that Tori had kept all of this a secret.

"Did she have a car pick you up at the airport and drive you to all these places?"

"I'm proud to say I made it from the airport to the hotel and then to the salon on my own without any problems," he said. "I took cabs. Tomorrow I'm going to tackle the subway."

"Hotel?" I scrunched up my face to show him how I felt about that. "You don't need one of those. Stay with me."

"I didn't want to presume I could stay with you, especially since I need to talk to you about the ranch."

Reality landed with a thud between us. "Have you put it on the market already?"

"No. I talked to my siblings about it, like you said I should." He ran a hand over his clean-shaven jawline. "They were frustrated with me because I didn't tell them Silver Sage was in trouble. All three want to help keep it going."

"That's wonderful." Their support wasn't a surprise to me,

but Matthew had convinced himself he was alone in the fight to save the ranch. Sometimes our perceptions are more powerful than reality. "I'm so glad you opened up to them."

"Me too," he said. "I guess I shut them out of ranch business because I was ashamed I couldn't fix everything by myself. I've had to take a hard look at my attitude toward asking for help."

"Asking for help can be hard," I agreed.

"Yeah, it's not my strong suit. Turns out, my siblings are committed to keeping Silver Sage in the family. Bowie wants to move back to Wyoming to run it with me, which was a shock, and Faith wants to be more involved, too. Sam has always done his part with the horses. Obviously, we still have a cash flow problem. That hasn't changed."

The server delivered a bottle of Spanish wine Tori had pre-ordered for us, and I had to wait through the tasting and pouring, my curiosity ramping up with each passing second.

"What do you plan to do with the place?" I asked when the server was gone.

"That's why I'm here." He cleared his throat and straightened his shoulders, his expression turning serious. "Lauren Cozzi, the Hart family would like to make you a business offer."

This certainly was a night of surprises. "What kind of offer?"

He reached inside his leather bag and pulled out a plastic portfolio, which he set on the table in front of me. Under the transparent cover was a title page with a color photo of the stables. "This will tell you all the stats about our nearly four hundred acres, including the bank's valuation of the property, our property taxes, several land surveys, and a lot of other things that I have a feeling you're going to enjoy reading."

That made me smile because he knew me so well. I lifted the portfolio's cover. "I'm itching to read it."

"We want to keep the property in our family," he explained as I flipped through the pages, "but we can't make that happen without an investor. Faith, Bowie, Sam and I would like to offer you part ownership of the ranch. You would buy half the ranch after we negotiate a price, based on all the information presented here. Then we'd work together to make it a great place to visit again. It would be a Cozzi/Hart family business. I told them your ideas, and they were onboard."

"Even with the TV show filming there?" I asked cautiously. It wasn't necessarily a dealbreaker, but it felt like the perfect way to connect the two halves of my life.

He nodded. "Yep, even the show. Turns out, Faith is a fan."

"Wow."

"We have one stipulation though. We want to reserve two weeks of the summer for families to visit the ranch. That way, the people who have been coming for years can still spend time at Silver Sage, and hopefully we can attract new families, too."

I tried to wrap my head around his proposal. "And you would stay on and run the ranch, I assume?"

"Our roles would be written into the contract," he said. "I was thinking we'd have a leadership team consisting of all five of us, and we can each focus on a specific area, like expeditions or guest relations. I'd like to keep on as many current staff members as possible—Tyler, Walt, Raelynn."

"And what about Chef Damon?"

Matthew shifted in his seat. "He's at a rehab facility in Denver where he's getting the help he needs. I told him that, assuming we stay open, I'd try to keep him on staff. Maybe that makes me a soft touch, at least according to Bowie, but I feel for the guy, and he cooks outstanding meals. Let's give him a chance to redeem himself."

He looked like he was waiting for me to disagree. "I think

you've got a kind and loyal heart, and that's one thing I like best about you."

He let out a long breath, as if he'd been holding it. "Thank you. I think he's going to be okay, I really do. When I visited him at the treatment center, he told me he's committed to the program. Hopefully, this is his turning point."

I opened the file again and looked down at what the ranch was worth. The number was big and a little scary, but my heart already knew what it wanted to do. Still, I had other questions that needed to be answered before I said yes.

"What about us, Matthew? I'm not saying my answer hinges on that, but I need to know where we stand with each other. Is this just business?"

"That depends." A smile twitched on his lips. "Do you think you could stand at least part of a bitterly cold winter shacked up with this old rancher? I can't promise you exciting nightlife, but we've got warm fireplaces, cozy beds and pretty views. I've also ordered a kit so you can make matcha lattes at home, although I had one this afternoon at a cafe near my hotel, and it tasted like a mug full of grass." He flared his nostrils to show his distaste for my favorite hot beverage. "I think I could make you some of that tea from what we have out in the meadow."

I laughed, imagining him puckering at the taste. "And if I move to the ranch, would you take me out two-stepping, sir?"

"Yes, ma'am." He reached across the table and took my hand again, interlacing our fingers. His warm, firm grip reassured me that our story might not be perfect, but it was going to be beautiful. "I'll take you two-stepping and to bingo night, and all the other exciting events Three Rivers has to offer. What do you say, Mrs. Wagonblast? Are you in?"

I gazed into his eyes, the color of faded blue jeans, and then I grabbed hold of the reins, steering my life onto a new path. "Mr. Hart, it looks like you've got yourself a deal."

MATTHEW'S EPILOGUE

THREE MONTHS LATER

"Good morning!" Lauren padded into the kitchen in her bare feet, wearing one of my flannel shirts and a pair of sleep shorts. Unlike those of us raised on a ranch, our new Director of Finance and Marketing didn't always get up with the sun. I wrapped my arms around her and kissed her hair. How did she always smell so good?

"Good morning, sweetheart." Man, it felt good saying that to her. Every time Lauren walked into a room, I lit up inside. At some point, the shine on our relationship might dull a little, but I still couldn't imagine that happening. The more I got to know her, the deeper I fell in love.

"Hmmm..." She hummed as she pressed up against me. "You smell like...horses."

"Just for that, I'm waking you up early tomorrow and making you go on the morning ride." I gave her behind a squeeze, eliciting a delighted squeal from her, right as Bowie appeared in the doorway.

"Excuse me," he grumbled. "I thought the kitchen would be a safe space."

Lauren's cheeks turned pink as she pulled away from me. "Sorry, Bowie."

"You don't need to apologize to him," I said. "We live here too."

Over the past three months, so much had changed in my life. First off, we'd signed the contract to make Lauren half owner of Silver Sage. Then Bowie, our new Director of Expeditions and Maintenance, moved down from Alaska and into my house—our house now—and we got started on ranch renovation projects. My new title was Director of Operations and General Manager, which sounded like a big job, but now that I had Lauren and my siblings helping out, they'd actually taken a lot off my plate.

Adjusting to our new roles at the ranch came with some challenges, and the biggest one for me was cohabiting with Bowie. Even when Lauren was back in New York, he and I butted heads as roommates. We had different temperaments and were both largely set in our ways; however, I had a plan to rectify that situation soon enough.

Bowie opened the cabinet and pulled out a frying pan. "I'm making second breakfast, and then I'll get out of your hair."

Bowie's first breakfast, before he and I went out to the stables to help Walt, looked like something you'd eat in Scandinavia—strong black coffee, weird looking dark bread with smoked fish, and a bowl of fruit with plain yogurt. His second breakfast, after we'd done our chores, was always a cheese and spinach omelet. Although my eating habits were less quirky than his, I'd had to increase my calorie intake, too, so I could keep up with chopping wood, shoveling hay and tearing out rotted drywall. At least I was in good shape for a guy my age.

"I'm sorry we don't have much privacy right now," I whispered to Lauren.

Right on cue, another Hart brother strode into the house.

"Good morning!" Sam, now our official Director of

Veterinary Services, entered the kitchen with Jake trotting at his side. Ella was right behind them.

"Ever consider knocking?" Bowie asked.

"Sorry, buddy, we're on a mission," Sam said. "The Dude has been kidnapped again."

Jake pranced around the kitchen in his plaid coat and black booties like a miniature Sherlock Holmes, waiting for someone to drop a treat.

Lauren looked perplexed. "You mean the stuffed marmot from the bar?"

"That's the one," Sam said.

Ella's cheeks were rosy from the cold, and her eyes shone with excitement. "Every six months or so, The Dude gets taken from the bar. A few days later, he's back, and all these photos of him in various places get uploaded to an Instagram account called TheDudeTravels. Isn't that wild?"

"That is one of the weirdest Wyoming things I've ever heard," Lauren said. "Do you have any guesses who's taking him?"

"I have no idea," Ella said, wide-eyed. "Sam and I are looking for clues. Do you guys know anyone who's leaving on a trip soon?"

None of us knew a thing, but Ella didn't look defeated.

"That's okay," she said. "We'll solve this mystery eventually. I wish I got to travel as much as The Dude does."

"I'm starting to think travel is overrated." Lauren stifled a yawn. "I wish I didn't have to go back to New York so often."

Lauren was still the CFO of Ms. Match, but she was in the process of training someone to take over most of her duties so she could focus on the ranch. She and Tori were currently deciding how they would advertise and run their retreats. Then, there was the reality show about dating out west, which was still in pre-production, whatever that meant. Gigi was thrilled about the show and kept asking if she could be an extra when they filmed at the ranch. The answer to that was a hard no.

"You won't be wishing you were here in February," Ella said. "There's so much snow, Sam has to dig a path for Jake to go pee in the yard. Otherwise, he'd sink, and we'd never find him again."

"Don't forget about your snot freezing," Sam added. "And your hair, if you go outside with a wet head."

"And the wind." I shivered thinking about the cold wind that seemed to blow constantly in Wyoming.

"She'll be fine," Bowie said with a smirk. "She's got her cashmere blanket and matcha tea to keep her warm."

I could tell he liked Lauren because he razzed her about her luxury items. Teasing was Bowie's love language.

"Yeah, I saw you on the couch the other day taking a nap under my pink cashmere blanket," Lauren shot back. "Snoring away under there."

Everyone laughed, including Bowie. "It is soft," he admitted.

"What are you doing for Thanksgiving, Ella?" Lauren asked. "You're welcome to join us."

"That's sweet of you," Ella said, "but my mom is part Shoshone, so we don't celebrate Thanksgiving."

Her mom, Patty, was taking a new MS medication and doing much better, and Ella had taken up residence in the apartment above the bar instead of living at her parents' house.

"She'll eat pumpkin pie later, though," Sam said. "I sneak some to her every year."

Ella gave us a guilty smile. "What other time of year can you get pumpkin pie?"

Lauren picked up her mug and took a sip. "I hate to break up this party, but I need to take a shower. Ella, good luck with your marmot mystery." She blew me a kiss as she walked out of the room.

Bowie tilted his head to the side and stared at me. "What on earth does that lovely woman see in you?"

"That I bathe regularly, for one thing," I shot back. "Maybe the marmot is hiding in that mangy facial hair of yours."

Ella and Sam laughed, but it was hardly a joke. His beard was grazing his chest, and it definitely needed grooming. "Are you gonna clean up for our Thanksgiving meal? You look like you wandered in off the highway."

Bowie cracked two eggs into a bowl, one in each hand, like a magic act. "Don't worry, Mom, I'll trim it up a little."

If our mom were alive, she'd make him shave that thing off or at least wear a hairnet over it in the kitchen.

"I need to get started on the cooking," I said. "We have to set up the dining room, too. Walt is taking Gigi and the other kids on a trail ride to keep them busy today."

We were a big party for Thanksgiving this year. Faith and her daughters, Vesper and Lyric, were staying at Cottonwood Cottage, and they'd invited Gigi to bunk with them. She was beyond thrilled to spend time with her older cousins. Lauren had family staying with us at the ranch, too. Tori, her boyfriend Nick, and his three teen daughters were lodging in the Bluebell cottage. When Lauren invited her sister for Thanksgiving, I didn't really expect her to say yes, but Mama Cozzi was on a cruise with Rocco and his partner, so the timing was perfect.

Sam backed up toward the door. "I have to see a few clients this morning, so I'll have to come back later to help with the cooking. I'm bringing pumpkin and pecan pies, three of each. C'mon, Jake!" His little pal ran to his side, long ears flapping.

Ella waved to us. "See you soon!"

"I can move around the furniture in the dining room so we can seat everyone." Bowie poured his eggs and vegetables into the pan. "Do you want me to set the tables, too?"

"That would be great. Lauren, Faith and I can do most of the cooking. Faith is also going to work on making centerpieces."

There was another knock at the door as Faith appeared with a basket full of plant clippings. "Was that Sam I saw leaving?"

"You'll be shocked," I said, "but he managed to get out of helping us chop wood and move furniture."

Faith laughed. "Give him a break. He's probably going to put his hand up a cow's butt later today. That's much worse than chopping wood." She started reaching for the pull on one of the upper cabinets. "Do you still have Mom's vases in here?"

"Probably." I reached up to open it for her, then followed her directions to take out all the vases she needed.

"I touched up all the tablecloths and napkins with an iron yesterday," she said, "and we're preparing enough food for a small army. Vesper is making hot cider. Lyric wanted to make a charcuterie board for appetizer hour. I told her I wasn't sure if we were doing apps, but then I figured, why not?"

"Charcuterie board?" Bowie lifted his eyebrows. "This is the New Yorker's influence."

"Says the guy who buys imported Swedish bread." My phone buzzed with a text from Sam, which I quickly scanned. "Sounds like we need to set two more places. Sam just remembered he invited Cal and Austin to join us."

"He what?" Faith's voice hit a shrill note.

"He ran into them at the feed store yesterday, and they were going to be alone at the ranch this year." I looked back at his message. "I'm supposed to text them the time."

"And he's telling us this now? On Thanksgiving day? Flipping Sam." That was the closest Faith ever came to swearing, and it meant she was seething, which seemed like an outsized reaction, but I wasn't going to be the one to tell her that.

"Do two more people really matter?" Bowie asked, as Faith folded her arms on her chest. "You said we have a ton of food."

Quick as a rattlesnake strike, her disposition changed. "You're right." She turned her back to us and began plucking through the greenery in her basket. "We can make room. It's good he asked them."

Bowie and I exchanged knowing looks because we'd lived with our mercurial sister for eighteen years in that house. Maybe she was feeling the pressure of feeding so many people, although she wasn't doing it alone. We were certainly all pitching in and doing our part. Bowie and I had both tried to convince her to move back to Three Rivers, suggesting she take on a position at the ranch dealing with staff or hospitality, but she kept resisting that idea. I was hoping this trip would make her change her mind because if anyone needed a fresh start, it was Faith.

"I'm going to shower," I said. "Then I need to check that turkey."

I'd brined the bird the day before in a mixture of salt and citrus, the way Chef Damon had directed me by email. I tried to get him out to the ranch for Thanksgiving, but he'd taken a job as a personal chef for actors who lived in a six-million dollar Brooklyn brownstone, and they wanted him to cook their holiday meal. They were sober, too, which worked out well for him, and he sounded happy with his job, at least as happy as a curmudgeon can be. They only needed him for six months, so he'd be available in time for summer season at the ranch. Before Lauren fully committed to re-hiring Chef Damon, she'd had lunch with him in the city to check on how he was doing and, according to her, clean living agreed with him. She said he looked ten years younger and even smiled a few times.

Lauren was still in the shower in our bathroom, which

was good luck for me. The air was steamy, but I could make out her form behind the foggy shower doors.

"Any room in there for me?" I asked.

"Sure," she said. "Come join me."

"Someone told me I smell like horses." After shucking off my clothing, I stepped into the steam with her. "Help me get cleaned up?"

She grabbed the pink bathing sponge she'd brought with her and pumped some sweet smelling lavender soap onto it. Before Lauren, I washed with my parents' ancient washcloths and bar soap from The General Store, so this was a new, perfumed world for me. Lauren began rubbing the soapy water over my chest, but this wasn't merely a seduction on her part. She was serious about her job of getting me clean, which made me smile. You didn't become a multi-millionaire entrepreneur by getting sidetracked from your purpose.

After my chest and neck, she addressed my armpits, shoulders and arms, and then she went back to my chest.

"A little lower," I told her, keeping my voice serious.

She looked up at me and smiled, trailing her washcloth to my stomach. "Right here?"

I tilted my head. "That's good, but a little lower."

She laughed and followed my lead, moving the washcloth downwards. "Hmmm…right here?"

"Now that you mention it"—I leaned my head toward hers—"that spot needs a little attention." Our mouths met and the pink sponge fell to the floor. Lauren's hands wrapped behind my neck, pulling me down into a deep kiss.

"Dad!" A little hand banged on the bathroom door. "Daddy!"

I groaned as Lauren and I stilled. "Sorry," I whispered, but she just laughed. "What is it?" I called out to Gigi.

"Elijah is hurt! He got into a fight last night, and Walt just found him. He's got a bad cut on his side and his ear is injured, too. We called Sam, but I want you to come with me to the barn."

"Okay, give me one second. I'm getting out." I laid my forehead against Lauren's, the warm water still running over us. "I'm sorry. It's not always this crowded around here."

"It's fine," she said. "Honestly, I love having everyone here. Did you tell Bowie our plan yet?"

"Not yet, but I will."

There was more knocking on the door, less furious this time. "Are you coming, Dad?"

I sighed and kissed Lauren one last time before getting out of the shower. "We'll revisit this later."

LAUREN'S EPILOGUE

$\mathscr{O}$ur stomachs were full to capacity, and we still had Sam's pies warming in the ovens for dessert. My generation remained seated at the dining tables, a few of us having removed a belt or opened a top button on our pants as we digested our huge Thanksgiving dinner. The children —some of whom were actually young adults—offered to take charge of cleanup, and, with the door propped open, we could hear their laughter and music inside the kitchen. The fact that Nick's daughters were welcomed into the Silver Sage family made me so happy, but I wished Serge and Julien were with us, too.

My sons had traveled to Switzerland for the long holiday weekend to visit their father and grandmother. I'd urged them to accept Freddy's invitation, to which Julien had been especially resistant. They'd lost a lot of respect for their father in the past few months and, as much as he deserved their disappointment and censure, it hurt my heart to see them estranged. After our marriage went sour, I never spoke ill of Freddy to our boys because I didn't want to poison them against him or turn our problems into theirs. Instead of harping on his deficits, I emphasized things like how he could deftly sail a boat in high winds and speak three languages. For all his faults, Freddy loved his sons, and it wouldn't make me happy to take that away from them.

"Best Thanksgiving meal ever," Sam proclaimed as he rubbed his midsection. "Thank you to all the chefs."

"You baked the pies," I said. "They smell delicious."

"Thank you to those who made the long trip out here," Matthew added. "It's been wonderful having our New York friends with us."

"We were thrilled to be asked," Nick said. "It's fun to see my girls acting like children again instead of trying to be sophisticated teenagers."

"I enjoyed the trail ride with them this morning," Walt said. "I was told I have rizz, which turns out to be a good thing."

As we all laughed, a parade of kids drifted out of the kitchen with pies, plates and serving utensils, and everyone began circulating and switching up seats to find new conversation partners.

"Explain to me again how everyone is related," Tori said as she sat down next to me. "Austin is Callum's son?"

"No, he's Callum's nephew," I explained. "Cal is a bachelor who owns the cattle ranch next door. He's been friends with the Hart family for years." I chuckled at the glint in her eyes. "I can already guess what you're thinking, and I doubt he'd want to be on *Ms. Match Goes West.*" We'd decided on the name and format of our new show. Tori would travel to rural areas of Wyoming, Montana and Colorado, to towns where it was hard for women to meet eligible men. She was going to use her skills to find these women the loves of their lives, which we were told would not be easy. That type of warning only made us more excited for the challenge.

"And why not?" she asked. "Cal is exactly the type of bachelor I'm trying to find out here, and maybe he's looking for some help in the love department."

"For one thing, he's way too private and reserved to agree to be on a reality show and, from what Matthew says, all efforts to introduce him to women have been rebuffed. He hasn't dated anyone in years." Faith was on the other side of me and appeared to be listening in so I turned to her and asked, "Do you think Cal wants to meet someone?"

"Oh…" Faith's eyebrows shot up. "I have no idea. He and I don't keep in touch."

Tori leaned over me to address Faith. "I think Austin and your daughter are hitting it off. The matchmaker in me senses some chemistry there."

I grabbed Tori's hand. "I noticed that too."

We all looked over at Vesper and Austin who were standing by one of the large windows overlooking the meadow. Vesper, who was tall and boyishly slim with long blonde hair, was saying something to Austin while he listened intently.

"The dining room could burst into flames around him," I said, "and he wouldn't even notice."

"Really?" Faith pursed her lips. "I hope she doesn't lead him on. She's just a friendly girl, that's all."

"Maybe they'll hang out when she's at the ranch this spring doing her research." I turned to Tori to explain. "Vesper is getting her Master's degree in ecological restoration at Colorado State, and she's coming here to do research for her final thesis."

"Smart girl." Tori tilted her head suggestively. "Sounds like they'll be seeing each other again soon."

Faith tossed back the last sip of wine in her glass, clearly not thrilled about the prospect of Austin and Vesper getting closer, which seemed strange to me. From what Matthew said, and from my own observations, Austin was a lovely young man. Maybe it had something to do with her daughter potentially meeting a guy who was invested in staying in Faith's tiny hometown? At any rate, it was none of my business, but that didn't mean I wouldn't stay curious.

"If you really want a challenge, Tori"—I pointed toward the other end of the table—"try finding a match for Bowie over there. He's a self-proclaimed lone wolf."

Tori waved her hand dismissively. "He's just hiding his true feelings behind that grizzled facial hair. There's someone out there who can break through that overgrown pelt of his. Remember, I thought I was going to be single my whole life until I met Nick. Every lone wolf can be tamed. Even him."

"Is that true?" Faith's eyes darted down the table where Cal and Bowie were seated together. "I feel like some men are happier on their own little islands, so to speak."

"Some people just lack the right relationship tools to be successful," Tori said. "We're going to have singles retreats here this summer. Did Lauren already tell you?" Faith shook her head. "Maybe you can come to one of them as a secret shopper. We'd love to have an insider tell us how it went and what we need to change."

"You'll be up here to visit Vesper anyway, right?" I said. "Maybe you could stay a little longer and do a retreat. It would really help us out." Matthew had mentioned that Faith needed to get away from her controlling ex-husband in Texas. Maybe a retreat at the ranch would do her good.

"I'll be visiting," she said, "but I don't think I could do the single mingle thing. Just the thought of that makes me feel queasy."

"What about you, Bowie?" Tori asked. He was sitting directly across the table from her, stroking that god-awful beard. "Would you be willing to go to a Silver Sage singles retreat as our mole?"

"A singles retreat? No way. I'm kind of a—"

"Lone wolf," his family finished for him.

Bowie was completely unfazed at everyone ganging up on

him. He crossed his arms on his broad chest and smiled. "Exactly."

"What about you?" Tori asked Sam, who was sitting to her left. "Are you a lone wolf too?"

"He's more like a lone squirrel," Bowie said, before his brother could answer. "Always chattering."

"Some people enjoy good conversation," Sam shot back at him. "We're not all lonely hermits like you. I'd probably enjoy the hell out of a retreat full of single women but, unfortunately, I don't have that kind of time on my hands. Besides, would it really be fair to the other bachelors?"

In response, there was a chorus of groans.

"That's three strikes," Tori said. "How about you, Cal? Want to come meet some eligible women and possibly find true love?"

"Uh…" Callum looked completely flustered by her question. "No, thank you, m'am."

"This western matchmaking is proving to be difficult," Tori said, "but I've faced harder challenges."

"Maybe Ella would do the singles retreat, if you can drag her away from work," Faith said, her voice infused with sincerity. "I know she'd like to meet someone."

"She already did." Sam's expression soured. "She's been dating some old geezer from Laramie named Harrison Forkwell."

"Please don't call him old," Matthew said. "I happen to know Harrison through the Chamber of Commerce, and he's only in his early fifties."

"Ella is thirty-nine though," Sam argued. "That's a big age gap. Too big if you ask me."

"She didn't ask you though, did she?" Bowie challenged, clearly enjoying what appeared to be some jealousy on Sam's part. "You're a little too invested in Ella's love life."

Sam was saved from having to answer Bowie's challenge by Jake yipping at his feet. The little scamp had been roaming the dining room all evening, gobbling up every scrap of food that dropped to the floor.

"Jake needs a walk," Sam said. "Anyone want to come with us?"

His invitation started phase two of the party, where people split off into groups. Some left to play card games in the Round Room while others went to watch football at Matthew and Bowie's house. As Sam dressed Jake for the outdoors, Faith offered to join them on their walk.

Matthew pulled me aside and got close so he could whisper. "Can we get some alone time? I thought we could take a walk, but not with Sam and Faith. Just the two of us."

"I'd love to." I leaned up on my toes and kissed his cheek, my lips brushing up against his scruff. Matthew was growing in what he called his *winter beard*, but he promised it wouldn't be wild like Bowie's. I had a feeling I was going to love the way it looked.

We strolled back to the house so I could put on a pair of thermal underwear, as well as a puffer jacket, gloves and a warm beanie. Matthew was right that Wyoming winters were no joke. It was only late November and already I needed layers to go anywhere outside. Matthew waited for me on the porch, unbothered by the weather, his breath visible in the cold night air. His outer layer consisted only of jeans, a quilted flannel jacket and his cowboy hat.

"You don't even want a coat?" I asked incredulously.

"You know my logic. If I dress too warmly now, I won't have anything to work up to later this winter. I start out light." He extended his bent elbow toward me. "Shall we?"

I took his arm, loving the way his sturdy bicep felt under my hand. "We shall."

As we wound our way up the trail that would lead to a hill overlooking the ranch, we were both quiet, taking in the starry night sky. It felt wonderful to stretch my legs and breathe in the fresh air after a long afternoon of sitting around in a warm room, eating way too much food. When we got to the top, we paused to take in the view. Matthew put his arm around my shoulder, and I melted into him.

"It's been a perfect day," I said with a sigh. "Or it would have been if Serge and Julien were here. I miss them."

"Once we're moved into our own place, we'll get all the kids out here," Matthew promised.

We turned to look back into the distance from where we'd come. Matthew got quiet, and I saw him reach into his pocket. My breath caught in my chest when he pulled out a small jewelry box and placed it in my hands.

"What's this?" I wasn't worried that he was prematurely proposing. We'd already discussed our feelings on engagement and marriage, and we were in agreement that, for now, we were happy to leave things as they were. At least I thought we were...

I lifted the cover off the box to find a keychain with a leather strap that could be held in my hand or worn on my wrist. The name Silver Sage was embossed on the leather, and five keys hung from the keyring.

"You're a co-owner," he said, "so you need a set of your own keys to everything. I wanted to make it look nice for you."

I held the keys in my hands, emotion flooding through me. "Thank you. You always know how to make me feel at home here."

He reached over and touched one of the keys. "This is the master key for all the main buildings—the office, kitchen, dining room, and pool house." He touched another key and gave me a knowing look. "This one is for the wine cellar." He touched the third key. "Front gate so you never have to sleep on the ground again unless you want to, and" —he touched the fourth key— "this starts up the Suburban, which I'll teach you how to drive."

I'd lived in New York City so long, using public transportation or riding in hired cars, that I wasn't a confident driver anymore.

"Oh, gosh, that huge thing?" I took a deep breath, reminding myself that I was Lauren Wagonblast out here. "What am I saying? I can definitely learn to drive the Suburban."

"That's my girl."

I touched the last key. "What's this one?"

"That's the key to Bluebell Cottage. I'll make sure we're moved in by the time you get back here in January."

We were spending Christmas in New York so the next time I came back to Silver Sage would be the new year. A new year, a new house, a new life…

Matthew gazed into my eyes. "We're moving pretty fast here, and I want you to know that I'm going to take care of your heart. I won't hurt you the way that other guy did."

Tears clouded my vision. "I'll always take care of your heart, too. I promise you that, Matthew."

A little over four months ago, when I was drowning in humiliation and self-pity, I thought my life was over. I was right. That old life had to die for this new world to open up for me. As much as I wished it had happened earlier, it had to be this way. Timing was everything in life, and it had brought me to this wonderful man standing in front of me, asking me to put my trust in him.

Matthew leaned down and kissed me, and it was as sweet as the first time. He pulled me into his arms and held me to his chest, where I could feel his heart beating. The love we felt for each other burned as brightly as a meteor shower on a dark Wyoming night.

"Should we see how the card games are going in the Round

Room?" Matthew asked when we were nearly back to the house.

"Sounds good to me." I grabbed his hand and pulled him toward me for one more quick kiss. "I might need some tea. I always get sleepy after a big meal."

Matthew pointed to a patrol car pulling up to the ranch's main office, spotting it before I did. "What's the sheriff doing out here?"

We walked faster as a knot of worry tightened in my gut. The sheriff, a middle-aged woman with closely clipped hair, stepped out of the car and put on a hat that matched her brown uniform.

"Evening, Matthew." She looped her thumbs on the thick belt around her waist. It was impossible not to notice the gun hanging at her side. "I need to speak to your brother Bowie."

Matthew and I were only a few feet away from her now.

"Is he in some type of trouble, Sheriff?" he asked. "Can you tell me what's going on?"

"I need to speak to Bowie directly," she said. "I have someone with me who I'm told belongs to him."

"Someone who belongs to him?" Matthew repeated. "What are you talking about?"

"Look inside the squad car," she said. "I'm supposed to speak to Bowie about this but you can draw your own conclusions. It's a tale as old as time."

Matthew and I looked at each other then peered into the dark depths of the back seat of the car. When I saw who was inside, I gasped.

~

Buckle Up, Buttercup, book #2 in the Silver Sage Ranch series, will tell Bowie's story of coming home to Three Rivers. Be sure to follow Jill's newsletter, website or social media so you don't miss her next book release!

ALSO BY JILL WESTWOOD

BETTER THAN EVER

Least Likely Two

Our Nerdy Secret

Baby Be Mine

FOSTER'S CREEK

Homewrecker

Control Freak

Drama Queen

AUTHOR'S NOTE

In the summer of 1994, right after college graduation, I took a job as a housemaid at a guest ranch in southeastern Wyoming. Never before had I experienced such wide open spaces with endless skies, meteor showers, and double rainbows. That summer I learned to two-step, drank beers at the local honky tonk, rode (and fell off of) a horse, got followed by curious cows, and watched a man pass out drunk on the bleachers at a rodeo. It was a wild adventure. Those four months live in vivid color in my memory, and I knew I wanted to write about the ranch someday. Silver Sage Ranch is based on that place and those experiences; however, the Hart siblings are entirely fictional, as are their romantic partners and all the other characters in my series. Unlike Silver Sage, the place where I worked appears to still be a thriving family-owned dude ranch, and I'm so grateful for the inspiration that their beloved ranch provided for this book series.

I owe a big thank you to Nicole Lisa for being an amazing critique partner and the best friend a person could have. Sarah at Okay Creations produced my beautiful book cover, and I'm so excited to work with her on the covers for the rest of this series. Finally, thank you to all my readers for leaving reviews and telling your friends about my books. Now saddle up and get out there because love and laughter don't end at forty!

ABOUT THE AUTHOR

Jill Westwood is the author of romantic comedies about strong women and the sexy men who fall head over heels in love with them. She likes her books steamy, smart and a little bit wacky. Her goal as a writer is to make readers laugh and swoon.

She's a New Yorker who grew up on Long Island and later moved around the country in search of a place to put down roots. She now lives in North Carolina with her family, but you will often find her daydreaming about living in the English countryside. That's probably because her mother raised her on Masterpiece Theater, Cadbury chocolate bars and novels by Frances Hodgson Burnett.

If you would like to know more about her, please visit www.jillwestwood.com.